THE WILD

Mahendra Jakhar is an ex-journalist currently working as an independent screenwriter and author based in Mumbai. He started as a journalist in Delhi with *The Times of India*, where he worked for six years before moving to Mumbai to pursue his dreams of being a scriptwriter.

His first novel *The Butcher of Benares* was published by Westland Publications. It was rated as the Best Crime Fiction Debut Novel of the Year by *Mint*, *The Economic Times*, and was an Amazon Rising Star. The book has been adapted as a Netflix series *Mandala Murders* by Yash Raj Entertainment.

His other novels include *The Swastika Killer*, *Chakra Warriors*, *Housewife* and *The Diary of a Prostitute*.

As a scriptwriter, he wrote the script for the Hindi feature film *Manjhi—The Mountain Man* directed by Ketan Mehta, and starring Nawazuddin Siddique and Radhika Apte. Earlier, he has written scripts for Mahesh Bhatt's *The Killer*, starring Irrfan Khan and Emran Hashmi, Tigmanshu Dhulia's *Shaagird*, and many television shows including *CID*, *Maano Ya Na Maano*, *Seeta aur Geeta*, *Dwarikadhish*, and others.

His film script *Bhiwani*, based on the boxers of Haryana, was selected for the International Film Festival of India, for the competitive section at Film Bazaar.

Mahendra also conducts workshops on screenwriting, to help discover the creativity, imagination and ideas hidden in every person. He's a TEDx speaker and has taken creativity workshops for *The Times of India*, IIT Kanpur and IIM Ranchi, among others.

You can reach him at:
mahenjakhar@gmail.com
X (formerly Twitter): @mahenjakhar
Instagram: @mahenjakharworld

THE WILD

MAHENDRA JAKHAR

RUPA

Published by
Rupa Publications India Pvt. Ltd 2025
161-B/4, Gulmohar House,
Yusuf Sarai Community Centre,
New Delhi 110049

Sales centres:
Bengaluru Chennai
Hyderabad Kolkata Mumbai

P-ISBN: 978-93-7003-935-3
E-ISBN: 978-93-7003-257-6

First impression 2025

10 9 8 7 6 5 4 3 2 1

The moral right of the author has been asserted.

Printed in India

The greatest happiness of life is the conviction that we are loved; loved for ourselves, or rather, loved in spite of ourselves.

Victor Hugo

1

Shweta Chaudhary, editor-in-chief and star anchor of News World, appeared on her daily show *News Line* from 9.00 p.m. to 10.00 p.m. five days a week. People loved her show—she grilled top politicians, bureaucrats, film stars, army generals, social activists, CEOs and industrialists, among others. Most of her guests would be on the edge. There was no telling when she would rip them apart on live television with the entire nation watching.

That night, she spoke of the daring daylight attack by Naxalites on a CRPF camp in Chhattisgarh, and followed it up with her take on the ill-equipped forces, the half-hearted action taken by the state against the Naxals, and the indifference of hidebound politicians.

The expression on her face and the tone of her voice were perfect for the occasion—neither too emotional nor too dramatic. Years of training had taught her to strike the right balance.

Shweta finished the first round of analyses and announced a short break. Forty minutes into the show, she had given only eleven minutes to her eminent panellists to express their opinions on the outrage.

The video footage of the massacre was sold by the Naxals to the highest bidder. Shweta had quoted a price no other news channel could match. The attack had taken place at 11.30 a.m., her channel received the footage the same evening, and she aired it on her show at 9.00 p.m., peddling it as 'EXCLUSIVE'.

The attack came as a shock to the entire country which was waiting for the results of the general elections. The ratings of Shweta's show skyrocketed. The channel bosses were happy; she was minting money for them. It never pricked their conscience that the huge amount of money paid to the Naxals for the footage would be used to buy more arms, resulting in more attacks and deaths.

After the break, Shweta was back on the screen, analyzing the political parties in the fray, the number of seats won, and the possible candidates for various cabinet posts. The question every Indian on the street was asking was, 'Who will be the next prime minister?'

The panellists screamed, begged and protested for their turn, but Shweta went on and on. For the last five days, she had been living in the office, and had anchored for over twelve hours each day, covering just about every aspect of the general elections.

When she was not in front of the camera, she would be on the phone with reporters across the country, shouting at them to get her exclusive visuals, bytes and reports. While on the phone, she would also amble into the graphics department, and yell at everyone, 'I want it loud and big! The colours are all hogwash. Look at the map. Where's the ticker? I want a band under the map. Think of a better headline.' When no one could come up with anything better, she would do so on her own, making everyone feel foolish.

During the 26/11 Mumbai terror attacks, she anchored continuously for three days till the siege ended. Later, she had to be hospitalized due to over-exhaustion, but she was out in two days and back to grilling army officers, top brass in the police, and politicians and intelligence officials for the security breach that led to 26/11.

Shweta's voice never faltered. Like a seasoned actor, she had the right modulation for each story. Her diction was perfect as she articulated the mood of the nation.

That night, she was happy with the exclusive footage News World aired of the Naxal attack. She ended her show at 11.45 p.m. The smile on her face was perfect—neither too pronounced, nor too subdued. Everything about her was just right, everything.

Shweta was thirty-seven, but didn't look it. Of medium height and build, she had straight black hair that fell over her shoulders. Her sunglasses were always perched atop her head, a style statement none of the ladies in the News World office dared copy.

The perfect trophy wife, she drew a salary of over five crore rupees per annum, had a luxury car, a sea-facing penthouse in the most expensive building in Worli, all-expenses-paid international trips twice a year, an expense account for dining out, local travel, gym, spa, beauty treatment, hair, make-up, a fancy wardrobe, books, and a multi-crore insurance policy.

This is what a woman should be—beautiful, sexy, successful, glamorous, with a solid social standing. However, the thought of her as a wife scared most men off.

At 12.30 a.m., she said goodbye to everyone in office. As soon as she came out of the studio, she changed into a short black dress presented to her by a Bollywood designer. Then she stepped out of the building with her unlit cigarette still dangling in her right hand. Prabhakar Morey, the old security guard, came running to her. Taking out a lighter, he lit her cigarette. He could see the little flame dancing in her eyes as she smiled at him.

'Thank you, Morey,' she said, and walked to her car.

This was the moment Morey waited for each day—to light

her cigarette. It had become a ritual. The flame of the lighter in her eyes gave him a sense of purpose, something to look forward to in his otherwise dreary life.

Parked right outside the main entrance was Shweta's gleaming silver Mercedes. It had been presented to her by the channel's owners. As the car moved, she rolled down the window and flicked out the cigarette ash that flew away into the night.

She seemed content with the extensive coverage of the general elections, especially with the exclusive video footage of the Naxal attack thrown in. For the last ten months, News World had occupied the number one spot. Not for a moment had she let the team slacken. Her motto was to keep everyone on their toes, and drive them to work by instilling a sense of fear. Always ready to axe people, she, in fact, had sacked many reporters and production executives for even minor mistakes. And in an environment of recession, no one wanted to lose their job.

She believed that lies were best told with a straight face and a hint of arrogance. She did that every day, facing the entire nation.

The silver Mercedes sped through the darkness of the Worli Mills compound that had been converted into an ultra-luxury commercial hub. News World also had its office and studio there. Shweta's sea-facing apartment was hardly a twenty-minute drive from the studio. At times, she stopped at the Worli sea face to take a walk along the long promenade at night. The Bandra-Worli Sea Link would be lit up, looking hauntingly beautiful, while the cool sea breeze would act like a balm for her aches and pains.

She would stop here to gather her thoughts, plan strategies for the next day, make notes on her smartphone, shoot mails to the research team, talk to reporters in far-off states, discuss marketing and publicity with the business team, and think of a new design element that the channel could incorporate to make it stand out. And in those few minutes, she would smoke at least seven to eight cigarettes.

In the rear seat of the car, she closed her eyes for a moment to shift gears from this night to the next day. She had learned to programme her mind this way, and soon, she focused on the tasks of the morrow.

Familiar with the drill, the driver turned the car to the left and was slowly inching towards her favourite spot when a message appeared on Shweta's smartphone. She cursed out loud as she had told everyone not to message her unless it was urgent.

She opened the message and read, 'Your life is about to change.'

Deleting it, she cursed again, 'Fuck off!'

Slowly, the car came to a halt. The driver, who also served as Shweta's bodyguard and kept the street urchins and lechers at bay, stepped out and held the door open for her. As she readied to step out, another message popped up.

She was annoyed. She really didn't want to be disturbed during her mental calisthenics.

As she opened the message listing, she could only see the first two words, 'Welcome to…' She pressed the delete button, cursing again, 'Fuck, fuck, fuck.'

2

Ambar Apartments, the sixty-five-storeyed high-rise, stood like a giant amidst other inferior blocks of concrete in Mumbai. This was *the* address for Mumbai's crème de la crème who controlled the city and the country's finances. Even Bollywood A-listers couldn't easily pick up an apartment here despite offering to pay a premium. Most residents were top CEOs, political bigwigs, and founders and owners of the latest unicorns. Only one Bollywood actress had managed to get an apartment here, thanks to the favours of a corporate honcho she was friendly with, and of course, the sixty-fifth-floor penthouse was occupied by Shweta Chaudhary.

The channel bosses had zeroed in on a small bungalow for Shweta in Pali Hill, surrounded by residences of actors and actresses. But she had put her foot down; only the penthouse in Ambar Apartments would do or she wouldn't take up the job.

The penthouse was an eight-thousand-square-foot space, almost 180 metres above ground level, making it difficult to even see it from the street below. Everything in the penthouse reeked of luxury—Italian marble flooring, expensive paintings adorning the walls, Italian lighting, glass panes imported specially from Germany to withstand pressure fluctuations at this height, Persian rugs, antiques, and artefacts acquired during extensive travels across the world.

The noiseless elevator capsule with piped jazz took less than a minute from the lobby to the sixty-fifth floor. Shweta hated the elevator as she lost the network connection on her smartphone for that minute. She often complained that the elevator was too slow.

It was 1.15 a.m. when she reached her penthouse. She inserted a card in a sleek slot. A green light beeped and she gently pushed open the door. The whole place was flooded with light. Dressed in a casual linen shirt and blue jeans, Aakash Khurana, her husband, sat on the sofa watching a food show on the state-of-the-art smart TV.

Irritated by the lights and the deafening noise of the TV, Shweta headed straight for the dining table that was covered with delicacies, and placed her bag on it. Then she switched off most of the lights. She loved only a hint of light—a faint glow on the wall, with lamps on the tables and the corners casting abstract patterns everywhere. Then she went straight for the TV remote and lowered the volume.

Used to her behaviour, Aakash said nonchalantly, 'I recorded this show today. It was awesome. I created a whole new recipe— Spice-o-Clay Fish.'

'Hmmm,' Shweta said, fiddling with her smartphone.

At five feet eleven inches, thirty-nine-year-old Aakash was slim and fit, with a soft, pleasant face. The typical teachers' favourite and quintessential all-rounder, he was just the person one hated by the time one reached college. He always maintained a neat haircut, clean-shaven face and well-manicured hands as these made it to the close-ups on his YouTube channel Foodgasm where he posted a recipe every day. The channel had over 100K subscribers, mainly women who would be glued to the show. His Instagram account was also a hit with women, raking in over 500K followers. He also had a weekend show on a local Hindi news channel, *Badi Khabar*, but now he was looking for his big break on a national TV channel.

Shweta sat on a side chair without even noticing her

husband, and switched the channel to News World. She looked at the mutiple bar-charts, map and the ticker moving across the screen. She spotted a typo and immediately called up the desk reporter and blasted him for being irresponsible. Come what may, even past midnight, she was not going to let the ratings slip.

'What the hell. You don't even look at me or say hello,' Aakash protested.

With her face still turned to the TV screen, Shweta said curtly, 'Hello! Does that offer enough food for your male ego?'

Irritated, Aakash got up. 'Even I work. But you're obsessed with your channel.'

'Really? Well, you just copy recipes from some old book and plonk them on your show. And you call that *work*?' Shweta reacted with a smirk.

Aakash stood there stunned. 'Wow! So you are the one who really works?'

'This is news. Not a food show where you stand in a kitchen and cook. In news, every second matters,' she impressed upon Aakash.

'I also have my own pressures of being a television show host,' Aakash said.

Shweta sneered at him. 'Do you call that a TV show, where you teach old aunties to make chutney, *murabba*, cakes and silly new recipes?'

'You sit on a chair and read out from a script like a schoolgirl reading from a textbook,' he said.

This infuriated Shweta, but she managed to hide her anger. 'There's a difference between cooking and anchoring on a news channel. Even our maid cooks,' said Shweta nastily.

Aakash snatched the remote from her hand and switched off the TV. 'My cooking is an art. Look, I cooked all these Italian dishes for you. I thought we'd have a nice dinner.'

Shweta went up to the wine rack stocked with the choicest French wines. She selected a bottle and poured herself some wine. She lit a cigarette and walked out to the sundeck.

It was a beautiful penthouse, in fact too beautiful, the kind that was photographed for interior design magazines but not truly *lived in*. With five sprawling bedrooms, it had a study stacked with books from top to bottom—mostly untouched. In spite of a shared bedroom, husband and wife had their separate rooms.

The interiors had been done by a Bollywood star wife who was once an actress. Now she had taken to designing homes. Well, she had definitely turned their penthouse into a museum. None of the guests dared touch anything lest they break it. In fact, no one came to their penthouse. A busy couple, they didn't even have time for each other. How could they be expected to entertain guests, relatives, or even family?

With the wine glass in hand, Shweta stood on the sundeck of her sixty-fifth-floor penthouse, looking out at the sea, and at Mumbai's skyline glittering in the night.

Slowly, Aakash inched close to her, and placed his hand on her shoulder. 'I'm sorry. Let's have some food.'

'Stop doing all this. We have a maid to cook. You do your cooking on your food show, not in my penthouse,' Shweta snapped.

'But I've cooked all this so that we can spend some time together.'

'Did you ask me? You can't start taking decisions on my behalf,' Shweta turned around abruptly and walked back inside.

Aakash tried his best to hold on to the lava that was stirring deep inside him. He was his wife's man, not his own. He knew that she could be nasty, that there was no telling what she would say next. He had learnt to handle her, put up with her tantrums, adapt to her temper, even to her abuses, her smoking, drinking, her taunts and comments, to be able to live together. That is, if this could even be called *living together.*

To change her mood, Aakash tried again. 'Once these elections are over, I want us to go on a holiday. We need some time to ourselves, away from all this. I think Italy would be the perfect getaway.'

Shweta flashed her large eyes in anger. 'Did you even ask me? How can you plan or cook something without even bothering to check with me? When will you grow up? How long will you remain as though you were still in college, you bloody good-for-nothing cook?'

The words stung Aakash physically. The lava inside rose to the head and flowed over. Aakash picked up a plate of pasta garnished with colourful vegetables, and flung it at the wall. The plate shattered; like frayed nerves, the pasta splattered on the wall before dripping on the artefacts below. Then he picked up a bowl of soup and smashed it to the ground. This was followed by a bowl of salad, more plates, wine glasses, wine bottles, photo frames…whatever was within reach.

'I'm just a good-for-nothing cook!' Aakash fumed.

Shweta tried to stop him but the lava was now flowing in full spate. Aakash pulled open the fridge door and reached for the exotic vegetables, milk cartons, sauces…everything inside, before trying to topple the fridge. But instead of crashing to the floor, it balanced precariously on its open door, holding on for dear life, as it were.

As Aakash turned upon the chairs and glass tabletops, Shweta, in her attempt to stop him, tried to push him back, scratch him and hit him, but to no avail. Aakash picked up a chair and smashed it on a glass table.

They hit each other violently. They knew that their failing

marriage had turned them into bloodhounds. They had given up everything dear to them for glory, for triumph over lowly creatures, for the adulation of people they didn't know and never would, who watched them on television day in and day out, and were in love with their images. Reduced to their digital selves, they had lost touch with each other. Whenever they tried to reach out to each other, at the slightest touch they exploded into a million pixels.

The penthouse of dreams had fast turned into a house of horrors.

'I'm just a maid. See what a maid does,' shouted a crazed Aakash.

Their lives rested on rusted hinges. Things could collapse anytime.

Shweta looked around despondently. The living room ressembled a battlefield—a grotesque collage of smashed crockery, scattered glass pieces, pasta and salad peeling off the walls, milk flowing from a tilted fridge, mixing with red wine while an array of sauces smeared crushed vegetables.

'This is what you are, a brute! You're an animal,' Shweta spoke coldly.

Surrounded by a trail of destruction, Aakash stood still, trying to control his rage. He knew nothing was left in their relationship. They had been married for over seven years now. Their conversations had become stilted, punctuated with long silences, senseless repetitions and inconsequential chit-chat. Even the lightest remark drew out their hidden rage towards each other. Both had turned into hollow companions. Still, they were living together, *trying to be together*. But how long could one love an empty shell?

Away from each other, they communicated through inane messages: 'So, going? Coming? Ok! Done! See you. Later.

Don't wait. Will be late. M out. GNite.' The very marriage that had brought them together had now turned into a prison.

Shweta picked up a bottle of wine that was still intact. Teetering in her high-heeled sandals over the glass pieces, she returned to the sundeck, taking long swigs from it. Aakash picked up a bottle of Scotch and drank from it.

The fancy Italian lights cast ghastly shadows everywhere. The sixty-fifth-floor penthouse towering over the rest of Mumbai had just been blown apart by the darkness festering within two people who were *once in love with each other*. The fantasy had crashed.

'I want a divorce,' Shweta mumbled matter-of-factly.

'I'm going to file for it first thing in the morning,' Aakash agreed.

Shweta took another swig. She looked at the war zone and said coldly, 'I want you out of this place. This is my place. I got it from my channel. Go and cook your food somewhere else. I have maids to do my work.'

Aakash glared at her with bloodshot eyes. The lava had settled somewhat. He nodded quietly and drank from the bottle.

The smartphone in his pocket beeped. He didn't want to be bothered with a message. Still, he took out the phone and read the message. 'Your life is about to change.'

'Is there anything left to change?' he slurred in his drunken stupor.

Shweta came in and sat on the sofa. She curled up her legs and continued to drink till the wine bottle was empty. Then she stretched out on the sofa and closed her eyes.

Aakash slumped to the floor with his back against the wall. He had already polished off half the bottle of Scotch, and was now fighting to keep his eyes open.

'I'm going to move out in the morning,' he thought aloud.

Through the years, they had made everything outside look perfect because nothing inside was.

They didn't realize that they were two different beings, with different outlooks on life. From the beginning, Aakash was soft-spoken, submissive and more of a people-pleaser, while Shweta was arrogant, egoistic and proud. As the years passed, these differences were magnified, the cracks widened, and love turned into bitterness.

Shweta never let up an opportunity to put Aakash down. She would publicly compare him to other men, and poke fun at him in front of her colleagues and friends. It was a hurt buried deep in Aakash's soul. A tiny scratch on the surface unleashed the hidden pain that turned into uncontrollable rage. Two successful professionals, two beings that were part of the upper crust of society, had turned into animals.

'What has come to an end must end,' Aakash thought bitterly as an alcohol-induced sleep overwhelmed him. At least while they slept, they could be humans again.

Aakash's phone beeped again. He fumbled for it. He tried to read the message but it appeared blurred. So he slipped back into his nightmares.

In the midst of the battlefield was a cryptic message, 'Welcome to the wild.'

3

Sunlight spread on land like oil slicks on water. As the sun rose higher, it reduced the colours of the land into a pale canvas of pastels. The dash of green merged into the vastness constituted by varying tones of yellow—camel with spots of brown. The sky too became colourless.

Soon the hot wind stretched its limbs. It geared up to blow over the land. Not a living being was in sight. A few insects crawled out of their hiding, leaving telltale marks on the ground. An eagle circled the sky, its eyes scanning the horizon. It spotted life near a keekar tree, with its small green leaves and long thorns. In fact, the tree had more thorns than leaves. Yet, goats and camels skilfully managed to eat the leaves. The eagle shrieked, gliding towards the tree. Two figures lay on the ground, close to the tree trunk. Nothing stirred. The wind let out a slow and dull howl. Then that died as well.

There was a slight movement near the two figures. The eagle swooped down with lightning speed and scooped up the lone rat with its claws, letting out a loud, victorious cry before flying off with its prey.

The two figures near the keekar's trunk woke up with a start. The sun shone right into their eyes as if someone had turned a spotlight on their faces. Their eyes narrowed. The ground beneath them felt warm, as did the rough tree trunk that supported their backs.

Slowly, they opened their eyes. The first thing Shweta and Aakash did was look at each other. Then they stared at the barren wilderness. They looked around; everywhere, it was the same barren wilderness.

They tried to move and realized they were chained to the tree.

For miles, they could see nothing but hillocks, ravines, dry grass, shrubs, a few small trees followed by another endless stretch of nothingness.

'What the hell is this?' Shweta shouted nervously.

Aakash noticed they were wearing the same clothes as the night before when they fought and drank themselves to sleep. They didn't have any footwear. And with each passing minute, the ground was getting hotter.

Both reached for their phones but couldn't find them. Their pockets were empty now. No phone, no credit cards, no cash, not even a single coin. Even the strawberry-flavoured lip balm Shweta usually carried was gone. Gone too were the expensive watches they had gifted each other on their last anniversary. The sunglasses perched on Shweta's head were missing. Shweta and Aakash were just two bodies and two souls shrouded in dusty clothes, both feeling as barren as the land they lay on.

Shweta tried to get up but was held back by the heavy chain. She cried out in frustration. 'I have to be there for my edit meeting.'

Aakash stared around blankly. Not a person in sight. After a while, he cried out, 'Help!'

The eagle returned stealthily.

4

In the vast emptiness, Aakash's cries for help echoed far and wide only to bounce back to him. The eagle circled the keekar and on seeing the two figures struggling to free themselves, smiled before taking flight back up in the sky.

The heavy steel chain wound around the tree trunk with a series of knots had handcuffs on each end that were fastened around Aakash and Shweta's wrists. As Shweta tried to free her hand, the handcuffs scraped it, leaving long red marks. Aakash braced his foot against the tree trunk in a bid to free his hand, but to no avail. Clearly, this was the work of an expert; there was no way out of here.

Shweta kept screaming for help, but her pleas fell on deaf ears. Aakash tried to uproot the tree to free themselves, but all their attempts failed. Within an hour, they were dead tired. The harsh sun seemed to focus all its attention on the two lone figures.

Shweta lay on the rough ground, her dress covered in dust. She shut her eyes, mumbling, 'This can't be real. I'm dreaming. Soon, I'll be back in the studio. I have to be there for the general elections. The winning party will announce the prime minister and cabinet ministers, and I have to be the first person to interview the next PM, exclusive.'

'I hope it's a dream,' Aakash said slumping down.

'Maybe I mixed too many drinks. I'll have to go for a full body bleach, hair treatment, and my lips are dry. Damn, where's my lip balm?' As though hallucinating, Shweta stretched out her hands, and rummaged through her dress. All she found was dust.

'This is the same lime-green linen shirt and the same jeans I was wearing at home. Even you have the same dress on,' Aakash said.

'Yes, it's a dream. Just close your eyes, and soon, we'll get up and this'll be over,' Shweta said, shutting her eyes tight.

Aakash looked around, his eyes wide open. There was an eerie silence. The entire landscape seemed to come charging at him. He had never seen such a place—barren land dotted with hillocks, dry grass, narrow alleys between hills, and the wind rushing through them like a hissing snake. He looked at the tree and realized it was a keekar. It didn't bear any fruit and could survive in harsh conditions.

He had read that this tree was found mainly in dry and arid regions. So they could be in Rajasthan, Gujarat, or some part of Haryana, Punjab, Uttar Pradesh, Madhya Pradesh, Maharashtra or even in one of the villages near the Indo-Pak border. In short, they could be anywhere or nowhere.

'You need to wake up,' Aakash said. 'Wake up! This is not a dream. This is a real tree with real thorns. This is a real chain, and this is a real place. We are real and we can feel the pain.'

Shweta kept her eyes shut. 'It will end. I know it will end. I'll be at my edit meeting soon.'

'Open your eyes,' Aakash shouted, irritated. 'Look around. Pinch yourself.'

'No, no, no... I'm not opening my eyes.'

Aakash turned towards her and slapped her across the face.

A stunned Shweta looked at him angrily. 'How dare you slap me, you bloody male chauvinist pig? You guys think you can do anything to a woman? I'm the editor-in-chief of News World and you dare slap me just because I'm your wife. I'm going to report this to the police. You're going to rot in jail, you bastard.'

They had tried hard to hold on to their marriage—endless counselling sessions; sex; more sex; exotic vacations; spa treatments; shopping sprees; parties; posting happy pictures on social media; reading all the books on marriage and relationship advice.... But to no avail. They wanted to hold on to each other. Yet, they had drifted apart. They tried their best to maintain the façade of a beautiful marriage, but that too was crumbling.

They forgot that chains do not hold a marriage together. Through the years, threads—hundreds of tiny threads—weave people together. Aakash spoke calmly, trying his best to hide the anger boiling within him, 'This is not a dream.'

The shock of the resounding slap shattered Shweta's reverie. She was frozen to the spot with her eyes scouring the place. Even the view of the horizon was blocked by hillocks. She tried to tug at the chain once again and felt the handcuff stinging her wrist. The more they tried to free themselves, the more fiercely the handcuffs tore into their skin.

'Who would do this to us? And why?' Aakash wondered.

'It's a reality show,' said Shweta. 'One of those reality shows on TV. The team from *The Gamechanger* had approached me to be on their show, but I refused. It has to be something like that. I'm sure they've planted cameras all around us, and people across the country are watching us.'

Aakash looked around thoughtfully.

Shweta yelled, 'Hey guys, enough of this. We know you're hiding behind these hillocks. Time to come out. I'm not playing these games. I want out.'

There was no answer.

'They can't kidnap us and tie us to a tree in the middle

of nowhere without our permission. No TV channel or show works like that,' Aakash observed.

Shweta turned to him. 'You don't know these reality shows. They'll do anything to get ratings. Now they have the country's top news anchor and her husband tied to a tree. The whole country must be glued to their screens.'

Aakash tried to spot hidden cameras or the crew tracking them. There was no sign of life anywhere.

Soon, Shweta was screaming hysterically at the supposed crew, 'I'm going to sue you all! I'll make sure your channel loses its license! Now get us out of this chain! I'm not taking this anymore!'

There was no response. Even the dry grass didn't move. The wind howled as if to shut her up.

Tears rolled down Shweta's cheeks. The sun was getting increasingly harsh. Their throats were parched and their skin had started itching. At uneven intervals, the wind rushed through the ravines, hissing and returning with loads of sand that it dumped on them. Their hair, their clothes and their insides were layered with sand. They had no idea where they were.

Finally, they slumped down, once again resting their backs against the keekar trunk. Their eyes were watering. It wasn't afternoon yet.

Shweta shut her eyes as tears trickled down her cheeks. 'I'm telling you it's a dream...'

Despite being chained to Shweta, Aakash felt alone, the way he always felt in their luxurious penthouse. When they started dating, Shweta worked as a production assistant in a TV production house in Delhi while Aakash was still looking for a job. Even then, Shweta would argue, fight, scream and call him names. At times, she would leave him stranded in the middle of nowhere and drive away. Aakash was convinced that it was her high-pressure job. So, he absorbed all the abuse, the gaslighting and the public humiliation, and blamed himself. His self-esteem hit rock bottom. He started to believe that he was truly good for nothing; the only motto in his life was to please his wife. Maybe in the process, he would earn a word of appreciation from her, but that never happened. Even after all these years, nothing changed. He failed to recognize that essentially people never changed.

Chained to the tree, Aakash knew deep down that he would be blamed for this as well. He still hoped that despite her abusive behaviour, someday she would listen to him, understand him. But at times, his hidden rage erupted like a volcano.

But the wild was ready to embrace them both.

5

Perhaps it was noon. The sun seemed to mock Aakash and Shweta. They didn't dare open their eyes again and see the wilderness. The hours dragged on like an injured cockroach across a slippery floor.

Moving in and out of sleep, at times they dozed off due to sheer exhaustion, and at others, they hallucinated—they were walking on water or sitting in their studios preparing for their shows. A few more hours went by till the sky started to turn grey and the sun transformed into a giant ball of fire. With only alcohol in their bodies and not a drop of water in sight, both of them were getting dehydrated. The temperature dropped slightly and the wind also stopped howling. It seemed to have had its share of fun and escaped through the ravines, turning gentler with every twist and turn.

Shweta felt something crawling up one of her legs. On seeing a scorpion trying to find its way into her dress, she cried out in terror, 'Aakash! Aakash! Look at that! I don't want to touch it! It could be venomous.'

'If you don't, it's sure to bite you,' Aakash snapped and flicked back the scorpion with his fingers as the steel chain jangled in the silence of the wild. The scorpion fell on the ground, turned to look at them for a moment, and scurried away.

'So this is for real,' Shweta said.

'No, we're dreaming. Why don't you let the scorpion bite you instead? Then maybe you'll feel the reality,' Aakash said, irritated.

Suddenly, Shweta noticed her bare fingers. 'Where the hell is my diamond ring? They took it away.' She started to shout, 'Thieves! Show your faces!'

The land was silent as ever. The sun ducked farther down behind the hills before disappearing from sight.

'Why would anyone do this to us?' Shweta cried.

'Must be one of those politicians you keep grilling on your show in the name of press freedom,' Aakash said sardonically. 'I had warned you so many times not to go after them.'

'You were always a coward. Only good at standing behind the kitchen counter baking cakes and pastries. I highlight issues that affect the common man, and in that fight, I won't be cowed by a politician.'

'When did you last travel in a local train, a public bus or even an autorickshaw? You sit in your studio and pretend to be an opinion-maker. Actually, you news anchors are no less than politicians. They do everything to garner votes while you do everything to garner ratings.'

'We don't stand in a kitchen making *paani puri* and coming up with new fish recipes. We bring change in society. We are the change-makers and that's the power of the free media!' Shweta shouted at him.

Aakash laughed out loud. 'This constant yelping about free press is nothing but a license to peddle scandal, crime, sex, sensationalism, hate and innuendos, backed by someone with deep pockets and a sinister agenda.'

'Don't you dare say anything about my work and the media! I know you well. You flirt with those girls on your show. It could be either a boyfriend, a father, or an uncle who has got us into this mess.'

'That's all you can do and have always done—blame me,' Aakash snapped back. 'It's all because of you that we're here.

A chef doesn't have such bitter enemies. But being married to you, I have also been thrown in this wild!'

'Then you should've walked away long back. Why did you stay on with me?' shouted Shweta. 'Bloody coward. You don't have the balls to do anything worthwhile. You're only good for cooking in your kitchen—your safe zone. You were always scared to go out there on your own. You wanted to piggyback on me and stay put in my penthouse.'

'I wanted to save our marriage!' Aakash snapped, boiling with rage.

'Our marriage has long been over. Now better focus on saving our lives,' Shweta said mockingly.

Their frustration and bitterness would soon reach boiling point. Luckily, they were not in the penthouse. They were chained to the keekar in the middle of the wilderness; this could stop them from clawing at each other.

As they looked around, the reality of their situation dawned on them. Fear filled their hearts. Fear is a potent weapon. When nothing works, fear does. Through the ages, battle-planners, kings, soldiers, teachers, bosses, parents and even loving partners have used fear to command respect. Something about fear, particularly, the fear of losing one's life, makes everyone fight to survive. Fear makes the world go round.

Fear calmed Aakash and Shweta's nerves. They watched the wilderness change colour to different hues of grey, much like an ocean at night. Silence descended on them from all sides like a ton of bricks.

Aakash looked at the chain and the lock on it. He tried again to free his hand only to end up with more gashes on his wrist.

Shweta, looking at the hill facing them, cried out excitedly. 'Look, someone's there!' She started to shout. 'Hey! Here, please help us! Hey!'

Two figures came down the hill towards them. Shweta was suddenly filled with hope. 'Please hurry, help us!'

As the figures drew closer, they looked like two boys dressed in tattered trousers and torn t-shirts. One seemed to be in his late teens, perhaps seventeen, while the other was much younger—around ten. The boys looked at Aakash and Shweta quizzically.

Shweta pleaded with them. 'Please help us! Please get us out of these chains.'

'Dimple, it seems they've been kidnapped,' the older boy said looking at them.

The younger one looked terrified. 'Babloo Bhaiyya, if it's kidnapping, we can't free them. It could be any of those gangs, and if they get to know we helped them escape, they'll kill us.'

Aakash tried to explain the situation. 'We have no idea who got us here. If you help us out of these chains, I'll give you money, lots of it.'

The two boys looked at each other. 'Dimple, if they don't know who kidnapped them, maybe we can take a chance. How much should we ask?'

'Hey!' Shweta called them out. 'I'm Shweta Chaudhary. You must've seen me on television. We're from Mumbai and yes, we'll give you lots of money. Please help us.'

Dimple grew excited. 'Mumbai? Babloo Bhaiyya, I've heard all film heroes and heroines live in Mumbai. They eat burger, pastry and drink only Kala Cola.'

Babloo looked excited. 'Didi-ji, I always wanted to be an actor in movies. You don't have to give us money, but please take me with you to Mumbai and make me an actor.'

Shweta said hastily, 'Yes, I'll do that. I know Shah Rukh, Salman, Hrithik and all. I'll introduce you to them all, and you'll be a superstar. Just help us out of these chains.'

'Babloo Bhaiyya, show them your Salman Khan style,' said Dimple.

Babloo launched his act—first Salman, then Shah Rukh, followed by Hrithik and Aamir. 'I'm very talented. Now everything depends on you making me a star.'

'Yes, we'll do that, but first you'll have to help us out of these chains,' Shweta cried.

'Arrey Babloo Bhaiyya, show them the dance that you did on Jahmru's wedding.' Clearly, Dimple was enjoying himself.

Initially, Babloo looked bashful but when Dimple sang in his childish voice, Babloo began to dance. He jumped, cartwheeled, rolled on the ground, twirled, following it up with a series of pelvic thrusts that culminated in an enticing snake dance. 'This is my original number,' Babloo said proudly.

'Really, you're so talented. You have all the qualities of a superstar. If you want to come to Mumbai with us, you'll have to free us first,' Aakash reminded the boys of their condition.

Dimple walked up to them and peered at the chain. 'This looks very strong. We'll have to go back to the village and get a saw to break it.'

'Bhaiyya-ji, by the time we go to the village and return with the saw, it'll be late in the night. By then, all those packs of dogs and wolves will be out,' Babloo said.

'What?' Shweta cried incredulously. 'Dogs and wolves come out in the dark here?'

'Yes, Didi. This is a dangerous place. Even big gangs don't come this side. God knows who kidnapped you and left you here. Maybe they're not looking for ransom but want you to be eaten alive by those dogs and wolves,' Babloo said.

'It's a sort of punishment in this region, but you're from Mumbai. Why would anyone want to do this to you?' Dimple said.

Aakash tried to get up. 'What the hell is this place? Where are we?'

The boys looked at each other. Then they burst out laughing. 'You don't even know where you are,' said Dimple.

'No idea. Someone kidnapped us from Mumbai, and when we woke up, we were chained to this tree.' Shweta looked around frantically.

'This is Chambal,' said Babloo gravely. 'You must've heard its name.'

'Chambal?' Aakash looked puzzled.

'The Chambal they show in movies? *Bandit Queen, Paan Singh Tomar*, and all?' Shweta asked nervously.

'Yes, this is the land of Phoolan, Paan Singh, Maadho Singh, Mohar Singh, Chhabiram, Malkhan Singh, Maan Singh, Nirbhay Singh Gujjar, and many other dacoits,' Babloo said proudly.

'How the hell did we end up in Chambal?' Shweta shouted.

'Did you ever do a report against any dacoit?' Aakash asked.

'I have nothing to do with dacoits.'

'Don't worry. I'll get you out of this chain,' said Babloo. 'Dimple, just place a hard rock under the chain so that I can see it.'

'Really, you're going to free us? Thanks!' Shweta cheered up.

Babloo took out a country-made pistol from his waistband. 'I'm going to shoot the chain and break it, just like in the movies. Dimple set the chain straight.'

Aakash and Shweta looked at the pistol, and trembled. 'Do you even know how to use the pistol?' Shweta asked.

Babloo smiled at them and pointed the pistol at the chain. 'This is Chambal. Here, boys learn to shoot instead of playing with marbles. Just turn away from each other so I can take aim.'

Wound around the tree and tied to their wrists, the chain

gleamed in the dark. Dimple placed a stone under it so that when the bullet was fired, it would break the chain instead of hitting the tree.

Babloo smiled at them. He spat on his hands, rubbed them together, held the pistol again, and took aim. 'I'm freeing you on one condition—you'll take me with you to Mumbai.'

Dimple said excitedly, '*Jai ho* Babloo Bhaiyya!'

The sound of the shot echoed through the wild, travelling through the hills, the narrow alleys, the ravines and the crevices, before returning to them with a resounding boom.

Aakash and Shweta opened their eyes to see the chain still intact. Pistol in hand, Babloo was lying flat on the ground with blood flowing from his head.

Dimple bent close to him and shook him, 'Babloo Bhaiyaa! Babloo Bhaiyaa!'

'What happened?' Shweta asked.

'The bullet must've hit the stone and ricocheted, hitting Babloo Bhaiyya in the head. He is dead,' Dimple said, with tears in his eyes.

'What the hell is going on?' Shweta cried. 'I can't be trapped like this in Chambal.'

The blood flowing from Babloo's head was absorbed by the sand. The land was thirsty for blood. Suddenly, Dimple got up, looking around with fear-filled eyes. It was dark. 'I'll have to leave. Soon, the dogs and wolves will smell the blood and they'll be here.'

'Please, you can't leave us here,' cried Shweta in despair.

Dimple looked at them. 'You better get out of this chain. I can hear the wolves and dogs. They are already on their way.' Then Dimple ran off with the country-made pistol.

Darkness descended on Chambal like a thick blanket. Aakash and Shweta couldn't make out anything. A few stars from a faraway galaxy shimmered in the sky. They waited helplessly as they tried to figure out how to free themselves from the chain.

Suddenly, the stillness of the wild was shattered by the howling of wolves and the barking of dogs. Chambal had come alive.

6

Blacker than black, the darkness enveloped them like an impregnable wall. Standing barely two feet apart, Aakash and Shweta couldn't see each other. They had never witnessed such darkness. Mumbai sparkled with millions of lights at any time of the night.

In Chambal, barring the stars a few light years away, the sky was absolutely dark. Aakash and Shweta felt as though they had been thrown into a deep, dark pit. The only relief was that the land had cooled down, the hot and howling wind had stopped blowing, and the dust seemed to settle down as if it also needed rest.

However, another kind of howling started; it could be the wolves or dogs. The sound seemed to be coming from all directions, like nature's own surround system, amplifying each sound to great effect.

Shweta Chaudhary, the hotshot news anchor known for her fearless journalism and blunt questions, shivered in the dark. On hearing the sounds of nature, Aakash, the celebrity chef, crouched like a foetus.

Somewhere in front of them lay Babloo's lifeless body. They couldn't see it in the dark but for the first time in their lives, they could smell death in the blood on the ground. It had drawn out all the four-legged creatures.

'We've got to get out of these chains,' Shweta shook her hands vigorously.

Aakash strained his eyes to see the stone under the chain.

He picked it up and started to hammer away at the chain. Soon, the stone was split into two.

Shweta started crying. 'I don't want to die like this. I don't want to be eaten alive by dogs and wolves.' The hard-nosed agnostic folded her hands and looking heavenwards, cried out in despair, 'God, please help us!'

The cool wind rushed to their ears as if to whisper, 'See, it was so easy, you just had to ask.'

Suddenly Aakash said excitedly. 'This is not a huge tree. The chain is wound around the trunk. Somehow, if we can uproot the tree, we can free ourselves. C'mon, we need to dig.'

Shweta looked at her slender fingers and manicured nails.

'Hurry up! Those beasts will be here soon,' Aakash said with a sense of urgency.

Mustering up all their strength, they started to dig under the tree with their fingers. Shweta quailed at the sight of her filthy hands, but the threat to their lives made her dig even harder.

They kept digging till they reached the roots. Aakash gently shook the tree, trying to uproot it. Finally, the keekar leant to one side before falling to the ground. Hurriedly, they unwound the chain from around the trunk. The cries of wolves and dogs drew nearer. Aakash and Shweta had no choice but to run blindly into the unfamiliar darkness of Chambal. The wind tickled them, nature laughed out loud, and the darkness carried them further into an even more expansive ocean of darkness.

∽

The sound of their own breathing pursued Aakash and Shweta like a wild animal. Still held together by the chain, they ran till they stumbled and fell. They went tumbling down a hill, over dried bushes, rocks, sand and thorny shrubs, till they finally stopped. They had reached somewhere; only it was nowhere.

Chambal is overrun with natural formations like hills with craters, or circular hole-like features, mud mounds as high as hills, and serpentine, narrow pathways. Night in Chambal filled each pore with darkness, heralding the time for wild animals to leave their lairs and for dacoits to emerge from their hideouts. Even the police never ventured here at night. There was a time when entire police teams were massacred in these ravines in the dark.

Aakash and Shweta couldn't see the bruises that covered their entire bodies, but the excruciating pain they felt at various places marked the injuries.

'Did someone really kidnap us? Or is it some sort of revenge?' Many such thoughts crossed Shweta's mind.

Meanwhile, a pack of wolves tore apart Babloo's body as the dogs stood at a distance, awaiting their turn. The first light of day would also bring vultures and eagles. Once they had their fill, it would be the rats' turn, and then worms would tear into the remains. Soon the wind would scatter the parched bones, and all would finally turn to dust.

Unable to figure out which direction to go, Shweta and Aakash lay on the ground staring at the night sky. The stars made faces at them. Aakash had his ear to the ground; he could hear the sounds—like those of a hundred horses galloping towards them. Prowling the place like the nocturnal guardians of Chambal, the wolves had sensed trespassers.

'Get up, we need to run,' Aakash shouted.

At first, Shweta didn't budge. She found comfort in the cold earth, and had shut her eyes. Only when the sounds of the sprinting wolves grew louder did they scramble to their feet.

Aakash and Shweta fled through the darkness, their bare feet bruised and battered. Thank God, the ground was cooler at night.

As they ran for their lives, something came alive. Other than their own breath, something within them reinforced their will to survive.

They had no idea how much distance they had covered, whether they were going around in circles or headed in any particular direction. Nothing seemed to matter so long as they were alive for the moment.

Suddenly, everything became still. The howling of wolves stopped. The only sound was that of crickets chirping. Like a giant serpent, the wild seemed to have swallowed up Aakash and Shweta. They ran in all directions, looking for an opening into the light. There was none. Aakash and Shweta got sucked deeper and deeper into the dark.

'I need to stop for a moment,' said Shweta, completely out of breath. Unable to see Aakash, she could only hear him breathing, and was assured that he was still there, tied to the chain.

Aakash tried to feel the ground with his bare feet. 'Could be flat ground. Let's sit here.'

'Don't worry, soon it'll be morning. We'll definitely find a way out of this,' Aakash tried to reassure Shweta.

They had nodded off for what seemed like an hour when Aakash heard the growling of wolves once again. He froze—many yellow and black eyes glared at them from a few feet away. He shook Shweta. As usual, she cursed, 'Let me sleep.'

Aakash pinched her hard till she got up crying, 'What the hell?'

'The wolves are here,' Aakash whispered.

Shweta saw their gleaming eyes drawing closer and closer.

'Run,' whispered Aakash.

As Aakash got up to run, Shweta tripped on the chain and fell face down on the ground.

The first wolf readied to spring on them. Suddenly, a lit wooden torch sliced through the dark and landed in front of the predators. It was followed by a heavy voice. 'Back off or I'll kill you all.'

Aakash and Shweta turned to see an old man walking through the darkness. Picking up the lit torch, he stood in front of the wolves. 'Back off!'

The wolves crouched down in fear, unable to meet his eyes. Suddenly, they turned and fled.

Dressed in a *dhoti* and ragged kurta, with a heavy turban wrapped over his head, the old man spoke softly. 'It's okay now. They won't trouble you. I'm Gadariya, the shepherd of Chambal. Please follow me.'

With a staff in one hand and the lit torch in the other, he guided them over the hill. A small bonfire burnt on the other side of the hill. Gadariya invited them to sit near the fire. Then he handed them a small clay pot filled with water. 'You must be thirsty.'

Snatching the pot, Shweta started drinking. They hadn't had a drop of water since they dozed off drunk in the penthouse. She drank her fill and washed the dust off her face and eyes. Suddenly, she realized that she had finished more than half the pot. She handed the pot to Aakash, who took long sips and poured some water over his head before handing the pot back to Gadariya. Both thanked him.

Gadariya was almost sixty years old, with deep-set lines crisscrossing his face. His eyes shone in a way that was possible only with years of experience of the wild. They seemed lost, yet focused.

She raised her arm to show the heavy steel chain that bound her and Aakash together. 'We are from Mumbai. Someone kidnapped us and tied us to a tree here in Chambal. We managed to uproot the tree and run, but we are lost. We have to get out of here.'

Gadariya nodded quietly. He walked to the edge of the hill, and stood there looking into the darkness. 'You better rest now,' he advised. 'Daylight will show you the way out of this.'

Exhausted, Aakash and Shweta lay on the ground close to the bonfire. Their stomach rumbled as they hadn't eaten anything for a while. Gadariya was still standing at the edge of the hill staring into the darkness. The wolves and dogs howled in the distance.

Suddenly Gadariya yelled in the dark, '*Chup!*'

The entirety of Chambal came to a standstill. The wolves and dogs stopped howling. Even the crickets stopped chirping. Darkness hung over the land like a thin veil ready to be pulled off. Lulled by the weight of their droopy eyelids, soon Aakash and Shweta drifted off to sleep under the night sky, with the stars watching over them.

Gadariya looked at them and whispered to the wind, 'Welcome to Chambal.'

7

Shweta came from a well-to-do family in Gurugram while Aakash, an orphan, was brought up in Amritsar by his maternal grandparents who ran a *dhaba* on the highway. Aakash had perfected the art of making *kulche*s but his *kachori*s were a hit with truck drivers. It was his father who had taught him the secret recipe of kachoris. Aakash's parents had migrated to London in the early '80s, but they were killed there in a race riot. The orphaned boy was sent back to his maternal grandparents in Amritsar.

While in college, to pay his fees Aakash worked at a small eatery in Kamla Nagar, making the same *kachori*s that soon became a hit with all college students. Even Shweta loved them and would get them packed by the dozen for her family. They spent some memorable time together in college.

Often, they would go to Nirula's and buy a tomato soup that they shared, and sit there for hours, talking and laughing. Later, when they ran out of things to talk about, it was difficult to imagine that once they had whiled away hours just talking and laughing. Even the Nirula's manager recognized them, and would enquire about them if they missed even a day at the outlet.

Aakash bought a cheap second-hand motorcycle, and Shweta and he would scrimp to fill petrol in the bike. Then they would ride aimlessly all over Delhi and Gurugram. Those were fun-filled times. Later, when they had the luxury cars and SUVs they once dreamt of, they hardly spoke to each other, let alone go out on romantic drives.

With their hearts brimming with love, they got married when they were hardly twenty-five. Looking back, they thought theirs was a child-marriage.

Shweta had rapidly climbed the ladder to the post of a senior journalist in a news channel, while Aakash worked his way through the kitchen of a five-star hotel in Delhi. Both worked long hours, and were determined to reach the top.

They lived in a rented flat like roommates meeting occasionally. That irked Aakash. He wanted to spend more time together and start a family. Shweta was totally against having a child.

'Look at the population in our country,' she would tell him. 'Why do you want to bring another person into this world?'

'We got married to have a family,' Aakash rebutted.

'The two of us are also a family,' she would counter. 'You have some old-fashioned ideas, and need to get a life, Aakash. Where are you in your career? You wanted to be a head chef but you are still chopping vegetables and cleaning utensils in the kitchen. I mean, who does that?'

With Shweta's constant barbs, he planned to leave the job and open his own restaurant. When Shweta heard his plans, she lost her temper and started calling him crazy and delusional.

'I thought we were both responsible for running this place,' reminded Shweta. 'Now you want to put the entire burden on me and resign from the job.'

'You told me it was a good-for-nothing job, so I planned to do something else,' Aakash explained.

'Then get a better job. I mean, a well-paying job where you're not washing utensils and chopping vegetables.'

Aakash sent out his résumé to other restaurants in the city in search of a high-profile job, but nothing came of it. The moment he would discuss this, Shweta would start calling him names. He kept taking it all without countering her.

When Shweta bagged the position of editor-in-chief, News World, she did think of freezing her eggs for the future. However, the very thought of carrying a child for months, motherhood, and losing out on precious time that would set her career back by years, made her decide against it. She didn't want to lose out while men enjoyed all the power, prestige and glory.

For Aakash, there was no other option but to give in, and focus on building his career. At least that way, their marriage would remain intact. He buried his pain deep inside; it turned into resentment, while Shweta's growing bitterness turned into deep contempt for him. With the social media boom, Aakash created his own YouTube channel and had a loyal following. Still, he was not considered among the top chefs of the country. Occasionally, a few local television channels invited him as a guest but that didn't catapult him into stardom. Meanwhile, much younger chefs were turning into wonderkids with their fusion of Indian and European dishes.

While Shweta became known across the country for her fiery debates and caustic remarks, and her show enjoyed the highest ratings, Aakash only managed to get an afternoon show on a lesser-known local TV channel that targeted housewives and senior citizens.

Often, they would sit down to talk. But soon, that would turn into a heated argument that would turn into a shouting match that would turn into a nasty fight. At times, they became violent, flinging things at each other, smashing plates, vases and lamps, or slashing paintings.

It was difficult to live together but they carried on like carrion.

∞

As light flooded the valley, Chambal woke up to its deathly glory.

Pain shot through Aakash's ribs before reaching the chest; his groin hurt badly as he ran out of breath. He screamed in his head, its sound echoing in his cranium and through the rest of his body. His wide-open eyes glared at the harsh sun shining right into his face. He heard muffled shouts. Then he heard a loud shriek and saw Shweta doubling up in pain.

A man dressed in a tattered police uniform and holding a rifle was kicking them and shouting something. He raised the rifle butt and hit Shweta in the abs, making her eyes bulge out in pain, before kicking her in her back and head. Regaining his breath, Aakash yelled at the man, 'Don't you touch her again, else I'll kill you.'

The man turned to Aakash, who was on his knees. He pointed his rifle at his face. 'You two killed Babloo, he was from my village. Now it's your turn to die.'

Aakash froze in the spot. Shweta looked around for Gadariya but he was nowhere to be seen. She mumbled, 'We didn't kill anyone. Someone kidnapped us and brought us here. We're from Mumbai and have nothing to do with anyone here.'

'Dimple told me everything,' shouted the man. 'Babloo and Dimple saw you tied to the tree and Babloo wanted to free you but accidentally took a bullet in the head. I couldn't even cremate him. He was devoured by wolves and dogs. Now you'll have to pay for it.' He cocked the rifle.

'Listen to us, please listen,' cried Aakash, seeing the rifle pointing between his eyes. 'We didn't kill him. He wanted to help us by shooting at the chain. Instead, the bullet ricocheted and hit him in the head.'

'Yes, it was a freak accident,' pleaded Shweta.

'Accident?' shouted the man pointing the rifle at her now. 'He was like my little brother.' Then he sat on his haunches, and holding the rifle, ranted, 'Babloo loved to watch films. So many times I took him to Gwalior. He wanted to become a film hero. My Babloo, little brother of Bhoora dacoit, was hit by his own bullet. This Chambal has cursed me.'

Aakash and Shweta looked at each other nervously. 'You are a dacoit?' Shweta asked.

'Dacoit?' Suddenly, Bhoora sprang to his feet. 'Have you never heard of Bhoora dacoit? The entire Madhya Pradesh police was after my gang. They bribed some of my gang members who betrayed me, and the whole gang was wiped out. I'm the only one left now, but soon I'll rule over Chambal.'

'Is there a city nearby?' Aakash asked, trying to hide his excitement.

Bhoora looked at both of them and then at the heavy chain that tied them together. 'Where do you think you are? The Chambal is spread across Uttar Pradesh, Madhya Pradesh and Rajasthan.'

'Please, you have to help us. We don't even know who got us here. Just get us out of here,' Shweta pleaded with him.

Bhoora nodded his head and said, 'Surely, someone with a personal grouse against you kidnapped you and left you in Chambal.'

Shweta yelled impatiently, 'I'm a journalist from Mumbai. You must have seen me on television. I have never met anyone from Chambal in my entire life.'

'Yes, I too am a chef and have a television show where I cook food,' Aakash added. 'Just help us get out of this place. We have to be back in Mumbai.'

Bhoora started to laugh. His rough, knotted hair flew about his face as he mocked them. 'Who would want to kidnap a cook and a reporter?'

'Well, all top politicians know me very well. If you have a cell phone, I can call the home minister. He'll send a whole army to rescue us,' Shweta spoke with pride in her voice.

Bhoora walked up to her. Bending close to her face, he laughed out loud, 'O Madam, there's no signal in Chambal. To make a call, we'll have to go to the nearest town.'

'Please take us there. We'll be grateful to you,' said Aakash with folded hands.

'In Chambal, there are no free lunches. Everything has a price. Since the time most gangs surrendered, were arrested or killed, dacoits here kidnap people for a ransom. In spite of there being no cell phones in Chambal, news spreads like wild fire. Soon, many gangs in Chambal will be fighting to capture you both for a fine ransom,' Bhoora told them.

'We're ready to pay you whatever you want. Just get us out of here,' Shweta mumbled.

'First thing, oye Madam, keep your voice low or I won't hesitate to shoot you. Here, the dacoits love TV people. Okay, let's talk money. How much are you willing to pay to get you out of here?'

'You'll have to get us out of here to the nearest town so that we can make a call to the police station. For that, we can pay you a lakh,' suggested Aakash.

Bhoora raised his rifle and pointed it at Aakash's head. Then he aimed it at Shweta's head. 'You don't seem to understand. It's not about getting out of Chambal but about getting out of here alive. It's about your life. You think one lakh is good enough to buy your life?'

'Okay, five lakhs,' Shweta interjected.

'I like it. You seem to understand,' said Bhoora. 'Dimple said that you had told the boys you knew all those film stars in Mumbai.'

'Yes, most of them come to my studio for interviews. We attend their parties, film premieres, launches, and I'm close to many of them. If you're interested in a film role, I can also get that for you,' Shweta tried to bait him.

Bhoora nodded, 'Dimple told me that they eat burger and drink Kala Cola in Mumbai. Is that true?'

'Mumbai is not a city on another planet. It's also part of this country,' Aakash said, irritated.

Bhoora smiled, 'Chambal is also a part of this country but just look around. Does it look anything close to Mumbai? Here, dogs and wolves fight among themselves just like the gangs. Everyone is ready to kill everyone else. There is no TV, no cell phone, no film stars. Some did come to shoot here and promised to improve our lives, but eventually left us high and dry.'

Aakash and Shweta were quiet.

'Do you have a house in Mumbai?' Bhoora asked them.

'Yes,' Shweta replied.

Bhoora asked, 'Are you both married?'

'Yes,' Aakash answered.

'Who could've kidnapped both of you and tied you with this chain in Chambal?' Bhoora mused.

'We have no idea,' Shweta said sharply.

Bhoora turned to Aakash, 'Tell your madam this is not Mumbai where men are used to women shouting. Next time she raises her voice at me, I'll shoot her. You seem to have given her too much of freedom. These women need to be kicked and kept in place. I won't hesitate to teach her some manners.'

He then turned to look at Shweta and checked her out from toe to head. Her short black dress was torn in many places. Suddenly, Shweta felt conscious of herself. Bit by bit, Bhoora's lusty, lecherous eyes were stripping her bare. In Mumbai, she had always flaunted her curves and flawless skin, but here in the wild, she wanted to hide herself.

'Do all women dress like this in Mumbai?' Bhoora asked laughing. 'I'll have to go to Mumbai. Come, follow me.'

Bhoora started to walk as Shweta and Aakash walked behind him.

'So where are we going right now?' Aakash asked.

'First, to my village Kutwar. It's close to Morena. You must've heard the name of Morena,' said Bhoora.

'I've heard lots of stories about Morena; it's featured in many Bollywood movies,' replied Shweta.

Bhoora smiled. 'It's just a small town.' He thought to himself, 'They have everything in the world. Yet they want to give me only five lakh. Bloody hell, they think the dacoits of Chambal are beggars or what. I won't let them off for anything less than a crore. Let them call the home minister and the army. This is Chambal; this is my land. Let them come!'

Legend has it that those who enter Chambal don't get out alive. Even dead bodies don't leave this land. The only thing that travels out is bad news.

8

One of the largest wastelands in India, Chambal has been a haven for dacoits for over a century. With its maze of hillocks, ravines, narrow alleys, and sparse vegetation, it was the perfect hideout for dacoits. Oftentimes, police teams chasing dacoits in these ravines lost their way. Most died of hunger while those who survived were captured and killed by the dacoits.

Till the 1980s, dacoits reigned supreme in Chambal. The last infamous dacoits of the wild were Phoolan Devi and Nirbhay Singh Gujjar. Most dacoits preferred to call themselves *baaghi*s or rebels as they belonged to lower castes and were forced to take up arms to fight caste oppression and the feudal system that had prevailed in the region for centuries.

The current gangs operating in Chambal were largely petty criminals, with a handful of dacoits who were still revered in this region. In the 1970s, dacoits considered themselves Robin Hood-like figures who robbed from the oppressors and distributed the bounty among the oppressed. Even police officers of that time would reminisce with pride the time they stood face-to-face with the likes of Daku Maan Singh, Chhabiram, Madho Singh, Mohar Singh, or even Phoolan Devi.

In the wild, Shweta and Aakash walked behind Bhoora. Like a police officer leading criminals, Bhoora wasn't bothered that they would run away. He knew there was no place to run to. He was their guide, their saviour. All around them was hostile land.

'How far is your village?' Shweta asked, walking barefoot. The dirt road was getting hotter.

'It's close by,' Bhoora said without turning.

'We've been walking for over two hours and you've been saying it's close by. How much more do we have to walk?' Aakash cried, fatigue weighing down his body.

Bhoora marched on with the rifle on his shoulder. 'Well, you don't want to walk, you can stop here. I need to reach my village.'

Aakash and Shweta tried to keep pace with him. The chain between them kept jangling. They had not eaten a morsel since they were chained to the keekar. The sun, the sand, running through the ravines, and now this long walk had drained them of their energy.

'Can we get something to eat?' Shweta asked feebly.

Bhoora turned to look at her and smiled, displaying his crooked tobacco-stained teeth. 'You want to eat, then keep walking.'

Both Aakash and Shweta looked at him dumbfounded. Bhoora laughed. 'There's nothing here. That's why we have to reach the village.' He kept walking ahead and said, 'You know, there were times when police teams got lost in these ravines. Many of them died as they started to eat mud out of hunger. Only a dacoit can survive in Chambal.'

Aakash and Shweta had no idea how they were still walking across the wild. Their feet felt numb with pain; their heads were no longer working. They seemed to be on autopilot.

Life in Mumbai, and their sixty-fifth-floor penthouse in Ambar Apartments, had alienated them not only from the rest of the world but also from themselves.

Chained as they were, each time Shweta stopped for a breather, Aakash had to stop too. Bhoora kept walking ahead briskly. Often, Aakash and Shweta had to break into a run to keep pace with him. The sun shone relentlessly over their heads, while the sand heated up mercilessly under their feet. Even keeping their feet on the ground was becoming impossible; they were forced to hop. Bhoora wore tattered brown canvas shoes. His khaki police shirt with a burnt-out hole had a big bloodstain at the back.

'How come you have blood on your shirt?' Aakash asked, trying to slow him down.

Without stopping, Bhoora replied, 'I killed a police constable who was chasing me in Etawah. I hid behind a truck and shot him in the back. This uniform, these shoes and this rifle—all belong to him. I just took them.' He laughed. 'Now I'm the police.'

'You killed a policeman?' Shweta said, looking stunned.

'So what do you think we dacoits do here? We kidnap and murder. It's the business of Chambal just like you do yours,' Bhoora said nonchalantly.

'You are wearing the policeman's shirt with his blood on it?' Aakash asked, horrified.

'In Chambal, we call them medals. The moment someone spots you in this uniform with a bullet hole, they know you've killed a policeman. They fear and respect you all the more for it. I just have to get together a few more youngsters and form my own gang. Maybe with your money, I'll reign over Chambal once again,' Bhoora said loftily.

To prevent her feet from getting burnt, Shweta tried to take longer strides. Instead, she tripped and fell down.

'What the hell are you doing, Aakash? You can't even walk properly or what?' She yelled.

'You can't blame me for everything,' Aakash said.

'I told you that we'd move in a rhythm so that we don't pull each other down. You never bothered. In fact, you've never bothered.'

Bhoora stopped to watch the husband-wife spat.

Aakash extended his hand to Shweta. 'C'mon, get up. We have to reach the village.'

'I don't need your hand or help. I've never needed you in my life. God, why did I even get married to you? Bloody useless, good-for-nothing man. You're better off cooking in the kitchen,' Shweta spat fire. 'Now don't keep standing on my head.' She struggled to her feet and pushed him away. 'Now better walk in step. Don't break the rhythm.'

Aakash nodded quietly. Even in the wild, with a dacoit watching them, Aakash felt embarrassed as if the eyes of a hundred men and women were on them. He looked crestfallen. This was not the first time. They had got into arguments and quarrelled at all kinds of public places—restaurants, weddings, movie theatres, gyms, swimming pools, and even on vacations at the most exotic places. There was something wrong with them.

Looking at Aakash, Bhoora shook his head. 'If my wife had behaved like that with me, I would've shot her and buried her right here. You're not a man. If you want, I can help you. This is your chance to get rid of her.'

'What the hell are you saying?' Aakash shouted.

'See, no one knows that both of you are in Chambal. If you really want a happy life, finish her off. You can also give me the money and go back to Mumbai and have a great life. Or else, this woman is going to make life hell for you,' Bhoora said with the cold-heartedness of a seasoned killer.

'Enough! She is my wife, and I'm not a killer like you. Let's go. We have to reach the village,' Aakash fumbled for words.

'Think about it. I'm ready to help you. It takes just one bullet in the head for a quick kill. I'll somehow manage to get you out of the chain. We can bury her here. No one will ever get to know. It's a superb idea for a stress-free and happy life.'

'Keep quiet, please,' Aakash entreated him. 'If you want your money, just take us to the village.'

Bhoora smirked. 'Nowadays, no one values a good piece of advice. They prefer to be humiliated by a woman.' He raised his voice. 'Arrey, you don't know these women, they have destroyed civilizations. The Mahabharata and the Ramayana all happened because of women. They use their bodies to entice us hook, line and sinker. Then they turn us inside out. We also need to use their bodies and discard them. That's my policy in life and I'm happy. I'm not bound to anyone, especially not to a wife. Have you ever seen animals doing all this? They keep moving from one female to another.'

'I'm not an animal,' said Aakash.

Bhoora turned and started to walk again. 'You said Madam has connections right up to the home minister? Is it true?' He asked mockingly.

'Yes,' Shweta shot back. 'By now, the entire Mumbai Police, and politicians across party lines must be on the alert. They might have put the entire paramilitary on the job to find me.'

'Do they know where you are?' Bhoora asked.

Shweta became quiet.

Bhoora laughed. 'If they don't even know your whereabouts, how will they search for you? Yes, they'll be busy searching for you in Mumbai. I've heard that the number of murders, robberies, kidnappings and rapes in Mumbai are far higher than in Chambal. Maybe, after a few days, the police will show a decomposed body with your handkerchief thrown in to say they've found your body.'

'They can't fake my death. I'm a famous journalist and news anchor,' said Shweta.

'That's what the police usually does. They can sense when a missing person will never return. For a high-profile person like you, they have to show results. So a decomposed body would work marvels. They've also done that for many dangerous dacoits whom they could never capture,' Bhoora said.

Fear gripped Shweta. Like a millipede, it crawled from her head to her guts. 'Let's not speculate. Soon, I'll be in Mumbai to clear everything. Let's please hurry up.'

This is exactly what she did on her TV show, in *News Line*—speculate. Even when there was no issue, she created one, adding drama to it. She had invented the novel concept of a news show on which everyone shouted at each other exactly the way a husband and wife quarrelled at home. And the viewers and the audience lapped it all up. Only now, it was being staged between politicians, police officers, sportspersons, senior journalists, activists and more. She had successfully turned every living room into a battleground.

For a fleeting moment, Aakash and Shweta forgot their hunger. They just wanted to reach the village and somehow bribe Bhoora to help them get back to Mumbai. Fear kept them moving.

They must have walked for another three hours when suddenly, Bhoora pulled out his rifle and pointing it at one of the hillocks, shouted, 'Who's there? This is Bhoora dacoit. Come out or I'll shoot.'

Covered in dust, Aakash and Shweta looked at the hillocks and mud mounds. There was no sound. 'Who's there?' Aakash asked.

'Ssssh!' Bhoora gestured to him to be quiet. With his rifle pointed to the sky, he moved stealthily, peering at the hilltops. Then he said softly, 'Seems like other gangs have come to know about you two. They might attack us to get you both.'

'Why? What have we done?' Shweta asked, puzzled.

Bhoora smiled at her. 'You are the ones kidnapped from

Mumbai. That means big money for all the gangs. They'll be ready to give an arm and a leg to get their hands on you. Even one of you is good-enough booty for a gang.'

Aakash and Shweta looked at each other nervously.

'Don't worry. No one can take you away from Bhoora,' he looked up and fired a shot, yelling, 'Run.'

They ran through the ravines of Chambal with death closing in on them from all sides. Unable to keep pace with Aakash, Shweta kept falling. Finally, Aakash grabbed her by the hand and both ran for their lives, hand in hand.

9

The shot echoed across the ravines, drowning their loud screams. Bhoora laughed, following it up with a victory dance. 'Got him,' Bhoora cried triumphantly.

Aakash and Shweta saw a figure somersaulting downhill. Then it slid over the slope and fell nearly twenty feet, hitting the ground with a loud thud.

The sight of the battered figure brought the ravines to a standstill. For a moment, even the howling wind seemed to stop and take a look before sprinting through the ravines to announce the event to the entire valley. Aakash and Shweta stood shell-shocked. The pool of blood that had engulfed the body was soon soaked up by the thirsty land.

The boy with his face down was wearing dirty shorts, a shirt and rubber *chappals*. Bhoora walked up to him and with one leg, flipped him on his back. The boy hardly looked ten. Blood oozed out of the hole the bullet had made right above his stomach. The boy opened his eyes and looked at Bhoora. He tried to say something but it sounded garbled.

Aakash and Shweta rushed to the little boy. Aakash tried to remove his shirt but it got stuck on the handcuffs. Somehow, he tore off the shirt sleeve and pressed it on the boy's wound. In a matter of seconds, the shirt was soaked in blood.

'We need to get him to a hospital,' Aakash yelled at Bhoora.

'In a few more minutes, he'll be dead. Let's wait till he dies,' Bhoora said coldly, bending down to check the boy.

Shweta was furious. 'You couldn't differentiate between a

little boy and a dacoit. You shot at him without warning.'

'O Madam! What if it was really a dacoit? Had I taken my time, he would've shot all of us. In Chambal, you can't take chances,' Bhoora said without an iota of guilt.

Raising his hand slowly, the boy pointed to the hilltop. On it stood a goat. It looked down at the boy and bleated, as if crying for him. The boy had tears in his eyes.

'Damn! He had come here looking for his goat that must have lost its way,' Bhoora said. He gently slapped the boy's cheek. 'What's your name? Who's your father?'

The boy's hand slumped to the ground. Soon he turned cold. He was dead.

Aakash couldn't fight back his tears. Shweta placed her hand on his shoulder trying to calm him down.

Bhoora got up, looked around and said, 'The boy could be a Yadav. If they get to know about this, they'll attack our village.'

'What do you want to do?' Shweta asked.

'We'll have to bury him right here so no one finds his body. That way, we'll all be safe,' Bhoora said.

'This is crazy,' shouted Aakash. 'At least we should hand over the body to his family.'

Bhoora shook his head in disagreement. 'This is not Mumbai where a body needs to be properly cremated. A dead person in Chambal is a dead person. The moment the family sees his body, the first thing they'll do is shoot you dead. Now get to work. We need to dig a grave for him.'

He started to dig with his bare hands. 'What the fuck are you two doing just standing there? I need your help here,' Bhoora said, chiding them.

Aakash and Shweta walked up to him. Slowly, Aakash bent down and reluctantly started to dig with his sore fingers that had lost all skin.

Bhoora got up, muttering impatiently, 'This way, we won't finish before night. You'd better put some energy into the digging while I get the boy here.' Saying that, Bhoora walked away.

Aakash and Shweta started to make a pit in the ground. With broken nails and bruised fingers, digging was torure for Shweta.

If only someone had shown her a mirror, Shweta would've cried out in horror. Her straight black hair was knotted and caked with mud, the eyes were puffy and nose looked swollen. Tear lines crisscrossed her cheeks. The perfect woman with a perfect life looked very different now.

Like a captured animal, Aakash looked fear-stricken. None of the housewives who sat through the afternoons watching him cook, who shared his recipes, and adored his soft voice, his smile, his gentleness, had ever seen the brute in him—the brute that surfaced during many of the gladiatorial fights between Shweta and him. Now in the wild, even the brute seemed to have lost his spirit. Like a broken horse, he stood meekly, ready to be flogged.

It was late afternoon. The sun was beating down on Aakash's bare back. Shweta and he dug the grave slowly and painfully. Their bodies broke out in sweat. Even the wind had abandoned them. They had turned into grave diggers—the scum of the earth. After a long time, they were neither shouting at or abusing each other, nor were they smashing things.

Dragging the body of the boy to the grave, Bhoora shouted, 'You can't even dig a bloody hole in the ground. Make it deeper, else the boy won't fit in.'

'You killed an innocent boy.' A devastated Aakash pounced on Bhoora.

Almost on cue, Bhoora hit him in the chin with the rifle butt. Aakash spun and fell on the ground.

'I might shoot you both and bury you along with the kid. If you want to get back to your lives in Mumbai, don't try to be a hero. It's usually the heroes who die,' Bhoora said menacingly.

Bhoora dragged the lifeless boy by his legs to the pit. He took off his blood-soaked shirt and flung it at Aakash. 'You better wear this,' he barked, before kicking the boy into his muddy grave.

Aakash looked at the shirt and recoiled in horror. 'I can't wear it.'

'Do you see the harsh sun right over us? By the time we reach the village, your whole body will be blistered and burnt,' Bhoora said angrily.

Reluctantly, Aakash put on the shirt. He ran his hand over the bloodstains, and looked at the boy lying in the pit peacefully.

He closed his eyes. It seemed as though the very core of his soul that held everything together, and gave his life some semblance of purpose and meaning, had been wrenched out. For a moment, his world collapsed in a meaningless heap.

Bhoora chucked the boy's slippers towards Shweta. 'See if these fit you?'

Shweta gave him an angry look and said flatly, 'I'm *not* wearing the boy's slippers.'

Bhoora laughed at her sense of outrage, and chucked the slippers into the pit. 'Okay then, fill it up.' With that, he started kicking in mud over the lifeless boy.

Out of respect for the dead, Aakash and Shweta started filling the pit from his legs up. Bit by bit, the boy soon disappeared into the earth.

Bhoora said while chewing on his tobacco, 'Madam-ji, if you are a TV reporter, you must've seen a lot of deaths.'

'I've never seen a little boy shot to death in front of my eyes,' said Shweta, aggrieved.

'It happens. Just try to forget it and don't mention it to anyone in the village, or we'll be in trouble. I am here to help you. Focus only on that.' Bhoora drove home the point.

'You want money, nothing else. Right?' Aakash asked.

'So you want everything for free?' Bhoora retorted. 'Look, I'm trying to help you, or you'll never get out of Chambal. Soon, other gangs will sniff you out. Once you're in the clutches of a big gang, no one will be able to help you.'

Aakash and Shweta stood close to the boy's grave while Bhoora resumed his brisk walk as though nothing had happened. They had to run to catch up with him.

'How far is your village now?' asked a breathless Aakash.

'Close by.'

Shweta wanted to curse out loud, but somehow managed to swallow her anger and kept walking.

Aakash and Shweta looked like slaves—chained together, with gashes on their wrist and bruises all over their bodies—to be sold at the marketplace to the highest bidder. The death of the little boy had crushed their spirit, and depleted whatever little courage they had. Captured and led by a dacoit through the wild, they walked helplessly, their heads hanging in shame.

No longer did they ask 'how far?'. For them, the very act of walking was an act of hope—they were moving towards a destination, the Promised Land that would help them out of their captivity and lead them back to their routine lives. Routine was bliss.

In Chambal, death stalked them at every step. They yearned to get out of the wild, but the wild seemed to have different plans for them.

Suddenly, Shweta raised her head and cried out, 'Gadariya.' Aakash also spotted the old man who had saved them from the wolves last night. Standing on top of a small mud mound, he was looking at them. Shweta raised her hands to draw his attention, 'Gadariya!'

'Shut up!' shouted Bhoora. 'That Gadariya is a lunatic. He

roams the entire Chambal. Don't get taken in by his stories.'

'He helped us last night and gave us water,' Aakash spoke up in Gadariya's defence.

Bhoora guffawed loudly. 'That Gadariya? The madman of Chambal? Almost forty years back, dacoits kidnapped his wife. Ever since, he's been looking for her across the Chambal Valley.'

'Forty years? Would she still be alive?' Shweta asked.

'Even the most daring dacoits don't live to be forty in Chambal. She must've been raped, killed and buried,' Bhoora said nonchalantly.

Aakash and Shweta looked at Gadariya who walked over the dry mud mounds towards them. 'Why would he still look for her after forty years?'

'Love—he was and still is madly in love with her. Only death will give him peace,' Bhoora said.

Aakash and Shweta looked at each other. They were two strangers thrown into a situation. They shared the same house but could never share their lives.

'How can anyone love one person throughout their life? A man should know how to handle his emotions, or he is likely to lose his head, like Gadariya,' Bhoora smirked.

Almost simultaneously, Aakash and Shweta looked up, but Gadariya had vanished as suddenly as he had appeared. It was as if they were hallucinating. They stood in a void, with nothing around them. They felt hollow inside, but then, life in Mumbai beckoned to them.

Without food or water, they dragged around their depleted bodies. They followed a dacoit who had killed an innocent boy, a dacoit who was now their saviour. They had no idea whether he was leading them out of Chambal or further in; they had no choice but to follow him.

Bhoora had a wicked smile on his face as he licked his chapped lips.

10

Their feet were covered with blisters and sores. Somehow, they kept walking over the dry, hard and cracked land. Walking on treadmills in air-conditioned gyms, wearing hi-tech running shoes, and watching videos on the screen in front of them, Aakash and Shweta were always short of time, like most people in big cities. Everyone was busy being busy.

By the time they reached the village, it was dusk. A dull greyness had enveloped the place. The land hadn't yet cooled down. Aakash and Shweta could see small mud houses, and a bunch of noisy kids running around. In the distance were a few brick houses.

As Bhoora led them into the village, the group of village kids gathered around them. Most were less than ten years old. All of them carried country-made pistols and fired in the air—a celebratory salute to Bhoora who had brought glory to their village, as he was one of the few dacoits who had survived more than two and a half decades in Chambal, being part of many gangs.

The kids noticed the steel chain that bound Aakash and Shweta together. In hushed whispers, they talked among themselves. 'Seems like a big party?' 'Why is she dressed in undergarments?' 'Look at all the blood on his shirt. Bhoora must have beaten him to pulp.' 'How much will he get for these two?' 'Bhoora won't demand less than five lakh.'

Suddenly, a little boy came running out of the crowd towards Aakash and Shweta. 'Didi, it's me, Dimple! You remember, I met you with Babloo?' He smiled at them. 'This is our village. Now you are in safe hands. There won't be any problems. I'll take care of you.'

'*Ae mauda,* just get out of here,' Bhoora shooed away the kids. 'Dimple, you take them to the house and give them some water. I need to check up on a few things.' Bhoora turned to Aakash and Shweta. 'This is Kutwar, my village. You take rest now and tomorrow morning, we'll go to Morena. You hand over the money to me and I'll get you out of this place.'

Aakash looked at him and said, 'We haven't eaten anything.'

Bhoora merely laughed. 'Dimple, get them something to eat.' With that he walked off, adjusting the rifle on his shoulder while proudly displaying the big bloodstain on the back of his shirt.

Clad in a cheap printed terrycot shirt with buttons ripped off, dark-blue shorts suspended from his thin waist, and rubber slippers, Dimple led them to a mud house. With tanned skin, large expressive eyes and teeth too big for his small mouth, Dimple's smile was still innocent—the kind only a kid his age could possibly have.

He made Aakash and Shweta sit on a charpoy outside and stood before them. The simple act of sitting down gave them some much-needed relief. Even soaking in the sauna after forty minutes of cardio didn't give them this much joy.

Dimple handed them a *surahi*. 'Here, have some water.'

Shweta drank directly from the surahi. The cool and refreshing water splashed all over her face, spilling into her nostrils. She splashed water on her face and poured some on her feet. A gleam returned to her eyes as she handed the surahi to Aakash. He also drank greedily and poured some cool water over his head, face and feet. The water tasted like the nectar of Gods. They could have given anything for it.

'You rest here while I get you some food,' Dimple said.

Aakash and Shweta lay down on the charpoy staring at the canopy of stars before closing their eyes. The cool breeze caressed their weary bodies like jets of water in a Jacuzzi. Even before their calculating heads could plan and strategize, sleep overcame them. And they slept on the same charpoy without a mattress, bedsheet or even a pillow.

Unbeknownst to them, they slept in the most ancient place in Chambal—the Kutwar village of Morena, a place associated with Kunti, mother of the Pandavas. Some 3,000 years ago, the 'Nag' kings had established their capital here. In the Mahabharata, this place was mentioned as the kingdom of Kuntibhoj, Kunti's father.

Shweta and Aakash were delirious; they constantly flitted in and out of dreams. Shweta cried in her sleep; tears streaked her face. She realized no one would even know where they had disappeared or where their bodies lay. She saw herself trying to call up all her contacts, but her phone seemed out of the network coverage area. Then she turned into a little girl playing with her father and her mother, calling out to them. She dreamt of her family, her home. Suddenly, she was pulled away from all of them, and flung into a deep dark hole. As she hurtled down, she screamed for help.

Aakash saw his father smiling at him as he drummed up heavenly dishes, and talked about the aroma, the spices, the perfect ingredients and the colours of the vegetables. He saw himself holding on to his father's finger while crossing the road. Then suddenly everything was engulfed in flames.

Both Shweta and Aakash sobbed in their dreams as memories escaped from the deepest recesses of their minds. They popped out like bubbles, gambolled over their heads, then burst and vanished.

They got up startled. As they opened their eyes, they found

themselves entwined in each other's arms, their faces covered with dark, sooty streaks of tears. They tore away from each other and turned to find that a large group of villagers had gathered around them. They had been watching the couple and giggling.

Still tied with the chain, Aakash and Shweta sat straight with their backs to each other. Dimple cut through the crowd with two steel plates. 'I've got food for you.'

Aakash and Shweta looked at the plate—two thick chapatis, a bunch of green chillies, and a piece of jaggery.

'How am I supposed to eat these?' Shweta looked puzzled.

'Take a mouthful of chapati, and bite into the chilli. If the chilli is too hot, there's jaggery. Get going or these kids might just snatch the food. My mother has made it especially for you,' Dimple said with the love and concern of a person who understood the value of a square meal.

The kids flocked around them as if Aakash and Shweta had snatched away their share of the meal.

Aakash started to eat the thick chapati and took a bite of the jaggery. Seeing him, Shweta started to eat as well. Soon she was eating the chapatis, green chillis and jaggery ravenously.

'This is really good, Dimple. Please thank your mother for us,' Aakash said chewing on the chapati.

'Arrey, you should taste the daal and *choorma* that she makes on festivals,' Dimple said with a smile.

Shweta looked at him and asked, 'Who named you "Dimple"?'

'My father. He was a constable in the police and loved Hindi movies. His favourite heroine was Dimple Kapadia, so he wanted to name his very first child Dimple. That's how I got the name.'

Aakash and Shweta smiled at him. 'How many brothers and sisters do you have?' Aakash asked.

'We were four brothers and two sisters, but now, I'm the only one left. They all died due to some illness or the other,' Dimple said as a matter of fact.

'Oh! What about your father?' Shweta asked, biting into a green chilli. It burnt her tongue but she loved it—the chilli made her feel alive. She followed it up with a piece of jaggery. The dryness of the chapati, the pungency of the chilli and the sweetness of the jaggery kickstarted something in them—perhaps life itself.

Dimple looked at them balefully and said, 'He was killed by dacoits.'

Aakash and Shweta looked at the boy, stunned. 'So now it's only you and your mother. Do you have land here in the village?' Aakash asked the boy.

'We have nothing. All our land was confiscated by the Gujjar family from whom my mother had taken a loan. Now she has to go to their house every night to work. I don't understand why she has to work at night. At times, Bhoora also visits her at night. Then they throw me out of the house.'

For a moment, Aakash and Shweta stopped eating. They didn't know what to say to Dimple. They weren't parents. In fact, they had decided never to have children as both wanted to focus on their careers and make a mark in the world. They wanted to be stars that shone so bright that they could be recognized by the teemimg millions. But they never realized that light from such stars never reached anyone, and like useless bulbs, they just dangled from the sky, looking down on everyone.

'I just want to grow up fast and be a police officer. Then I'll take my mother away from here,' said Dimple, his eyes filled with sorrow, yet gleaming with hope.

Indebted to the boy for the food and water, Aakash and Shweta felt utterly helpless. They nodded their heads silently like people in cities often do when they have nothing to say.

After wolfing down the chapatis, Aakash polished off the last bit of green chilli and licked clean the remnants of the jaggery that were still stuck to the plate. For a moment, both forgot they were tied with a chain and at the mercy of a cold-blooded dacoit from Chambal.

Suddenly, the sound of a *damru* filled the night air. Like the slow, steady and sharp beat of the wild, it echoed through the village. The kids who were smiling till now looked frightened. The sound of the damru drew closer. Then someone called out, '*Jai ho Chambal Maiyya ki!*'

The kids ran helter-skelter, screaming, 'He's coming! He's coming!'

As if appearing out of nowhere, he walked towards them holding the damru in one hand. The kids disappeared and the shepherd of Chambal came face to face with Aakash and Shweta.

11

A sudden hush descended on the village as if everyone had seen a ghost. In his flight to safety, Dimple dropped the surahi that shattered into pieces. The spilt water was leeched up by the dry earth as if it were sucking on blood. The wind was cool as it rustled against their ears, trying to whisper something. The stars above stared at them, twinkling like peeping toms.

Piercing the wall of darkness, Gadariya appeared with a staff in one hand. Barefoot, he quietly walked up to Aakash and Shweta. He sat down on one end of the charpoy.

'We saw you walking close to us,' Shweta blurted out.

Gadariya didn't react. He looked at them with eyes that could bore into their soul, wring it, shake it, and examine it. Dressed in the same turban, dhoti and tattered kurta, his face, body and feet showed no signs of fatigue. His hands looked strong, and he had long, slender fingers like those of an artist. With deep lines, his face seemed to be frozen in time, while the crow's feet around his eyes lent him the air of a jungle warrior.

He looked at the blood-soaked shirt Aakash was wearing. 'So you buried the little boy and the child's blood is all over you.'

Aakash, who had forgotten about the blood on his shirt, looked at it and said, 'That Bhoora killed the little boy. We had no choice but to help him bury him.'

Slowly, Gadariya resumed playing the damru. The sharp sounds emanating from it echoed in the silence. He kept looking at them and then suddenly stopped as though summoning the haunting silence to take over again.

'Did you have a choice? Could you have saved the boy? You choose to wear the shirt with the boy's blood on it. It's like the boy chose you in his death to share his blood. Now you are responsible for him,' Gadariya said.

'He's dead,' Aakash said, puzzled.

'But you carry his blood all over you. Someday, you'll have to clean this blood with blood,' Gadariya said cryptically.

'We aren't responsible for anything. You saved us last night from the wolves, but why did you leave us sleeping there? Now this dacoit Bhoora is demanding money to get us out of this place,' Shweta spoke up.

Gadariya looked at her with his deep, dark and shiny eyes. 'I didn't do anything. Things happen. The wind came and whispered in my ear to follow it.'

On the verge of losing his temper, Aakash spat, 'Maybe they are right. You really are a lunatic, the madman of Chambal.'

Gadariya had a gentle smile on his face. 'Yes, maybe they're right because I hear things they can't hear, I see things they can't see, I talk to the wind and the sand, I whisper to the ants, I dance with the darkness and this Chambal is my closest friend.'

Aakash looked at him, trying to control his anger. 'You say that this Chambal is your friend, then get us out of here. I don't trust this Bhoora. If you want money, we're ready to pay you.'

Gadariya laughed. 'I'm Gadariya, the shepherd of Chambal. I don't have any need for money but I'll show you the way.'

'Then just show us the way,' Aakash said, exasperated.

'Pray.'

'Pray?' Aakash was losing his patience. 'You want us to pray and wait for some miracle to happen and get us out of this situation? You're really fucked in the head.'

'We don't need prayers. We can pay our way out,' Shweta said.

'Bhoora told us all about you. You've been searching for your kidnapped wife for last forty years. Did you find her? Did your prayers help? Did God come down and point you in her direction? No. You've been wandering in this wild for the last forty–fifty years. What did you get? You got old and soon you'll die. That's the end of it,' Aakash said in a single breath.

'Everything comes on time to those who know how to wait,' Gadariya said, looking into the darkness.

Aakash almost burst out laughing. 'You've wasted your life waiting—giving it all your time and patience. Your wife must be dead and buried somewhere. These people call you a madman. The kids are scared of you and you are left with nothing.'

'I found love,' Gadariya said. 'It's the same love that connects us to this universe. It's also the love that brought you to Chambal, bound together by this chain. Why do you want to escape? Where to? What dreams do you want to fulfil? The only dream I had was to be close to my wife, my beloved. I would've been ecstatic had someone tied us together with such a chain. Inseparable, forever and ever.'

'You're a bloody nutcase. Just help us get out or get lost!' Aakash cried.

Shweta tried to diffuse the tension. 'We understand what you are trying to say, but please help us. I'm a journalist and a news anchor. This is the most important time for our country. Soon, they'll announce the new prime minister and the entire cabinet. I have this huge responsibility to present the truth. Please get us out of here. I promise to do a TV show on your life, and maybe a whole team will be deployed to help you find your wife or her body.'

Gadariya laughed till the wall of darkness shook and cracked. The wind also danced and laughed with him. Then he looked at them. 'I've already found what I wanted to find. Now it's your turn. You talk of the responsibility on your shoulders but the entire responsibility lies on His shoulders. Let go of the thought that you are managing something. There is nothing to manage. There was perfect order in the universe, but we men have disturbed that order in our pursuit of becoming superhumans. He laughs at us but forgives us again and again.'

Shweta sighed and said, 'We cannot leave everything to God. We have to work and create things. Look at Chambal. With a bit of effort, it could be turned green. But it certainly needs effort, planning, putting our heads together, and this wild could be a beautiful green land.'

'It needs nothing but love…to see the grass grow here, the trees dance in the rain, the flowers bloom…and it will all happen. In fact, a tree never makes an effort to grow, a flower never makes an effort to bloom. Nor must we make a huge effort to grow from babies into adults. It happens. All good things happen to us, we cannot plan good things in life.' Gadariya spoke as someone who had loved and lost and had then rekindled a love in his soul that would never be lost.

'Basically you don't want to help us,' Aakash said sarcastically.

Bewildered, Gadariya looked at them. 'Do you really need help? Well, this is a blissful state—to be tied together and away from the whole world that you've been trying to impress for so long.'

'You're fucking crazy!' Shweta shouted. 'You're enjoying our plight. I'm going to fight it out and get out of here. Now get lost!'

This is how she shouted at her team of reporters whenever they missed any breaking-news story. This was the way Aakash and Shweta spoke to each other when they quarrelled. This is how angry words turned into abuses, and marriages turned sour.

A similar psychological exhaustion ended in contempt for

each other as husband and wife. Aakash and Shweta could no longer stand each other, nor could they talk to each other like companions for life. Like two shadows living in the same house, they slid in and out of each other's lives, doing their best to *avoid seeing* the other.

'Those dacoits are better than you. At least they are clear in their dealings—that they want money to get us out of here.' Aakash gave vent to his bitterness.

'What makes you think I'm not a dacoit?' asked Gadariya with a smile.

Shweta laughed. 'You're nothing but a madman.'

Gadariya looked at them and took a deep breath. 'Have you heard of Daku Maan Singh?'

'Don't tell me you're Maan Singh?' Shweta smirked.

Gadariya laughed out loud. He looked at them and softly said with moist eyes, 'Daku Maan Singh was my father.'

Shweta and Aakash looked at him puzzled.

Gadariya took a deep breath, and bringing out long buried memories, said, 'All across Chambal and in the nearby villages, people adored him. He headed a gang of seventeen fearless dacoits who were credited with over 1,112 robberies and 185 murders.'

Gadariya looked at them, and smiled with moist eyes. 'The government wanted him dead, and declared a big *inam* on his head while he roamed free, addressing the locals and settling disputes. Finally, in 1955, while Maan Singh and his elder son Subedar Singh were sitting under a banyan tree in Bhind, a small village in Madhya Pradesh, they were shot dead by the troops.'

Shweta and Aakash saw a lone teardrop form under Gadariya's eye. He looked at them and suddenly flicked it away.

The wind in Chambal froze at the mention of Maan Singh's name. Even Shweta and Aakash had heard this name.

A Bollywood film was made on the life of this most wanted and dreaded dacoit of Chambal. They couldn't believe that they were sitting in front of Maan Singh's son Gadariya, a shepherd.

Gadariya closed his eyes. Memories flooded him. 'Today, Maan Singh has a temple in his honour in Khera Rathore, his village. The locals regularly offer worship at the Maan Singh Temple. No dacoit of Chambal leaves for any mission without offering obeisances at the temple. Those were the days when you could see battalion upon battalion of the police force marching into the Chambal to take on seventeen-odd dacoits armed with country-made guns. And the dacoits fought like lions. They were real baaghis. My father used to say there was no difference between a baaghi and a sadhu. Both gave up their worldly lives for a larger cause. Even today, the entire Chambal Valley refers to Maan Singh as *Chambal Ka Sher*—Lion of Chambal. There are many folk songs and *nautanki*s inspired by his life.'

Gadariya started to hum a song, '*Rasta chalta koi nahin loota, na bahino se chheene haar, jo bhi mila so baant diya, bahino ko pahinaye bhaat.*' (He did not rob harmless travellers, neither did he snatch the chains of sisters; whatever he got, he distributed to the poor and gave as gifts to the sisters.)

Aakash and Shweta sat in stunned silence, listening to Gadariya talk about Maan Singh. For a moment, they forgot that they were tied by a chain, or that they had been whisked away from their familiar world in Mumbai and were now trapped in Chambal.

The old man had tears in his eyes. He seemed like a schoolboy waiting on the steps outside school for his father to come and pick him up in his arms.

'It's been a long time since I've spoken about my father to anyone. Maybe you were meant to hear his story. It's his will,' Gadariya said, getting up.

'Wait, you told us that you were also a dacoit. So what's your story?' Aakash asked curiously.

Gadariya sat down looking at them. 'I'm the youngest child of Daku Maan Singh and the only one alive. My father wanted me to study, so he had sent me to a nearby school. I still remember those days when he used to drop me at school. Can you imagine Daku Maan Singh dropping his son to school?' Gadariya laughed. 'The entire school would stand at attention while my father walked up to the principal and hand him a wad of notes as donation for the school. He had great respect for teachers and never harmed one. He always told me that teachers, not politicians, could change society. I never understood it then, but now I know it's true.'

Aakash wiped the tears from his eyes. Gadariya looked at him gently. 'I can see you miss your father. We all do. In the end, all sons end up becoming mirror images of their fathers. Even today, I miss holding that finger, that hand of Daku Maan Singh, and being reassured by those eyes that I worshipped.'

'So, as your father told you that there was no difference between baaghis and sadhus, you chose to become a sadhu?' asked Shweta.

'Me, a sadhu?' Gadariya laughed. 'I was Sangram Singh—a name given to me by my father. By the time my father along with my brothers, uncles and cousins were shot dead, I had cleared highschool. There was a fire raging inside me to go out and kill each and every policeman, but somehow I controlled myself as my father had made me promise never to pick up a gun. So I studied further and came back to our village.'

Suddenly, he got up with a finger on his lips. 'Can you see that all of Chambal is listening to the story of Daku Maan Singh and his son?' He laughed till tears rolled down his cheeks. He started to weep, then finally became quiet and sat down again.

'In our village, I turned our house into a small school. At first, only a few kids trickled in. Then I went from house to house trying to convince parents to send their children to study. They preferred the kids working as manual labourers, or indulging in petty theft, to make quick money. I wanted to change all that. I spoke to the panchayat and the village elders. They listened to me because I was Maan Singh's son, but behind my back, they made fun of me for being a sissy, for not following in my father's footsteps. In the village, I fell in love with Radha. She was the most beautiful girl I had ever seen.

'Soon, we were married. We had so many dreams. She wanted to help me with the school, and slowly extend it to a highschool. She would visit the villagers and implore village girls to come to the school. Life was beautiful—as if I was living in a dream. One night, when we were having dinner, a gang of dacoits barged in. They thrashed me and forcibly took away Radha.'

Gadariya fell silent as he stared into the darkness. Minutes ago, his face had lit up while reminiscing about his beautiful wife. Now the pain etched deep on his soul surfaced once again. For a while, he sat quietly since he just couldn't string the words together into anything meaningful.

'I went from the police station to government officials, and then to the village panchayat seeking help. They all laughed at me derisively as if I was telling them a joke. For them, it was not unusual for dacoits to kidnap a young girl. They told me to forget her and find another girl. My heart ached with sorrow, a kind I had never experienced before.' Gadariya trailed off, fighting back his tears.

Aakash and Shweta waited for him to regain his composure, and cast the remnants of those memories into appropriate words once again to continue the tale.

Gadariya blew his nose. 'It had been almost a week after Radha was abducted. No one had any news of her. Early one morning, as I stepped out of my house, a few villagers walking by said that dacoits might have raped her and thrown her to the wolves. That changed me forever. All my sorrows turned into hate and anger. I thirsted for blood and revenge. I returned to the house, opened an old trunk in which my father had kept his stuff and took out his small axe. Yes, he had made me promise never to pick up a gun, so I picked up an axe. Then I walked out of my house, and headed for Chambal never to return home again.'

'So what did you do?' Aakash asked.

'What would you have done?' Gadariya countered. 'I wandered through the wild, looking for Radha, for the dacoits who abducted her. I sank into a deep, dark void and could see no other purpose to my life except to find them. So I started to hunt for dacoits—any dacoit—and started to torture them to extract information about Radha. I went on a killing spree. It didn't matter who these dacoits were. I just wanted to finish off all the dacoits of Chambal, as if the spirit of Daku Maan Singh had taken possession of me. Soon the dacoits were on the lookout for me, but each time, I managed to give them the slip. I could feel the spirit of Maan Singh guiding me, imbuing me with the courage, fearlessness and the killer instincts that only he had. The locals believe that Maan Singh's spirit still roams the Chambal Valley, that if you turn to him for help, he'll always come to the rescue. According to police records, my father Maan Singh had committed 185 murders. I went a few steps further and slaughtered more than two hundred men.'

Aakash and Shweta, who were jeering at him up to that moment, calling him a fool, shuddered. They had never met a mass murderer, let alone a man who had killed over two hundred men.

Gadariya's eyes had a faraway look as he continued. 'Still, I couldn't find my Radha. Finally, I learnt of the Tewatia gang who had abducted her. I crept into their hideout at night. They were all drunk and asleep. That night, I hacked each one of them to death with the axe. I went straight for their throats. Not a single one of them could utter a word. It was only when I reached the gang leader Deewan Tewatia that I woke him up and showed him the massacre. I wanted to see the horror in his eyes. He fell at my feet and pleaded with me to spare his life. I asked him about Radha and he told me that he had sold her to another gang which I had already finished off before. I chopped Tewatia into pieces and threw them to wild dogs. They were thirty-one men in all, and I killed them all in a single night.'

Gadariya fell silent for a while. Nothing stirred around them. The darkness also seemed to have frozen like ice. The wind dared not disturb them. There was not a single sound from the dogs or the wolves.

'That night, something happened to me,' Gadariya said. 'I was drenched in blood, and too tired to go on after killing thirty-one men. War-weary, I slumped to the ground and slept. When I woke up, I experienced a jolt within my soul that brought me into harmony with the entire universe. I was a totally new man.'

Aakash and Shweta looked at him, puzzled.

Gadariya smiled. 'My soul trembled with ecstasy, my mind was flooded with light, and my heart wept joyfully.'

'Does that mean you saw God or something like that?' Shweta asked the age-old question.

'I don't know that, but I experienced the one force that flows through everything. It was like electricity that powers the bulb, the fan, the cooler, the fridge, the television, the washing machine, the mixer, the computer, the music system, the huge machines in factories and so many other gadgets and appliances. All these are totally different, and have totally different functions, but it's the same electricity that powers them. I too felt that universal, life-affirming power that flows through everything, through each of us. Even calling it by a single name would be inadequate because it is in everything, it *is* everything. I don't know what to call it; some call it God. I don't know and I don't care. It flows through me and you and every being.'

Disinterested in Gadariya's spiritual blather, Aakash said, 'You killed so many people. Don't you feel any guilt or remorse?'

'No. I feel like a medium of the universal force that pushed me, under certain circumstances, to take such an extreme step. The police never bothered me because I was doing their work— killing the dacoits of Chambal. I was trying to create a sort of balance in the wild, and then the mindless killings totally upended my life. Like taking a U-turn. That is how sinners become saints.'

'So, like Maan Singh said, there is no difference between baaghis and sadhus; you became a sadhu,' Aakash sneered.

'I'm not a sadhu. The universal force told me to be the gadariya, the shepherd, and guide people towards love.'

'Did you find out anything about Radha?' Shweta asked.

'Once you experience this true love, you'll realize there is nothing to lose and that you never lost anything. Radha is still with me in my heart. At times, she calls out to me and we talk to each other. Radha and I are not separate; we are one.'

For Aakash and Shweta, the old man seemed to have lost his mind wandering in Chambal.

The wind started to blow gently. From the darkness of Chambal emanated a soft whistling sound. Suddenly, Gadariya got up and looked at the wild. Then he whispered, 'She's calling me. I'll have to go.' Soon he was off again.

Aakash felt the coldness of the raw steel gripping his hand and called out after Gadariya, 'Hey! Hey! You have to help us get out of here. You can't leave.'

'Please help,' Shweta cried too.

The sharp blade of the axe tucked into Gadariya's waistband glinted in the dark. He turned to look at Aakash and Shweta, and said, 'Pray.'

With that, he vanished into the ocean of darkness, as if it parted just to make way for him.

12

It was prime time for news channels. They bombarded the whole nation with their opinion polls, election trackers, and 'experts' putting forth their ridiculous theories. Each one had a different analysis and prediction for the election results. News channels had turned into political battlegrounds, with most news anchors turning into mouthpieces for their favourite political party.

The bosses of News World were having a tough time. Their star anchor, Shweta Chaudhary, who hosted the flagship show *News Line* had gone missing. The ratings of the channels hit rock bottom. The chairman, the vice-president and the MD of the media group were trying to locate her, but drew a blank. They didn't hear from her either. Meanwhile, advertisers shifted to other channels causing News World to lose out on considerable revenues.

Finally, the management decided to contact the police. A whole team was assigned to locate her. They tried to call her husband Aakash. He was also missing. None of their friends or family knew anything of their whereabouts. They contacted Shweta's family in Gurugram. Her elder brother Vikram Chaudhary told the management that being a rebellious child always, she must've gone on a secret trip abroad or a quick honeymoon. The management contacted the relevant authorities but there was no proof of them leaving the country.

Finally, the MD, along with senior executives, entered the sixty-fifth-floor penthouse to find the the place in a mess—

broken plates, stale food, wine and milk splattered all over the place, and shards of glass on the floor. Clearly, they had been attacked by someone, resulting in a major scuffle, and had possibly been kidnapped by the attackers.

Immediately, the police were called in. For them, it was a simple case of entry by force and abduction. According to them, they must've tried to resist and put up a fight but the kidnappers seemed to have been armed and kidnapped them with a knife or at gunpoint. But why would the kidnappers break plates, throw food on the walls, shatter glass tabletops and fling things around? Even the police didn't give it that much thought.

The security guards of the building were questioned but none of them had seen either Shweta or Aakash being bundled off by unknown men. In fact, no one saw any unknown person or persons entering the building. The police reviewed the footage from security cameras, but there was nothing. The kidnappers must have planned well in advance. There was a strong possibility that one of the security guards was involved. So all the guards were rounded up, interrogated, and even roughed up. Still no lead. In fact, the police had no idea what had happened, or how.

Shweta's family was informed about her possible kidnapping. Immediately, her brother, one of the real estate tycoons of Gurugram and Delhi, landed in Mumbai and met with all the top police officials and politicians. The police were under tremendous pressure to find her.

The management of News World suddenly realized that they had an exclusive story on their hands. They started to run the story of the kidnapping of their star reporter and news anchor Shweta Chaudhary and her husband. Senior reporters were tasked to gather material on them and compile it into a good sob story. Soon, other channels latched on to it; they also sent out their sniffer dogs to unearth exclusive stories.

News World ran an entire series on Shweta and Aakash's lives. They took bytes from housewives and aunties talking about Aakash and his gentle demeanour. They showed clips of him working in the kitchen, baking Danish pastries, talking about the rich Indian culinary tradition and his secret Spice-o-Clay Fish recipe.

For Shweta, News World got all senior journalists and editors talking about her professionalism, ethics and strong sense of morals. They talked about the time when she started as a production assistant, running up and down with tapes or walking into the most dangerous zones to get the truth. Her brother talked emotionally about her childhood, her rebellious nature and her adventurous spirit. In her college days, oftentimes she would run away from home to go on long treks in the Himalayas or to other college festivals.

The top political brass spoke of her steely spirit and no-nonsense attitude while asking tough questions. Political parties blamed each other for her kidnapping—Shweta must've stumbled upon some secrets of a top politician who then got the couple kidnapped. The Press Club organized a *hawan*, and pundits were called to do a *maha mrityunjaya yagya*.

With the election counting going on, and the new kidnapping case, the police were under tremendous pressure. They started to round up all possible suspects. Many local goons were caught, beaten and locked up. Still, the police had nothing to offer other than constant assurances that they were working on the case.

The good thing that happened to News World was that with the kidnapping story, they got their top ratings back. Advertisers returned in hordes and the management smiled again. The sickeningly sweet stories on Shweta and Aakash continued.

It was the third day since Aakash and Shweta went missing.

13

They sat on the charpoy with their backs to each other. In the vast wild, they were both prisoners. They could run in any direction but in reality, there was nowhere to run. The only hope was to wait and find a way out. They didn't know what to say to each other. All they could do was accuse and blame each other, get into arguments, shout, scream, fight, and break things. They wanted to comfort each other but both had long stopped doing that. There was a time when they had fallen in love with the most insignificant traits of each other. Over time, however, they could not stand each other's flaws and imperfections. They buckled under the weight of their expectations.

'Once I'm out of here, I'm going to find out who did this to us,' Shweta hissed in frustration as if talking to herself.

Suddenly, Aakash turned towards her as if he got the point he had been awaiting for such a long time. 'Could be one of your brother's rivals. He's part of the real-estate mafia, so they targeted us.'

'I don't have anything to do with him,' Shweta said curtly.

'Could be a politician, a businessman or a gangster whom you targeted,' Aakash said.

'My job is to bring out the hard truth, not serve chutneys and parathas to bored aunties.'

As accusations and counter-accusations flew from both sides, they screamed like wild animals clawing at each other. All the humanity in them was replaced with contempt, revulsion and hatred.

The very notion of being a companion for life became meaningless; the love they once had for each other had decayed. They were carrion, tied to each other.

'Don't you know that people laugh at you? Some men call you the bitch of news,' Aakash sneered.

'What about you?' Shweta retorted. 'The women who watch your cookery show call you *biwi ka naukar*. Have you seen your cartoons on the internet? They have put a tail in between your legs. Well, as a woman, I'm fighting hard in a male-dominated world while you're sitting pretty in a kitchen, baking and cooking. No woman would respect you for that.'

Aakash felt a sudden rage welling up in him. He wanted to somehow shut her up. Clenching his fists, he tried to control himself as his rage turned into tears that flowed from his eyes. This was the kind of nonsense with which they went after each other. The purpose was to humiliate, insult, shame, debase and degrade the other person to an extent that the other person would choke on their own tears.

Shweta was unstoppable. 'You're an utter failure, and I cannot understand how and why I stuck to you for so long.'

Aakash could feel his insides being riddled with humiliation. A deep anguish engulfed his soul like heavy mist. At such moments, Shweta turned into a monster—devoid of any shred of decency or decorum. Deep down, Aakash hated himself to the point of intense self-loathing for being somewhat dependent on her.

Right then, Dimple emerged from the darkness. Slowly, he crept towards them. He had brought a pair of worn-out rubber slippers for Shweta, and a pair of tattered brown canvas shoes for Aakash. The shoes had no laces but their soles were intact. Dimple looked around nervously to make sure no one was there before handing them the footwear. 'These brown shoes belonged to my father and I hope they fit you. And these slippers are my mother's. She is used to walking barefoot but you need them.'

Moved by Dimple's gesture, Aakash tried on the shoes. They were a size or two bigger but good enough for him to walk in. 'Your father must've been a tall man?'

'You should've seen him,' boasted Dimple. 'All these dacoits were scared of him and used to run for cover at the mere mention of his name—Constable Darbar Singh. He was shot dead by a dacoit. The government gave my mother a sewing machine and five thousand rupees. But nowadays, everyone buys readymade clothes, so she has to go out and work at night,' Dimple said with a tormented smile.

'I'm sure once you grow up, you'll take care of her,' said Shweta, trying on her slippers.

'Once I grow up, I'm going to track down the one who killed my father and shoot him dead just like he shot my father,' Dimple spoke with rage that was unusual for a normal ten-year-old boy.

The presence of the boy calmed both Aakash and Shweta. Their demeanour changed from bitterness and uncontrolled rage to genuine concern for Dimple. 'It would be better for you to study and help your mother. Don't get involved with these dacoits,' Shweta told the boy.

Dimple looked at her, and said innocently, 'Didi, why don't you take both me and my mother to Mumbai? I'm sure I'll get a job there. Then I won't let my mother work like this.'

'You're too young to work. First complete your education,' Aakash said gently.

Dimple looked at them and said proudly, 'You don't know me. I can carry more than fifty kilos of load on my back up and down a hill. I've heard many new buildings are being constructed in Mumbai. I'll carry all the load there. That's work.'

Aakash shook his head. 'You're a child, Dimple. You cannot throw away your life like this. What you need is education; you need to at least finish your school education, and then get to college. Which class are you in right now?'

Dimple laughed. 'I don't go to school. After they killed my father, I dropped out. If I stay here, my only aim in life would be to seek revenge.'

'Nonsense,' said Shweta. 'You cannot fritter away your life wanting to seek revenge.'

Dimple looked at them with vacant eyes and mumbled, 'Gadariya did it. The locals believe that it was the spirit of Maan Singh calling out to him to take revenge. He was shot many times but no one could stop him, and he killed them all. Now it's his spirit that roams in Chambal.'

'What do you mean his spirit?' asked Aakash, puzzled.

Dimple looked around in the darkness and whispered, 'Gadariya is long dead. He was shot dead by the dacoits and the police. It's his spirit that you see in Chambal.'

'So that's why you all ran away on seeing him?' Shweta said, surprised.

Dimple nodded his head still speaking in whispers, 'You can still see the bullet holes in his clothes and that axe tucked in his waistband. No one in Chambal dares stop him or stand in his way.'

'We met him. He sat with us and told us his life story. He can't be a ghost,' Aakash countered Dimple's story.

Dimple stared at them with eyes wide open with fear. 'People say that Gadariya only tells his story to those who are about to die and become ghosts. That way his secret never goes out of Chambal, and the villagers never talk about him, lest he haunt them for life.'

'Are you crazy?' Aakash said. 'Who tells you all this stuff?

We know he's not a ghost.'

'He comes and disappears at will. So many times, dacoits, policemen and villagers have tried to follow him but he disappears right before their eyes. Even wolves and wild dogs are afraid of him.'

'Okay, enough of all this. Bhoora will take us to Morena in the morning and from there, we'll go straight to Mumbai,' Shweta said, convinced that everything would be back on track soon.

'How far is Morena from here?' Aakash asked.

'In a jeep, about an hour,' said Dimple. 'It's a big city with a huge market, cinema hall, and lots of sweet shops.'

'Great, then we can directly go to the police station. They'll help us out,' Shweta chimed.

'Don't forget, this Bhoora is helping us only for money. So somehow, we'll have to convince him that we can't get him the money right here,' Aakash said looking at Shweta.

'You don't have to think about that. I'm going to call up the management from Morena and they'll sort everything out. Tomorrow morning, we'll be out of this godforsaken place,' Shweta said smugly.

'Don't trust this Bhoora,' Dimple said to them in a hushed tone.

Right then Bhoora appeared, totally drunk. Holding his rifle in one hand, he shouted, 'What were you telling them about me? I'm going to kill you and bury you right here, Dimple. Now get lost and send your mother here right now.'

Like a rat scurrying into a hole at the sight of a snake, Dimple disappeared.

Bhoora looked at them, licking his chapped lips with his tongue. 'We'll have to keep you safe. I've heard other gangs are also on the lookout for you.'

Bhoora pulled out a chain hooked to a block of cement on

the ground used to tether buffaloes. He picked it up and tied it to the chain that bound Aakash and Shweta. Then he put a heavy lock at the intersection of the two chains. There was no way they could be freed from it.

Bhoora looked at them and laughed loudly. 'Now you can sleep. In fact, I have informed the police so a police team will be coming in the morning to escort us to Morena.'

Tied to the buffaloes' chain, Shweta almost felt like an animal. Nonetheless, she heaved a sigh of relief. 'Thank God! At least the police will take us to the right place. Bhoora, I promise you'll get your money. Just get us out of here.'

Bhoora smiled at her. 'Madam, tomorrow you'll be in Mumbai in your house eating burger and drinking Kala Cola.'

Shweta lay on one side of the charpoy while Aakash lay on the other side, with their backs to each other. Both felt a sense of relief—finally, they would be going home. Shweta started planning for her show. She decided to blame politicians for her disappearance. She would use her sob story to get to the new prime minister, and soon she would be the star news anchor again. It would all be normal and beautiful, like it always had been.

Morning was still hours away. There was darkness all around. Bhoora stared at her legs. Her half-torn dress had rolled up to her thighs. Shweta was in deep sleep.

Bhoora inched closer to the charpoy, watching her. Then he extended his hand to touch her. Immediately, Aakash, who was still awake, warned him. 'Keep your hands off her.'

Shweta woke up with a start. Seeing Bhoora so close, she yelled as well, 'Don't you dare touch me! I will report you to the police!'

Bhoora stared at her for a while and then reached for an ant moving along the frame of the charpoy. 'I was keeping an eye on this ant or it might've bitten you.' With that, he put the ant in his mouth and chewed it.

'Get back to sleep. I'll keep a watch on him,' Aakash assured Shweta.

Both Bhoora and Aakash glared at each other. Bhoora picked up his rifle, cocked it, and pointed it at Aakash. 'It would be better if you stopped staring at me. My rifle is not used to being stared at either. If it goes off, I won't be responsible.'

Aakash turned his head and looked up at the stars. Moments later, he turned to look at Bhoora who was still staring at him, his rifle still pointing at Aakash's head.

Aakash closed his eyes, praying for the sun to rise.

14

The veil of darkness didn't lift an inch. Time seemed to stand still. Aakash kept an eye on Bhoora who took generous swigs of the country-made liquor from a bottle.

In the dark, Aakash saw a woman in a tattered saree walking towards Bhoora. To hide her face, she had covered her head with the *pallu*. She had a small build, tiny feet, and long dark hair that cascaded down to her waist. Meekly, she sat on the ground near Bhoora's feet and started to press his legs.

Bhoora glared at her. Then grabbing her by her hair, he slapped her hard. 'Bloody bitch, you want me to keep sitting here, waiting for you? Where the hell were you? Making out with someone else?'

The woman screamed in pain, waking Shweta.

'Now put some pressure on my feet,' Bhoora growled, tweaking her ear in disgust. Again, the woman cried out in pain.

'Don't you dare touch her,' Shweta shouted at Bhoora.

Bhoora turned to look at her and laughed maniacally. 'How does it affect you? This bitch here belongs to me. I can do anything to her. I can box her ears and slap her.' Bhoora slapped the woman hard again.

Shweta protested loudly, 'Bhoora, stop hitting her!'

Bhoora laughed defiantly. 'Do you want me to apologize to her and plead for her forgiveness?'

'You're a sick bastard! There's Gadariya who loved his wife so much that he has been wandering in the wild for forty years. That's love,' Shweta said.

'Don't be taken in by Gadariya's stories. He's a madman and will make you lose your mind too. You'd better focus on getting back to Mumbai, and don't forget my payment.' Bhoora turned to look at the woman and slapped her again. 'Move your bloody hands, you bitch!'

Outraged by Bhoora's actions, Aakash tried to get up but was pulled down by the chain tied to the block of cement. He looked helpless.

Bhoora smirked, saying, 'Why are you getting so restless? The show has just begun. Just sit back and watch.' Bhoora pulled the woman close and threw aside her pallu exposing her tattered blouse.

The woman was beautiful, with dark eyes and dark brown skin. She tried to pull back her pallu but Bhoora tore away her saree. Teary-eyed, she looked around for help.

Shweta shouted out at Bhoora, 'I'm warning you Bhoora, don't do that. I'm going to report you to the police.'

Bhoora didn't even bother to look at Shweta. He kept tearing the saree away. Soon the woman stood only in her petticoat and blouse. 'Why the hell do you want me to do all the work? C'mon, remove these,' Bhoora ordered her.

Aakash wrestled with the chain but to no avail. He groaned and writhed like a trapped animal. 'So this is why you tied us? Bhoora, I'm going to kill you! Let her go.'

Bhoora looked at them and laughed. 'What's wrong with you? Is she your sister, mother, daughter or what? If you're not interested, then close your eyes and sleep. Last week, I gave her a hundred rupees; it's time she repays me.'

The woman looked at them, begging for help with those innocent eyes which seared their souls. Aakash and Shweta both screamed at Bhoora, asking him to stop as he tore away her blouse.

In his drunken stupor, Bhoora slurred, 'These women are a criminal class. They are great con artists. They can turn a man into a dog and can keep them tied to their bedpost. They need to be tamed and harnessed like animals or they'll walk all over us.'

Bhoora hit the woman again and she fell down. Bhoora started to kick her in the ribs. She yelped in agony.

Dimple, the little boy, came running towards them and cried out, 'Amma!' He saw Bhoora kicking her and pounced on the dacoit. 'I'm going to kill you, Bhoora! How dare you kick my mother?'

The little boy punched and kicked Bhoora but one tight slap from the dacoit was enough to send him flying. Unable to help, Aakash and Shweta seethed in anger. They desperately looked around for villagers who could help but saw nothing but darkness.

Like a small bird trying to fight off a cobra, Dimple looked Bhoora in the eye and came charging at him. He started to punch him in anger. Meanwhile, Dimple's mother managed to grab her saree and wrap it around. She also tried to fight off Bhoora in an attempt to save her only child. The cobra played with them—teasing them, mocking them, at times taking their blows, and then hissing at them loudly, and even whacking them with its tail. Bhoora managed to grab Dimple by the throat, and started to strangle the boy with both his hands. The boy's eyes bulged out. Bhoora laughed sadistically, watching him gasping for breath.

'You know, I'm the one who killed your father. Yes, I killed Constable Darbar Singh. Look, this police uniform I'm wearing belongs to your father and I shot him in the back,' Bhoora revealed, taunting the boy.

The mother jumped on Bhoora, raining blows on him with years of pent-up rage and pain. Suddenly, Bhoora lost his grip on Dimple, and the boy fell down. Slowly, he sat up, gulping in as much air as he needed to fight the monster.

Bhoora punched the mother in the head and she fell to the ground. Seeing this, Dimple attacked Bhoora once again.

The cobra lay in wait for the little one to come at him. In a swift move, he picked up the rifle and smacked the boy in the head with the heavy butt. For a split second, Dimple froze in the air like a suspended statue with his arms spread out wide. Then he fell to the ground with a thud.

He lay there motionless. Shweta cried out, 'C'mon Dimple, get up!'

There was no reaction. Darkness covered him like a shroud. His mother rushed to him and shook him hard, repeatedly calling out his name, but the boy didn't react. Sobbing uncontrollably, she kept calling out his name while slapping him and shaking him vigorously. Suddenly, she leapt up and turned upon Bhoora like an injured animal in pain.

The rifle butt hit her abs with brute force and stilled her rage. She gasped for breath. Her legs wobbled and she crashed to the ground. Bhoora looked at Aakash and Shweta with a triumphant smile. 'Tonight, I'm putting up a free show for you. You won't see all this in Mumbai.'

Then he pounced on the woman like a snake on a rat. She had not even regained conciousness when he started to thrust inside her like a mindless beast.

Shweta let out a gut-wrenching cry. Aakash felt his soul being crushed. An innocent woman was being mercilessly beaten and raped in front of them, and all they could do was cry and close their eyes. They tried to smash the chain but that only aggravated the deep gashes on their wrists.

Bhoora kept looking at Aakash and Shweta defiantly as he grunted and groaned till he was spent. The woman protested feebly. She still had her eyes fixed on her son lying next to her. Somehow, she crawled up to him and hugged him. Her sobs turned into a loud wail. She picked up her clothes and wrapped the tattered saree around her. Then she started to drag her son away.

Shweta was benumbed with pain. This wound on her soul would never heal. She had done it all—reported from war zones, sites of terror attacks and genocides, but never had she witnessed anything so beastly, her own helplessness only highlighting the savagery. These are the depths a man could sink to. Was it only in the wild where a woman's cries for help went unheeded? Or could this also be happening in those air-conditioned bedrooms in big cities?

That night, something died in her. Her vanity, glory, self-esteem, self-righteousness, pride, beauty and intellect crumbled to dust. Like the brutalized woman, she also felt stripped, kicked around and thrown down into a whirlpool of tears and sorrow. There seemed no surfacing from it.

With vacant eyes, the woman dragged her lifeless son by one leg. Now there was nothing but darkness in her life. So, into the darkness she went with her only child.

15

The first rays of the sun dispelled the darkness, lighting up the monstrosity that was Chambal—covered by a blanket of silence and death.

Lying on the charpoy, Aakash and Shweta opened their eyes only to shut them as the morning light blinded them. Bhoora unfastened the lock that had chained them to the block of cement. 'C'mon, get up, it's time to move. The police are here to help us.'

Shweta and Aakash got up to see a few khaki-clad policemen standing in front of them.

'Madam, don't take tension. We'll escort you from here,' said the policeman closest to the charpoy.

Aakash looked at his pocket nameplate—Jai Veer Tewatia, Inspector of Police; he had three stars on the epaulettes. Two constables stood behind him.

'First, please arrest this dacoit, Bhoora. Last night, he killed a boy and raped his mother,' Aakash said angrily.

'Yes, we both saw it. We were eyewitnesses to the whole crime,' Shweta cried.

Tewatia looked at them and laughed. 'So what were you both doing? Enjoying the show? You must've dreamt up the whole thing. It happens to outsiders in Chambal. They get a fever, become delirious, and start to hallucinate.'

'We were not hallucinating!' Shweta shouted at him. 'This Bhoora had tied us to the block of cement here. Then he thrashed both the boy and his mother, right where you're standing.

The boy died after Bhoora hit him in the head with his rifle butt. Then he raped the mother.'

'The boy's name is Dimple. You can check with the villagers,' added Aakash curtly.

Tewatia nodded thoughtfully. 'Dimple. Hmmm. You could be right. The only problem is that Dimple and his mother both died four years back. The mother poisoned the boy and hanged herself. You must've seen their ghosts.'

'What?' Aakash blurted out incredulously.

Shweta looked at him; for a split second, a million questions sprang to their minds, but they couldn't utter a word.

'Forget all that. Ghostly spirits roam the Chambal and whenever they see someone new, they possess them. It is while being possessed that one starts to imagine and see things. But don't worry, they won't come back,' Tewatia assured them. 'You are lucky that we found you on our daily round of this village.'

Aakash and Shweta stared at him puzzled and horrified. Was Dimple real? What about his mother? What happened to Gadariya? Was he really a ghost?

'Ga-Gadariya?' Shweta finally managed to mumble the name.

Like a perfect host, Bhoora brought the policemen tea in steel tumblers from the village. Taking one, Tewatia said, 'It's all because of this Gadariya. He indulges all these spirits and communicates with them. He must've let them loose on you. I'll take you to Chambal Devi's temple. You bow down to her and she'll protect you from all such spirits.'

'I had told you to keep away from Gadariya. See, he managed to perform his magic on you,' said Bhoora, slurping the tea. 'Throughout the night, I was in the village trying to get in touch with Inspector-saab.'

Unable to make out what was real and what was imaginary, Aakash and Shweta were still not ready to come to terms with being abandoned in Chambal. What if all this was also a dream? What if they were actually hallucinating in their penthouse in Mumbai? They tried to reason it out, but had to accept the bitter truth—they were captives in this harsh land. The only way forward was to figure out how to get out of the place.

'Sir-ji, now relax. You'll be taken to Gwalior under police escort. From the airport there, you can take a direct flight to Mumbai. I've also informed the deputy commissioner, so everyone will be waiting for you. Madam-ji, everyone in Gwalior recognizes you from your TV show. And Sir-ji, my wife never misses your show. She's a big fan and has tried all your recipes,' Tewatia told them with a cheerful smile.

Finally, someone had recognized them for what they were— at least professionally. They could finally get out of the wild. The very mention of Gwalior, a big city, a direct flight to Mumbai, and the deputy commissioner waiting to receive them was comforting. There was a huge sense of relief as though their chain had finally snapped. After sipping the hot tea, Aakash said, 'We need to use the toilet.'

Bhoora guffawed. 'Saab, in Chambal there are no toilets. The whole wild is our home, our toilet, our everything. By all means, please, find a corner and relieve yourself. We'll wait here.'

Aakash and Shweta looked at each other. 'I'm not going out in the open here,' Shweta put her foot down. Both were silent for a while. Then Shweta realized the futility of her tantrum.

Together, Aakash and Shweta went behind the mud mounds looking for a secluded place to relieve themselves. A long and winding river flowed placidly through the ravines of Chambal, like a shiny ribbon meandering through the arid land. The morning sun glistened over its waters.

They ran towards the river, and like children, they jumped into its cool, refreshing waters. They soaked themselves and

scrubbed off all the dust and sand that had caked their bodies.
They playfully splashed water on each other. They were like
friends, like a young couple in love, having fun.

Standing atop a mud mound, Bhoora looked at them and
shouted, 'Hurry up, we need to get out of here.'

Shweta and Aakash turned to look at him. 'How are we going
to finish our job if you're constantly keeping watch over us?'

Bhoora waved his hand nonchalantly and walked away.
Shweta tugged at Aakash, 'I need to pee now.'

Aakash also had to find a suitable position to pee there.
They looked around at the wild and laughed at their situation.
Never had they thought that one day they would land up in
such a place.

Aakash looked at his blood-soaked shirt. The blood had not
washed off. He could see the boy lying on the ground, covered in
blood, his eyes pleading them for help. He saw himself carrying
the child to the grave and burying him. 'They're playing tricks
with us,' said Aakash.

'What do you mean?' Shweta asked.

'Bhoora killed that boy in front of our eyes and we buried
him. My shirt is soaked in his blood. Even Dimple was killed
by Bhoora, and he raped his mother. We're not hallucinating,
Shweta. These guys are confusing us. It seems even the police
are hand in glove with Bhoora,' Aakash shared his suspicion.

'But why would Bhoora call the police? After all, he needed
money from us?'

'Exactly,' said Aakash as if he had connected the dots. 'They
seem to have a different plan. We have to get out of here before
they get us.'

'Where will we go in Chambal?' cried Shweta.

'Let's get back to the river. The river will guide us,' said
Aakash, getting up.

Meanwhile, Inspector Tewatia, along with the two constables, had hot parathas brought to them by a villager, along with another round of tea. They weren't worried about the chained couple escaping from Chambal. They knew no one could escape from the ravines.

Aakash and Shweta ran along the river. 'The river will guide us,' said Aakash again. 'It must be flowing through a nearby town or city. Soon, we'll reach there.'

'How do we know we're going in the right direction?' Shweta wondered aloud.

Aakash continued, 'First, let's get out of here. Then we'll plan our next move.'

So, they ran and ran. They were completely out of breath when they spotted a vehicle in the distance coming towards them. They waved at it frantically, crying out for help. The vehicle slowed down; it was an old Mahindra Jeep that was common in these parts.

As the jeep drew closer, they noticed it was a police jeep. Then they saw Inspector Tewatia and Bhoora sitting in front, laughing at them. Aakash and Shweta turned around and broke into a run, with the jeep following them closely. Aakash pulled Shweta back into the river and they started to wade across it to get on the other bank.

The jeep stopped. Tewatia grinned at them and said calmly, 'Arrey, come back. The river is full of gharials, and they won't hesitate to eat you alive.'

Aakash and Shweta pushed through waist-deep cold water. As they moved forward, the water level kept rising till it now reached their chins. With all their strength, they cut through the underwater currents that kept pushing them back. Aakash wanted to reach the other bank and find an escape route from there.

Suddenly, pointing ahead, Shweta alerted Aakash, 'Look!'

A gang of dacoits was rushing towards them from the other bank. One of them shouted, 'There they are! I told you they are tied together by a chain.'

There was no way they could make it to that bank. Aakash looked back. With their rifles and guns cocked, Bhoora, Inspector Tewatia and the constables had taken position behind the jeep. Tewatia shouted a warning to Aakash and Shweta, 'Come back. If these dacoits take you to the other bank, we won't be able to help you.'

Aakash and Shweta had no choice. They were caught between dacoits on one bank and a police team they couldn't trust on the other. The dacoits pointed their rifles at them threateningly, 'Don't move or we'll shoot.' The ringleader called out to his men, 'Get them before they get away.'

Shweta had her eyes glued on the dacoits as they charged towards them. She was hardly able to move as her feet and her body went numb with fear. She didn't want to be caught by dacoits and held captive deep inside Chambal.

The dacoits jumped into the river with a splash, thrashing about the waters as they made their way towards the chained couple. Aakash realized that they couldn't take a chance with a gang of dacoits. It would be better to get back to Bhoora, Tewatia and his two constables. In life too, sometimes one had to choose between the brute and the corrupt. For now, the corrupt was the lesser evil. So Aakash and Shweta turned back to save themselves, if they still could.

Aakash pulled Shweta back. 'You stay in the front while I keep an eye on these dacoits.'

Shweta waded through the water with all her might. Aakash followed close on her heels. Bhoora stood next to Tewatia, grinning at the couple. 'C'mon, move fast,' Bhoora cried.

The dacoits were very close. As one of them pounced on Aakash, Tewatia shot him. With a gaping hole in the chest, the dacoit tumbled into the river. The waters turned blood red. Aakash and Shweta panicked and tried to wade faster through the water.

The dacoits from the other bank retaliated with gunfire. The bullets whizzed past Aakash and Shweta's heads, hitting the jeep with a metallic rattle.

The little time Aakash and Shweta had gained with the exchange of fire helped them move to the shallow waters and break into a run. Seeing them escape, the dacoits suddenly charged at the couple like an army, yelling instructions to each other. 'Grab them!'

Bhoora, Tewatia and the constables jumped into the jeep and drove up to the couple. Pulling Shweta along, Aakash cried out, 'Stop! Please help!'

As Aakash and Shweta ran towards the jeep, one of the dacoits pointed his rifle at Aakash while another shouted, 'Don't shoot! If they die, they're useless for us. We need them alive.'

Suddenly, Tewatia fired at the dacoits. Bullets flew from both sides again, riddling the jeep. Aakash and Shweta latched on to the side rails as the jeep sped off, with the dacoits giving a futile chase.

Soon they were far from the river. Aakash helped Shweta climb into the jeep. Then they closed their eyes, and thanked God for having escaped from the clutches of the dacoits.

Tewatia, who was behind the wheel, turned to look at them. 'You both are already famous all over Chambal. See, how many gangs want to kidnap you for a ransom. But why were you running away from us? Beyond the other riverbank, there is five hundred square kilometres of wilderness. You could be roaming there your whole life. I've come here especially to help you.'

Shweta shot back, 'You all were trying to make us sound like crazies. Bhoora *had* killed that boy Dimple and raped his mother.'

'Yes,' Aakash chipped in. 'We saw it all happen; it was not a hallucination. He also shot a boy while we were on our way to the village and forced us to bury him. All this blood on my shirt is that boy's blood.'

Tewatia looked at them. 'I am the SHO of Morena Police Station. If what you say is true, I won't spare Bhoora.'

Tewatia shouted at one of the constables, 'Put this Bhoora in handcuffs.'

Bhoora was handcuffed to the jeep amidst loud protests. He kept abusing Aakash and Shweta. 'You wretched ingrates! I helped you by calling the police.'

'So that gives you the right to kill a boy and rape a woman in front of us?' Shweta shot back.

Bhoora seethed with rage. 'I didn't rape any woman. You're dreaming things. I was only playing with her.'

Tewatia gave Bhoora a tight slap. 'Shut up. The next time you open your mouth, I'm going to shoot you dead.'

Tewatia looked at Aakash and Shweta. 'You two can relax and sleep till we reach Gwalior. I'll make sure you two are put on the earliest flight back to Mumbai.'

Aakash and Shweta looked at each other with tears in their eyes. Finally, they were out of the wild.

They closed their eyes. For a fleeting second, their pain and weariness vanished. They didn't want to see any more of this land. They wanted to be in their cosy world, in their sixty-fifth-floor penthouse from where they could look down upon the city.

But the wild had just woken up, and was spreading its tentacles to engulf them.

16

'Aakash, you could've got us killed by trying to cross the river,' said Shweta, her eyes still closed.

Aakash turned to look at her. 'How was I to know there was another gang waiting to jump at us?'

'That has always been the problem with you. Whenever it comes to decision-making, you falter. Most of your decisions in life have turned out to be disasters,' rued Shweta.

'Yes, the biggest mistake was marrying you,' Aakash shot back.

'Tell me one good thing that you've done. Nothing. That's why you got stuck with that local channel.'

Aakash swallowed his humiliation. 'Be that as it may, you never let up a chance to put me down. Even in the wild, you don't want to concede a point. It's always about you. I don't remember if you ever had a word of appreciation or encouragement for me.'

'Well, I don't think you ever did anything to *deserve* a word of appreciation. Your shitty channel would've thrown you out long back, but it's because of me that you could stay on there so long. You really think anyone is interested in your cooking and crap recipes?'

Aakash went quiet. They had argued fiercely several times in the past, but of late, they tired out too soon. They knew all their spats and runs-in were useless, that these would lead them nowhere. Finally, they were heading in the direction—to file for a divorce.

With one wrist handcuffed, Bhoora clung to the jeep's rail

and laughed. 'Saab-ji, I told you these women are a twisted lot. They'll ruin even the best of men. So never give in to them.'

'You shut up. You have no respect for women. I saw you beating and raping that woman,' Shweta cried out.

'Am I wrong, Inspector-saab?' Bhoora looked at Tewatia enquiringly.

Tewatia fumbled for words, and said politely, 'We should respect women. It is in our culture to treat women as mothers, sisters and goddesses.'

'Tell me about your wife?' Bhoora asked sarcastically.

'She is crazy; a madwoman,' Tewatia cried. 'From the crack of dawn till late at night, she's after my life for something or the other. She wanted to buy a new cooler and when I bought it, she complained that I don't fill it with water. Then she complained about my body odour. Arrey *behenchod*, I work all day in this sun, chasing dacoits. She can't even understand that and won't allow me to touch her till I've had my bath with her favourite perfumed soap. I hate that soap.'

Tewatia rambled on, giving vent to his anger and frustration. 'Whenever I become a bit romantic, she embarks on her endless complaints. At times, I want to shoot her at point blank range and shut her up forever.'

There was sudden silence in the jeep. Shweta shook her head in disappointment at the dismal conversation. 'For ages, women were oppressed and now, when they've started to speak up, men are complaining.'

'The problem is not with women. The problem is with wives. The moment a girl turns into a wife, she changes. She wants to control you, take charge of your life,' explained Bhoora.

'I'm telling you, never marry. In fact, the best marriage would be between a blind wife and a deaf husband.' The policemen laughed.

'You men are pigs,' Shweta shouted through the racket of the jeep on the dirt road. 'You men just want to eat, sleep and have sex. Even women don't need to marry an entire pig for a piece of sausage.'

Tewatia and the constables burst into laughter. Bhoora said seriously, 'Madam, I'm telling you the truth. That's exactly why Hanuman-ji never married. He was free to jump around and play.'

'There's a point in what Bhoora is saying,' said Tewatia. 'I look at my wife and feel that I have a companion for life. But no, she is a leech sucking my blood. There are times when I want to crush her but she's so smart that she understands even that, and plays tricks to divert my attention, bloody witch.'

'What happened, Aakash-saab? You've suddenly become quiet?' Bhoora enquired.

'Nothing, just waiting to reach home and sort things out,' Aakash replied.

'Don't forget my payment. See, I even arranged for police security or those dacoits would have kidnapped you and taken you deep inside Chambal,' Bhoora said.

'You'll get your money. Just get us to Gwalior Airport,' Shweta snapped at Bhoora.

For another half hour, they drove through the dusty roads. Finally, Aakash and Shweta would be free. Deep down, both had decided that they couldn't go on with this relationship. So the first thing they would do on reaching Mumbai would be file for a divorce.

Shweta wasn't interested in alimony. She was independent and could take care of herself. Unlike women who were dependent on their husband's income throughout their lives, she had her own identity, a successful career, a beautiful penthouse, luxury cars, and servants and maids to do her bidding. She would put everything behind her and concentrate only on her work.

Aakash and Shweta still had no idea who could've kidnapped them, chained them together and abandoned them in Chambal, and more importantly, why. They had never come across anyone from Chambal in their lives. They blamed each other, and drummed up various theories on the matter, but still drew a blank.

Suddenly, the jeep stopped with a jolt. Shweta looked around but couldn't see any city. 'Why have we stopped here?'

Tewatia opened the rear door. 'Madam, this is the last police chowki in Chambal region bordering Gwalior. DC Saab told me that a team of Gwalior police will be coming here to pick you up, and that I have to hand you both over to them.'

Aakash and Shweta looked at each other. Without protesting, they got down from the jeep and walked towards a single-storeyed brick structure plastered with mud. At several places, the bricks were jutting out. On one side, an old rusted board hung limply, with 'Police Chowki' scribbled on it as though by a child.

Surrounded by armed policemen, Aakash and Shweta walked towards the chowki chained like the 'most wanted' dacoits of Chambal.

As they stepped inside the chowki, they saw a gang of dacoits sitting there sipping tea from clay cups. Aakash and Shweta froze on the spot. The air was heavy with the smell of cooking oil. Two policemen were busy frying onion and potato pakoras while another served the dacoits.

The moment they saw Aakash and Shweta, they stopped munching and stared at them. In this part of Chambal, policemen and dacoits didn't get to see a woman for months, so when a half-dressed young woman turned up, they couldn't help but ogle at her.

Bhoora fell down at a man's feet and cried, 'Vishnu Baba, thank God you're here. Inspector Tewatia arrested me on false charges. I think he wants to finish me off in an encounter.'

Seated on the SHO's chair, Vishnu Baba looked every bit the gang leader. Almost fifty, he had unruly salt-and-pepper hair falling over his shoulders. Sporting a heavy beard and a moustache carefully twirled up at both ends, he wore a black kurta and a checked *lungi*. A grey sweat cloth hung from his neck. The other dacoits wore police uniforms and carried rifles and pistols issued by the police. A few of them even wore police topis.

Turning to Inspector Tewatia, Aakash asked, 'You told us that the Gwalior Police would be here to pick us up. Who are these men?'

Vishnu Baba looked at him and smiled. Patting Bhoora who was grovelling at his feet, he got up. 'You might not know me but I know everything about you.' Vishnu Baba walked up to them and offered his hand.

Aakash stared at him, puzzled. Vishnu Baba continued. 'Well, the entire Chambal knows me as Vishnu Baba. Just as Vishnu is the God of Gods, I'm the God of all the dacoits in Chambal. They all work under me; no one can commit a crime without my permission.'

'So it was you who had us kidnapped and chained us like this,' Shweta shouted, thrusting out her handcuffed hand.

'In fact, I'm more shocked than you that such a thing was done without my knowledge. But don't worry, we'll find out soon. Now you're in our custody,' Vishnu Baba said coldly.

'What do you mean?' Shweta asked, looking around desperately.

Vishnu Baba signalled to one of his men, 'Kallu, check them.'

A large man with massive hands, Kallu was as dark as coal. Poker-faced, he walked up to them, and started frisking Aakash from shoulder to foot. Then he pulled Aakash's hair as if it was possible to hide a weapon there.

Kallu turned to Shweta. She screamed, 'I'm not going to allow this man to lay his hands on...'

Even before she could finish, Kallu's hands were on her, patting her mechanically as though it was his day-to-day job to feel up young women. He shoved his massive hands inside her dress and felt her breasts, slowly moving them up and down. Shweta closed her eyes and bit her lips hard. When Aakash tried to protest, the barrel of a gun touched his head. Kallu moved his hands further down and slid them between her legs, and felt her all over before reaching down to her ankles.

Finally, turning to Vishnu Baba, Kallu said, 'Okay, ji.'

Tears rolled down Shweta's cheeks. Vishnu Baba flicked off a tear with his fingers. 'Please don't mind all this. I've heard they strip search all Indians and Asians at US airports, and no one says a word against them. If they're doing it for their security, this is also for our security. We need to be sure that you're not carrying anything that could be used as a weapon against us.'

Tewatia casually sat on one of the tables, smiling at the whole thing.

'What the hell are you smiling at?' Aakash shouted. 'Who are these dacoits? We need to be in Gwalior.'

Tewatia smiled. 'Sir-ji, you have been formally kidnapped. Till now, no one knew who had chained you and left you in Chambal, but hereafter, you have been kidnapped by Vishnu Baba.'

Shweta and Aakash turned to Vishnu Baba. 'We have been kidnapped?'

Vishnu Baba slapped Bhoora hard and asked, 'How much did you demand to get them out of Chambal?'

Bhoora recoiled and mumbled, 'Five lakh.'

Vishnu Baba spat on Bhoora's face. 'Look, they undervalue you so much. I know this girl is a well-known news anchor and you, Aakash Khurana, the chef at some local TV. I'm going to demand a ransom of five crore rupees from the government. If they cough up, you can go back to your past lives,' Vishnu Baba explained to Aakash and Shweta calmly like a teacher explaining school rules to students.

Shweta turned to look at Tewatia. 'So you fooled us all the way. You never planned to take us to Gwalior. How much are you getting from this deal?'

'Madam, in Chambal, the police have a fixed rate—twenty per cent on all deals. However, for Vishnu Baba, I've come down to fifteen. You know, my wife wants a bigger house, a bigger TV set, a new kitchen, new clothes, jewellery and all. You think I can provide her all this with my salary? We have to make deals. After all, I saved you from the other gang of dacoits or they would've kidnapped you. With Vishnu Baba, you're totally safe. That much I can guarantee,' said Tewatia.

'I think it's time we got going,' said Vishnu Baba.

'I'm not going anywhere with you,' Shweta protested.

Flicking aside his unruly curls, Vishnu Baba smirked at her. 'You don't seem to have understood that you're under my command. You've been kidnapped for a hefty ransom and till I get it, you'll do exactly what I tell you to do.'

Kallu picked up his rifle and shouted at the other dacoits, 'You guys went to sleep or what? Get up!'

Shweta sat down on the floor with Aakash chained to her, and said, 'Do what you want but I'm not moving.'

Suddenly a rifle butt landed on one side of Aakash's face. He fell to the floor with the impact. There was a gash on his head and blood trickled down his face.

Kallu looked at Shweta and said curtly, 'Next it will be your turn. Get up and start moving.'

Tewatia touched Vishnu Baba's feet. 'What should we do with this Bhoora?'

Vishnu Baba looked at Bhoora. 'He found them, so he'll come with us.'

Bhoora fell at Vishnu Baba's feet, ready to do anything for him. Tewatia removed his handcuffs and Bhoora felt like a whole new man.

Aakash managed to sit up. Shweta tore off a bit of his blood-soaked shirt and pressed it on the wound on his head.

As Vishnu Baba walked out of the police chowki, the other dacoits followed him. Kallu pushed out Aakash and Shweta and stood behind them, rifle in hand. Vishnu Baba looked at the police jeep and said, 'This is what they call breaking news. The top news anchor in the country has been kidnapped.'

He instructed his gang, 'For now, we'll take the police jeep and some guns from the chowki.' Then he looked at Kallu and said, 'The constables can be dispensed with.'

Kallu dislodged the rifle from his shoulder and shot the two constables. Then he walked up to to them and shot them again in the chest and the head.

Tewatia was too stunned to speak.

Vishnu Baba smiled. 'It's good for the police report. You can write that some dacoits attacked the police party, killed the constables and made off with the jeep and guns. Just wait till we get the payment, and you'll get your cut.'

Staring at the two dead constables, Tewatia nodded quietly. A few other policemen who had run out of the chowki stood behind a dilapidated brick wall, trembling.

Vishnu Baba climbed into the jeep while Kallu shoved Aakash and Shweta in the back and locked the door. The world collapsed before their eyes, leaving behind nothing but meaningless ruins.

Kallu got into the driver's seat. A few dacoits clung on to the sides while others sat on the roof as the jeep sped through Chambal Valley.

17

Back in Mumbai, Shweta's brother Vikram, along with top police officials and the management of News World, repeatedly watched her shows to look for a connection to her sudden disappearance. Vikram was sure one of the guests on her show whom she had grilled got her kidnapped. However, it was impossible to zero in on anyone.

No one had received any ransom call. If this had been done to harm her, it was doubtful that the police team would ever find Shweta and Aakash alive. They could have been killed and their bodies burnt or buried somewhere.

Vikram came up with a list of suspects, including three top politicians, a Bollywood star who was a paedophile, a pharmaceutical group which had been exposed by Shweta for manufacturing party drugs, and two of Vikram's competitors who could have done it to harm his family's business interests.

Despite spending sleepless nights, there was not a wrinkle on Vikram's clothes. Slim and tall, the thirty-nine-year-old hotshot wore designer suits and handcrafted Italian leather shoes. Always well groomed and perfumed, he had turned Taj Lands End into the base camp where he worked, and where he met all the sources who could have any information on Shweta and Aakash.

In Delhi-NCR, Vikram was known to be a ruthless maniac, addicted to cocaine, girls, wealth and power. In Gurugram, rumour had it that Vikram had bumped off many of his competitors and farmers unwilling to sell their land to him, and buried them in the foundations of the massive shopping malls he built there.

Somehow, no news channel or newspaper dared speak against Vikram. Most reporters were on his payroll. In fact, they lauded him for turning Gurugram, once a mere village, into a glittering metropolis.

Subhash Chaudhary, a small-time builder and their father, had constructed a few small buildings in Gurugram. However, he could never strike it rich. Vikram kept working with his father till the latter was killed in a road accident. Thereafter, Vikram started building his empire. Many believed it was Vikram who had his father killed as he was dead against taking over famers' lands.

Shweta totally kept away from the real estate business, and made a life of her own in Mumbai. She held Vikram responsible for their father's death, and hadn't spoken to him since. He called her persistently, but she never took his calls. A couple of times, when they met at a friend's wedding in Sainik Farms in Delhi, she gave monosyllabic replies to his questions before walking off.

Suddenly, her brother was trying to locate her.

Vikram had always hated Aakash, a chef, for marrying into their family. They had no idea about his lineage, so Vikram called him 'a bloody refugee'.

Vikram spoke personally to all the suspects on his list but couldn't get any information about Shweta or Aakash. He took it upon himself to find her. He was ready to do anything to get a lead on her. He bribed reporters believing they knew everything. Truth be told, most reporters had no idea what's happening in the city.

Another day was coming to an end. Vikram was getting increasingly restless. He yelled at the police officers and the management of News World for their incompetence. He had no idea that Shweta and Aakash were in Chambal with one of the most dreaded dacoits of that region.

18

Aakash and Shweta, who were hoping against all hope to escape from Chambal, were sucked back into the black hole. They travelled in the jeep with the dacoits for six to eight hours in Chambal. At one point, they had to get off the jeep and walk till the wild turned dark. The heavy chain still bound them together in spite of all the fights and arguments. The journey ended as they climbed and descended many mud mounds and finally reached the ruins of a temple.

The dacoits stretched out on the ground. One of them dug out a crate of country-made liquor they had buried behind the ruins. Kallu brought out a broken charpoy for Vishnu Baba, and spread a dirty mattress over it.

Finally, Aakash and Shweta sank to the muddy ground, with their backs to a broken wall, and closed their eyes. Within minutes, everyone was snoring.

Aakash and Shweta had lost all sense of time. Suddenly, they were jolted out of their sleep by Kallu kicking them. 'You have not come here to sleep. Get up.'

Vishnu Baba calmly lay on the charpoy. 'Kallu, don't be so angry with them. After all, you have felt her all over and in between her legs. Be gentle, she might allow you to do it again.'

The dacoits laughed crudely. One of them said, 'Baba, if you want them frisked again, I'll do a better job.'

Shweta felt violated; she wanted to bury herself alive.

'Arrey don't forget, we also have with us the great cook Aakash Khurana. He makes all kinds of English food on TV,'

Vishnu Baba laughed heartily. Then he turned to Aakash and asked, 'So what will you cook for us?'

Aakash quietly shook his head as if to say he had no idea.

Vishnu Baba snapped at Aakash, 'When I ask you something, you better answer, or the next time all these men will have their hands on your wife. So tell me.'

'Depends on the ingredients you've got,' Aakash said nervously.

'That's better,' said Vishnu Baba. 'Okay, where's Guddu? Did he get something for us?'

'I'm here, Baba,' Guddu called out as he hurried down a mud mound towards them. The young man was carrying a heavy sack. He approached Vishnu Baba and touched his feet. 'These are fresh for you.'

'Hand them over to our new cook from Mumbai. He has promised to cook us a treat today,' declared Vishnu Baba.

Guddu looked at them and smiled. 'This chain is a good idea.' He walked towards them. 'Usually I cook for Baba, but today you've got an opportunity to prove yourself. Who knows, Baba might be pleased with you and free you? He loves his food.' Guddu turned the sack upside down. Out tumbled two dead dogs with bullet holes in their bodies.

Guddu said proudly, 'I shot them from a distance of over a hundred metres. In the entirety of Chambal, there's no better shot than me.'

'Hey Guddu, let him cook now,' Kallu shouted. 'We're all hungry.'

Revolted by the sight of the dogs, Aakash mumbled, 'I've never cooked a dog.'

Guddu laughed. 'See Baba, your Mumbai cook has given up. He doesn't know how to cook a dog. Here in Chambal, I cook the best meat. I've cooked dogs, wolves, horses, buffaloes, snakes and grasshoppers.'

'Guddu, don't underestimate him. He comes on TV,' said Vishnu Baba.

'Okay, then let's have a competition and see who cooks better. This TV cook or this Chambal cook? What do you say, Baba?' Guddu spoke excitedly.

'Superb idea, Guddu,' another dacoit chimed in.

'Yes, let's have a competition,' cried the others.

Vishnu Baba looked at them and said, 'Okay, the competition is fine with me but what's the prize for the winner.'

Guddu took a few steps towards Vishnu Baba and said, 'Baba, if I win, I'll spend a night with the Mumbai girl.'

'She's my wife. Don't you dare touch her!' Aakash shouted angrily.

'Do you have a choice? These men could easily shoot you dead and do whatever they want with your wife. Now here's the chance of a lifetime. If you win, I'll set you free,' Vishnu Baba said enticingly.

'How can you set them free?' Kallu cried out.

'We have to be fair in competition. If Guddu wants the girl as his prize, Aakash should have an equally big prize too,' said Vishnu Baba as an equitable judge. Then he turned to Aakash and said, 'Are you happy with this? If you win, I promise, Guddu himself will escort you two out of Chambal and drop you off at Gwalior airport.'

There was sudden silence. Aakash and Shweta looked at each other. They were in no position to negotiate.

'I didn't hear your answer, Chef,' Vishnu Baba cried out. 'Are you ready for the competition or not?'

Aakash nodded nervously, 'Yes, I am.'

Suddenly, Vishnu Baba got up and started to clap. 'This will be fun. Finally, there's some excitement in Chambal. Guddu, c'mon, you're competing with the country's best chef Aakash

Khurana. Who knows, Guddu? One day, you might also have your own TV show.'

The dacoits sniggered. Vishnu Baba looked at them. 'It's good that you both are chained to each other. Now your wife can also help you.' Then he said, 'Munna, show them our kitchen and provide them with all the spices, oil and stuff. Meanwhile, let's get the drinks going.'

Hardly fifteen years old, Munna led them to the kitchen—a desolate corner of the ruins. A small glass bottle filled with oil and a burning wick was the only source of light. The sound of crickets chirping filled the air. Darkness stalked them like a sinister sentinel.

Stacked in the corner were a few pots and pans. There was no stove, gas or kerosene. Munna showed them the makeshift, open brick-and-clay *chulha*. For the fire, there was a pile of dry wood. Munna pointed to a few rusted cans. 'The spices and oil are in those.' He picked a long rusted knife with a wooden handle. 'This will help you chop and break the bones.'

Aakash and Shweta looked at each other nervously. Aakash had taken part in many cookery competitions on TV, but this was something he had never imagined. He looked at Guddu, who was a little distance away from them and had already got down to work.

Like an expert, Guddu made a long cut from the dog's chin up to the rectum and slit up the four legs. Then he started to peel the dog's skin.

Shweta couldn't get herself to skin the dog, and Aakash stood dazed as though his brain had been beaten to a pulp.

'Hey, we don't have all the time in the world. I am hungry,' Vishnu Baba shouted at Aakash.

With trembling hands, Aakash looked into the many rusted cans to check the spices. A plastic can had vegetable oil that had turned black with overuse. There were no powdered spices. Aakash took out a few turmeric roots, dried red chillies, cumin seeds and rock salt.

'We need to grind these.' Aakash turned to Shweta for help. He pointed to a stone grinder among the pots and pans and told Shweta, 'We'll have to use that. I mean you'll have to help me with this while I start to work on the dog.'

Shweta looked at him like a wife wronged. 'You know I have never done that.'

'Do we have a choice?'

Shweta nodded quietly while Aakash instructed her on how to move one stone over another. 'Just keep adding a little water till it turns into a thick paste.'

The chain restricted their movements. So they had to work closely. Aakash started to skin the dog the way he had seen Guddu doing it. He had cooked all kinds of meat, but never a dog. He turned to look at Guddu, who picked up the dog's severed head by the ears and showed it to them as though it were a trophy. Shweta would've puked, but somehow she managed to concentrate on the grinding. Aakash severed the head with great difficulty. The dead dog seemed to stare at him with its wide-open eyes. He started to cut it into pieces just the way he used to slice chicken.

Shweta was drenched in sweat. Her face became red and her eyes stung. The smell of dried red chillies made her nose run. She looked at Aakash and cried, 'This is all because of you. You agreed to have this crazy competition.'

'These men can easily shoot me or chop me into pieces. Then they can do whatever they want with you. Does that work better for you?' Aakash spoke as he angrily chopped up the dog's legs.

'Bloody useless man! Even at the police station when that

dacoit groped me, you just stood there like a corpse. Any man would have fought for his woman.' Shweta, the feminist, said bitterly.

'They held a gun to my head and wouldn't have hesitated to shoot me,' Aakash said, trying to suppress his anger.

Shweta smirked. 'You were always like this. You could never take a stand when the situation asked for it. Now we're in this hell all because of you.'

'Oh yes, it was me who chained us to a tree in Chambal,' Aakash retorted, looking at Guddu who was stoking the fire in the chulha.

Bhoora walked towards them with a steel tumbler filled with liquor. 'Aakash-ji, have this and you'll turn into a real man. These women ruin the best of men.' He looked at them with a sly smile and asked, 'By the way, who's the man between you two?'

Aakash closed his eyes for a minute, trying to concentrate on the situation. Then he said, 'We have to start the fire in the chulha.'

Shweta looked lost. 'How do we do that?'

Aakash picked some dry wood and put it in the chulha. He poured some oil over the wood, and with the burning wick, lit the chulha. Immediately, the dry wood caught fire. 'You need to be careful,' Aakash warned Shweta.

Guddu was already stirring the meat in the large pot on the chulha.

Aakash had to hurry up. Shweta had no idea what he was doing. It had been years since Shweta had cooked anything. She never needed to.

Soon Aakash also had the meat cooking in the pot.

Guddu tasted a piece of the meat and exclaimed, 'This is the best meat I've ever cooked. Tonight I am going to have some fun. What do you say, Madam-ji?'

As the smell of spices spread, the dacoits started to call out, 'C'mon, we're hungry. Let's taste some meat!'

Vishnu Baba announced that for the competition, he, along with Kallu, Bhoora and Chaubey-ji—one of the seniormost dacoits in the gang—would be the judges. All four would taste the dishes prepared by both parties and then decide the winner.

The four judges sat in a line on charpoys, with the other dacoits assembled around them in a semi-circle. Vishnu Baba called out, 'First, we'll taste Guddu's dish.' The other dacoits cheered, 'C'mon Guddu. This is your only chance with Mumbai *ki* Madam.'

Guddu walked up to the four judges with a steel platter. Vishnu Baba took a piece of the meat from it and started to chew on it. The other three followed suit.

'This is the best you've ever cooked, Guddu,' said Vishnu Baba. 'Let's hear what the other judges have to say.'

The other judges merely repeated what Vishnu Baba said.

Bhoora added slimily, 'Guddu, you better loosen your *langot* and get ready for the big night.' The entire place resounded with raucous laughter.

Vishnu Baba looked at Guddu and said, 'Don't forget, you're up against the TV-*wala* chef. Can you beat him, or will he get a chance to escape from Chambal with his wife?'

The air was tense. If Aakash won, it would mark not only Guddu's defeat, but everyone else's too. They would be left with no choice but to escort their hostages out of Chambal. Vishnu Baba called out Aakash's name. Aakash and Shweta walked towards the judges, matching steps, with Aakash holding the platter. Nervously, Aakash placed the platter in front of them.

Vishnu Baba looked at them. 'For the first time, we'll be tasting meat cooked by a TV chef. The question is, are you really that good?' He looked at Aakash with piercing eyes, and then turned to Shweta and smiled, 'Madam-ji, are you ready? Our little Guddu seems to be in love with you.'

Shweta tried to control her rage. Aakash looked at Vishnu Baba and said, 'You promised us that if we won, you'd let us go.'

Picking up a piece of meat from the platter, Vishnu Baba said out loud, 'The question is, will you win?'

Deep inside, Aakash knew that these dacoits were using them for their entertainment in the wild. They were both judge and executioner. There was no chance of Aakash and Shweta ever winning.

Vishnu Baba chewed on the meat and spoke like a judge on *MasterChef*, 'The meat is really juicy and soft. It has all the spices and it's lip-smacking.'

The dacoits looked at him dumbstruck. After a dramatic pause, Vishnu Baba continued, 'There's only one thing lacking in this dish—love. The dish Guddu cooked was full of love for this Madam, but the dish Aakash has cooked is filled with the desire to escape.'

'What do you mean?' Aakash shouted.

'It means that Guddu has won,' Vishnu Baba announced. He looked at the other three judges, 'What do you say?'

'You're absolutely correct. There's no love in his dish. Our Guddu has won,' Kallu proclaimed proudly.

'So, according to the rules of this competition, Guddu gets to spend a night with the woman,' Vishnu Baba announced. The dacoits cheered excitedly like schoolboys who had won a trophy, 'Guddu! Guddu! Guddu!'

Aakash held on to Shweta's hand. 'She's my wife and I won't let anyone touch her.'

Guddu started to walk towards them, brandishing a kitchen knife. 'If I have to cut you into pieces, I will.'

Holding Shweta's hand tight, Aakash turned around and

started to run. Guddu went after them. The dacoits cheered him while Vishnu Baba laughed. They ran over a mud mound only to be overpowered by Guddu. He looked like a hungry dog with his loins on fire. Pointing the knife at them, he said, 'She's mine.'

Aakash pushed Shweta behind him, and stood blocking Guddu's path.

19

The whole gang of dacoits cried out, 'Guddu, chop off his hands!' 'Chop off his head!' 'Look at the girl, she wants you!' 'This is your night, Guddu. Don't let her go!'

Guddu stood in front of Aakash and Shweta, brandishing the knife menacingly. Aakash tried to reason with him, 'Look, we are your hostages. If anything happens to us, you won't get your ransom money.'

Guddu dismissed Aakash and laughed lustily. 'I don't care about the money. Right now, I want this bitch. If you try to stop me, I'll cut you into pieces.'

With his bare hands, Aakash tried to wrench the knife from Guddu's hand. Hiding behind Aakash, a terrified Shweta watched everything.

Cheered on by the dacoits, suddenly Guddu made a dash for her. At the right moment, Aakash swayed back as if in a reflex motion and the knife sliced through the darkness. With each move, Guddu's lust for blood and the woman seemed to grow.

Aakash looked helpless. The cacophony of voices around him cheered Guddu.

Then Aakash shouted at the top of his voice, 'Vishnu Baba, you'll lose your ransom of five crore rupees if he does anything to us.'

'Don't worry about the ransom,' Vishnu Baba shouted back. 'I'll get the money in exchange for your dead bodies.' He called out to Guddu, 'Will you stand there the whole night or what? If you can't do it, I'm going to send Kallu.'

Kallu beamed with pleasure. 'Baba, please let me handle this since Guddu seems incapable of doing anything.'

'Let him have his chance,' Vishnu Baba said.

Guddu moved the big knife in his hand like an expert knife-fighter. 'I'll give you one last chance. You can look the other way while I make out with your wife, or you might lose your hands, head and your life. The woman is mine. Better put your hands down, or I'm going to chop them off.'

The world is a jungle. The question is who's the fittest, and shall survive? A man with a weapon is twice as powerful as the man without one, whether it is in Chambal or in the streets of Mumbai.

Tears trickled down Shweta's face. She closed her eyes and mumbled, 'God, you can't do this to us. Please, please help us.'

Guddu raised his hand to strike Aakash. At that very moment, the sound of the damru pierced the veil of darkness. In walked Gadariya, his staff in one hand and the damru in the other. From a distance, he looked at the gang of dacoits and at Guddu holding the knife. As he stopped playing the damru, silence descended on the ruins.

'Gadariya,' Vishnu Baba mumbled as he stood up from the charpoy. The rest of the dacoits stood up as well.

Gadariya looked at Guddu. 'So you were attacking these two who are chained and unarmed?'

Guddu froze on the spot. Then Vishnu Baba explained, 'Gadariya, our boy has won the woman in a competition. If he has to kill the man to take the woman, he will. You'd better not interfere.'

Gadariya looked up at the sky and shouted, 'Look, Maan Singh, what's happening in your Chambal! An innocent woman and her husband are being targeted by a gang of dacoits. These dacoits are ready to kill for the woman. Maan Singh, you'll have to do justice.'

The dacoits whispered among themseves, 'This Gadariya is a ghost. They say bullets can't hurt him. He can fly all over Chambal, and knows exactly what's happening where.'

'Shut up,' Vishnu Baba shouted at his men. 'There's no need to be afraid of him.'

Another whispered, 'I've heard he killed over two hundred men with an axe. If he slaughtered an entire gang in one night, he can easily kill us all too.'

Gadariya looked at them. 'Thank God, Daku Maan Singh is not here today or he would have lined you all up and shot you. He never raised as much as a finger on a woman, and you all are ready to tear her apart.'

'Maan Singh is dead and so are his stupid ideals. This Chambal belongs to me!' asserted Vishnu Baba.

Gadariya's laughter echoed through the ravines, making the dacoits shiver. 'This Chambal belongs to only one person and that is Daku Maan Singh. His spirit still lives here, and he protects and guards this Chambal.'

'This woman belongs to our man and if he has to kill the husband, he will,' said Vishnu Baba defiantly. 'If he wants to save his wife, let him fight.'

Gadariya looked at them and nodded. Then he brought out a small axe tucked in his waistband. 'It's unfair to fight an unarmed man.' He flung the axe towards Aakash, saying, 'Pick it up.'

Dumbfounded, Aakash first looked at him and then at the axe.

'Pick up that axe. Do you want him to take your wife away?' Gadariya yelled.

Aakash stepped close to the axe and grabbed it by its wooden handle. Gadariya smiled at him, and proclaimed loudly, 'This axe belongs to Daku Maan Singh. It's the same axe with which I killed more than two hundred dacoits in this very Chambal. Let's see what it accomplishes today.'

The dacoits stood still, their beastly rage thwarted by their sense of dread.

'You can't win against the axe of Daku Maan Singh,' declared Gadariya.

'Guddu,' Vishnu Baba thundered. 'Don't be scared. He's just a TV chef. He can't even hold the axe properly. C'mon, chop him to pieces, and the woman is yours.'

Sweating and trembling, Aakash held on to the axe as he watched the large knife sway in front of his eyes. Behind him stood Shweta, staring at this macabre dance of death.

Gadariya looked at Aakash. 'Remember, this is Daku Maan Singh's axe. They say the spirit of Maan Singh lives in the axe. Now you are Daku Maan Singh. Let the entire Chambal know that Daku Maan Singh is back. Tell them you are Maan Singh.'

As fear gripped Aakash's soul and sweat streamed into his eyes, his vision became foggy. He opened his lips to say something but no words came out.

'Go on. Say it. Cry it out to the wild!' Gadariya egged him on.

'I-I'm Daku Maan Singh.' Words tumbled out of Aakash's mouth like discordant notes of a symphony.

'Louder Aakash, louder! When Maan Singh spoke, Chambal trembled. Let your voice shake up the wild once again. Let Maan Singh speak through you. Conquer your fears and *become* Maan Singh!'

Guddu threateningly moved the knife through the air: 'I'm going to chop you up, cook boy, and have my way with your wife.'

Something stirred in Aakash; he felt a long-dormant courage

spring back to life. Suddenly, he cried with all his strength, 'I'm Daku Maan Singh!'

He cried again and again, the echoes of his cries piercing the dark night, and the deep ravines of Chambal. The yelping dogs and howling wolves suddenly fell silent, as if in reverence.

Gadariya smiled triumphantly, cautioning the dacoits with a finger on his lips, 'Maan Singh has returned.'

A mysterious energy charged the two rivals. They looked at each other, and made their first moves. The blades struck each other. Aakash knew he would have to fight. All his fears suddenly vanished.

Standing silently, the group of dacoits watched the duel transfixed. Vishnu Baba yelled, 'Guddu, just make mincemeat of that cook!'

Gadariya stood to one side and started to play the damru—like the drumrolls from wars of yore. There was something primitive about men ready to kill each other. Aakash could feel every nerve in his body tingling, like a great warrior on the battlefield. He had never felt this way.

They clashed. The knife struck the wooden handle of the axe. Guddu moved in closer, but Aakash managed to duck to one side.

Gadariya looked up at the sky and shouted, 'Maan Singh, you can't let a woman be torn to pieces by these hungry wolves. You have to show them that you are still the Lion of Chambal, that a pack of wolves can't scare away a lion.'

He turned to Aakash and cheered, 'Go for the kill, Maan Singh, go!'

The knife came hurtling down on Aakash. He ducked, and in that same move, swung the arm holding the axe with all his strength. The axe came up whirling from the bottom and hit Guddu under the chin.

Guddu's eyes popped out. He lost his grip on the knife and it fell from his hand. With the axe stuck under his chin, he moved aimlessly, looking at his gang for help. He looked at Aakash in disbelief and took a faltering step towards him. As Guddu freed the axe from under his chin, a fountain of blood spurted from the wound.

Axe in hand, Guddu charged at Aakash with a loud cry. He was about to bring the axe down with full force on Aakash's head but froze midway. The axe slipped from his hands as the knife sliced through his guts. It was Shweta. He couldn't believe this could happen to him. He laughed deliriously as blood spilled out of his mouth. He looked at Gadariya, and fell to the ground dead.

The dacoits froze in the darkness. Not a word escaped their mouth. Their Guddu, a skilled knife-fighter, had been knifed by a couple who might never have held a knife except to chop vegetables.

Gadariya looked at the dacoits. 'I told you, Daku Maan Singh still lives in this Chambal. His spirit still watches over the wild.' He bent close to Guddu's body and said, 'It's gone. The spirit has escaped this dreadful body.' He pushed the body from the mud mound. It went tumbling down, and fell close to Vishnu Baba.

Kallu and Munna rushed towards the body to see if Guddu was still alive. Overcome with rage and grief, Kallu raised his rifle and took aim. 'Gadariya, let's see who saves you.'

But Gadariya was gone. So were Aakash and Shweta.

20

Gadariya stood staring into the darkness with one leg entwined around the staff in his hand. Aakash sat close to Shweta, the chain making clinking sounds. They had put all their trust in Gadariya, and had no idea where they were. He had guided them through the darkness, through the narrow pathways and crevices, and over the hilltops, away from the gang of dacoits.

Aakash and Shweta were fascinated yet repelled by the inexhaustible variety of life. Something had happened to Aakash. He couldn't understand it. He had just killed a man, and experienced sorrow and joy in the killing. Shweta, on the other hand, broke down and wept.

'I can't believe I killed someone,' she cried as if confessing her crime to the entire wild.

Gadariya turned to her and said gently, 'If you had hesitated, he would've killed your husband and then you know what would've happened. You did well. This is exactly what was meant to be.'

'I feel horrible,' Shweta wailed.

Gadariya continued. 'A tiger stalks, chases, attacks and kills a deer. Do you think he goes through all these emotions before killing a deer? He acts because he has to. You did the right thing.'

'We want to get out of this place. Can you help us, please?' Aakash pleaded.

'Why do we have to go through all this?' Shweta cried.

Gadariya looked at her face streaked with rivulets of tears and smiled. 'Fate always acts with reason. We are the ones who are always judging. Things happen not by our will but as God deems fit.'

'Do you really believe in all this crap?' Aakash asked irreverently.

Gadariya looked at them and said, 'Once, during a village fair, Maan Singh had gone to Devi Bhawani's temple. Somehow, the police caught a whiff of it and surrounded the whole fair. A gun battle ensued, with Maan Singh fighting more than a hundred policemen. Finally, he was captured. The police decided to finish him off, so they tied him up inside a straw hut and set it on fire. There was no way Maan Singh could've escaped or survived. With no way out, he closed his eyes and prayed to Maa Bhawani. It rained. The fire was extinguished. The half-burnt straw hut collapsed and Maan Singh managed to escape.'

Gadariya looked at them. 'What would you call that? It's nothing but the will of God. Even a hundred policemen couldn't kill him. Maan Singh survived to become the Lion of Chambal.'

'I know for certain that it's not God who chained us and threw us here in the wild,' Aakash said bitterly.

Gadariya said, 'The question is not who did it but why? Look at it this way, the chain is not bondage. It kept you close together.'

'So that the two of us are tortured, and die in this wild?' Shweta said wryly.

Gadariya smiled. 'How long have you two been married?'

'I want to get out of this place and out of this marriage. Our married life is exactly like this wild—filled with fights, anger, bitterness, and totally barren and dry,' Aakash confessed.

Gadariya's laughter echoed in the dark. 'It happens. Marriage can turn one into a bitter person. In a marriage, two completely different people come together to share a life. The problem is they want to change the other person according to their expectations. Soon a blame game starts that turns ugly. It transforms marriage into a competition, a war where each wants the upper hand to prove that he or she is better than the other.'

'Did this happen to you too?' Aakash asked.

'Yes, it did,' said Gadariya. 'However, I soon realized that the two of us were just different. The only solution is to accept each other with all the differences. In fact, it doesn't need much effort.'

'So you seem to have a magic pill for this?' said Shweta.

Gadariya smiled. 'Yes, it's simple—love deeply and respect each other's differences.'

Aakash and Shweta both looked at him like students learning an important life lesson. They had met many new-age gurus and marriage counsellors, but they had never met someone like Gadariya. He apppeared to believe in the simplest of things— love—and seemed to have an answer for everything.

'We don't love each other anymore. How does one get this love back?' Aakash asked.

'Only love begets love; it cannot be rekindled mechanically. You have to start listening to your heart rather than your mind. The heart will tell you what to do. The heart is always right. Some call it intuition, but I call it the voice of God,' Gadariya looked at them and smiled. 'It was love that made you fight the dacoit and kill him to protect each other.'

Shweta and Aakash listened in silence.

'You seem to know the Chambal like the back of your hand. Please help us get out of here,' Shweta pleaded.

Gadariya replied, 'You should've asked God, not me, to help you. I'm a wanderer and could be wrong.'

'Enough of this nonsense. Can you help us or not?' Aakash said impatiently.

Gadariya looked into the dark. 'When the sun comes up, you'll see a narrow path leading straight ahead. Follow that and it'll take you to the highway.'

'Does a straight path even exist in these ravines?' asked Aakash.

'It's always the straightest path that takes us directly to our goal,' said Gadariya.

Aakash and Shweta were too exhausted to continue this exchange with Gadariya. They waited for the first rays of the sun to light the path leading to the highway. Crouched on a mud mound, for the first time in years, Aakash and Shweta rested their heads on each other's shoulders and slept.

21

In Chambal, dawn spreads fast, showing its true colours. The sun attacked the barren land with a vengeance, turning every grain of sand into smouldering ember. Then the cold of the night would swap places with an oppressive blanket of hot air. Again, the soothing curtain of darkness would be ripped apart, revealing nothing but unending ravines and hills.

As Aakash and Shweta opened their eyes, it all came back to them—the competition, the duel, Gadariya, his life lessons, and the path that would lead them directly to the highway.

They got up to look for the path. But blocking their view stood Vishnu Baba along with his gang of dacoits. He smiled at them. 'Arrey, why did you get up so early? You can sleep for some more time. I've heard people in Mumbai sleep well into the afternoon.'

'What do they do at night?' Bhoora asked mockingly.

'They party, dance, drink and sleep at five in the morning,' Vishnu Baba replied.

Sitting on the ground with his rifle in hand, Kallu sneered, 'Baba, I also want to become a TV hero like them. I can also sleep with all the heroines, drink *videshi* booze, and party.'

Vishnu Baba turned to Shweta. 'Tell me, can this Kallu ever become a film hero with his deadly looks?'

Everyone burst out laughing.

Vishnu Baba continued, 'Madam-ji, never mind what one says, our Chaubey-ji reads news like any other professional on TV. Chaubey-ji, let's hear the latest news. Who knows, Madam-ji might recommend you to her channel.'

An elderly man about sixty-five-years old, Chaubey-ji stepped forward in a torn vest and started to make sound and music with his mouth before getting on with the news. 'I welcome you all to my news show. First the breaking news—Vishnu Baba, the dreaded dacoit of Chambal, has kidnapped the renowned news anchor Shweta Chaudhary and her husband Aakash Khurana, and has demanded a ransom of five crore rupees, otherwise both hostages will be killed and their heads will be sent to Mumbai. *Dhanyavaad. Aaj ka samachaar yahin samaapt hua* (Thank you. That's the end of today's news)!'

Paralyzed with fear, Aakash and Shweta stared at the dacoits. Kallu leapt towards them and pointed the knife at Aakash. 'Baba, they killed our Guddu. I'll skin this bastard alive!'

'It was a duel, Kallu, and our Guddu lost. What can we do? It was that Gadariya who interfered in our matter. Next time, the moment you see him, kill him,' Vishnu Baba said angrily. Then he looked up and asked, 'Where's our computerwala?'

A lean man in trousers and a shirt stepped forward with a smartphone in hand. He walked up to Vishnu Baba and touched his feet. 'Baba, this time you have a big party.'

'Pappu, I want everything to be perfect.'

'Baba there's not a soul in Chambal or even the whole of Madhya Pradesh, who can go against your wishes. I've got everything you wanted,' said Pappu.

Vishnu Baba turned to look at Aakash and Shweta. 'Why are you standing? Please sit down. You are our guests and you have to look good and presentable. Pappu handles all our computer and video work. So we'll be making a video with you and sending it to Mumbai with the ransom demand. And don't think I'm angry that you tried to escape. Where will you go in this wild?

How far can you run? I'm happy that we are back together.'

He turned to address the gang. 'Everyone, get ready. It's time to show our Mumbaiwalas that you are no less.'

The whole place turned into a green room as Pappu untied a huge sack and pulled out costumes, caps, banners and flags. Aakash and Shweta stood there watching the preparations for their ransom video.

Dressed in a camouflage jacket, Munna turned to Aakash. 'How come all film heroes have muscular bodies?'

Too nervous to answer, Aakash shrugged his shoulders.

Pappu continued. 'I know they all take drugs. They look sculpted but they more are like balloons—full of hot air.'

Kallu placed a green banner on a rock. 'So what? They have all the beautiful women, cars, big houses, and eat pizza, burgers and cakes.'

'*Behenchod,* in Mumbai everyone is on drugs. They are always dancing, partying and having sex in movies,' Pappu said.

'What nonsense! Mumbai is like any other city, and normal people like you live there,' Shweta defended the city that had given her so much.

Amused, Vishnu Baba looked at her. 'She really loves Mumbai.'

Meanwhile, Kallu had straightened the banner. It had a message written in Urdu. The dacoits put on green *pathani* suits, and covered their faces with monkey caps. Pappu handed out Pakistani flags to two of them, and selected the right spot to film the video.

'Okay Baba, we're ready for the shoot,' indicated Pappu.

Vishnu Baba looked at the dacoits standing in front of the banner. He inspected their clothes and asked them to put some *surma* in their eyes. 'With this, the police, CBI, IB, CRPF and all other forces will be out looking for them. We can't take any chances.'

Aakash and Shweta couldn't understand what was going on.

Vishnu Baba made the dacoits rehearse their positions and shout 'Allahu Akbar!' Then he walked up to Aakash and Shweta. 'Now, you two better listen. You'll have to say that a terrorist group has kidnapped you and they are demanding a ransom of five crore rupees, and that you'll be killed if that's not paid. Make it a bit dramatic or I'll have to slice your throats to show them some blood.'

'You are not terrorists. This way, you'll never get the ransom,' said Aakash.

'Don't worry, we have our contact in Mumbai, so everything will be taken care of,' Vishnu Baba said.

Kallu, Munna, Chaubey-ji and the other dacoits were ready. They looked as excited and nervous as schoolboys waiting in the wings for their turn on the stage. Vishnu Baba pointed to a spot for Aakash and Shweta. Pappu adjusted the camera lens of his smartphone and focused on them.

Vishnu Baba ordered, 'Okay Pappu, roll.'

Pappu said, 'Action.'

Aakash and Shweta looked at each other and mumbled something. Vishnu Baba shouted, 'What the hell do you think this is? You want to do it or should I shoot you so you feel real pain?'

Looking at Aakash and Shweta, Pappu said, 'We need emotion. You both kneel down and all you guys point the guns at their heads.'

Munna asked, 'When do we cry "Allahu Akbar"?'

Vishnu Baba looked at him irritated. 'Asshole, once they finish speaking, only then will you speak.'

'What's the name of our terrorist group?' Chaubey-ji asked.

'It doesn't matter, Chaubey-ji,' Vishnu Baba yelled. 'Now, all of you shut up and get this done! Pappu, I hope your camera is working.'

Pappu smiled. 'Don't worry, Baba. I can beat the best film directors of Mumbai.'

Aakash and Shweta both knelt down with guns pointed at their heads. Pappu said 'action!'

Aakash looked at Shweta and started, 'Please help us! We have been kidnapped by this gang of dacoits in Chambal and they...' Before he could say anything more, Vishnu Baba came charging at Aakash and punched him. '*Sala*, these Mumbaiwalas don't understand if you talk to them nicely.'

Then he gave Shweta a resounding slap. 'You want me to strip this bitch and let my men rape her? It's not a film shoot like you people do in Mumbai. This is Chambal. Let me see who helps you here.'

Aakash and Shweta lay on the ground covered in dust. Slowly, they got up and took their positions again.

Pappu called out 'action!'

This time, they said exactly what they had been told to. And it ended with cries of 'Allahu Akbar!'

Vishnu Baba said, 'This is the problem with most people living in cities. You promise to build them a house, they don't believe you. You threaten to burn down their house, they do as they are told. Most people go through life trying to uphold the dignity they never had. The only one to enjoy respect is the one wielding the gun. Everyone bows to the powerful.'

The shoot over, Pappu was taking stock of the banner, monkey caps and pathani suits.

Taking off his suit, Munna asked, 'Baba, what'll we do with five crore rupees?'

'What five crores? Bloody fifteen per cent will go to Tewatia, ten per cent to our contact in Mumbai and another ten per cent to Bhoora. After all, he caught them,' said Vishnu Baba looking at Bhoora.

Bhoora smiled shyly. 'Baba, I'll be happy with whatever you give. I think a film should be made on your life as they did on Paan Singh Tomar.'

'Superb idea,' endorsed Kallu. '"Vishnu Baba"—the title itself is so powerful. We can get the same director who made *Paan Singh* to direct this film too.'

Vishnu Baba looked at them thoughtfully. 'Good idea. Once we're finished with these two, we can get that film director from Mumbai across.'

Everyone cheered, 'Vishnu Baba! Vishnu Baba! Vishnu Baba!'

22

By late evening, the video had reached the News World office. Even before they could put it on air, it was on YouTube. The entire city of Mumbai watched it on their smartphones, in local trains, in offices, in cafés, in roadside stalls, and in their homes. Those who missed it watched it on the prime-time *News Line* show. More than the threats and the demand for ransom, Aakash's blood-soaked shirt and Shweta's tear-streaked face did the trick. Somehow, the sight of blood and tears always worked.

Nalini, who was filling in for Shweta on *News Line*, spoke with a lot of emotion. 'This video confirms that both Shweta Chaudhary and her husband Aakash Khurana have been kidnapped by a terrorist group. They have demanded a ransom of five crore rupees for their release. The terrorists have beaten Aakash mercilessly to the extent that his shirt was soaked in his own blood, while they made Shweta watch the torture.'

As the video was picked up by other channels, references were made to the kidnapping and beheading of Daniel Pearl. Soon the entire security machinery was galavnized into action. News shows brought in their own armchair analysts for expert comments and opinions.

ACP Hemant Roy, Crime Branch, Mumbai Police, and his best men went through the video many times in the News World office. 'Terrorist groups usually never ask for ransom. They kidnap people and hold them hostage to get their own men released from prison. Most terrorist groups have a strong ideology, but in this video they come across as a bunch of small-time kidnappers. This video could be fake,' concluded Roy.

Vikram, who was present during the investigation in the News World office, shouted, 'After so many days, we have a lead and you're saying that the video is fake. We need to start negotiating with these terrorists and get Shweta and Aakash out of their clutches. I won't let my sister suffer anymore.'

Roy gave him a stern look. 'I understand your emotions but please don't interfere in my work.'

'What work have you done in all these days? At least the video proves that they've been kidnapped by terrorists but you are not even ready to accept that. I don't want to interfere in your work but then you better start working,' Vikram shot back.

Roy was known to be a no-nonsense officer while Vikram was an egoist, known to bribe top government officials to keep them in his pocket. With a heavy moustache and a robust physique, Roy looked like a wrestler, and not one to take crap from a businessman from Gurugram.

'Why is this man here?' Roy turned to his men, indirectly asking them to throw Vikram out.

Vikram started shouting, 'I'm Shweta's brother! You touch me and I'm going to get the whole media and tell them of your high-handedness! The only thing you have done is say that the video is fake. Can you prove it? Who else could have kidnapped her? She was the most popular news anchor and journalist in the country! They might have already taken them to Afghanistan while we're sitting here in Mumbai twiddling our thumbs.'

'If you want to be around, I don't want to hear a word from you, and I don't care who you are,' Roy snapped at Vikram. He looked at his team and said curtly, 'First, get the IT team working on the video. It was put on YouTube and mailed to the channel. Let's see if we can find the server. Then we might be able to point out the location of the kidnappers.'

'You don't have to worry about the ransom. If they want money, I'll pay. I'll arrange for five crores,' Vikram said soberly.

Roy turned to him with a finger on the lips. 'I told you not to interfere in our work. And remember, if the kidnappers make any contact, only a police officer, and no one else, will talk to them.'

'What makes you so sure that they'll try to contact someone else?' Vikram butted in.

'I told you these kidnappers don't look like terrorists. I think they are small-time kidnappers and it is possible that they're here in Mumbai,' Roy said.

'In Mumbai?' Vikram looked at the other policemen and the senior management of News World. 'If they're in Mumbai, then what are you all doing here? Why don't you go out and get them?'

Roy behaved as if he hadn't heard Vikram. He turned to his team. 'The banner in the video that those men are holding, with the message in Urdu...get that analyzed immediately.'

'Well, they could be real terrorists connected with Pakistani terrorist organizations and the ISI? Please don't discard that possibility. You know the ISI and their activities. What if it's the ISI itself?' Vikram sounded worried.

Roy looked at Vikram and said, 'Don't go by the stories you read in newspapers and watch on TV. Things are not what they seem.'

23

Vishnu Baba sat drinking from a steel tumbler. He enjoyed Old Monk rum and could polish off an entire bottle by himself. It had been a tough night chasing their two hostages in Chambal. Fortunately, everyone was back in the ruins. He was happy that they had found Shweta and Aakash, and made the video. Hopefully, it was now being watched all over the country.

As a young boy of seventeen, enamoured by one of the sadhus who frequently visited their village, Vishnu had joined his group. Vishnu travelled with him to all the holy places—Haridwar, Kashi, Allahabad, Badrinath, Amarnath, Kedarnath, and more. He even lived in Rishikesh for a few years. However, when they came to Delhi, Vishnu got addicted to liquor and women. Soon, he strayed into a ring of thieves and started breaking into homes and stealing things. That gave him a whole new high.

During a robbery at Vasant Kunj Enclave in Delhi, the owners of the house, an elderly couple, woke up and resisted. High on liquor and with his newfound temptation for robberies, Vishnu stabbed the old couple. While Delhi Police was under tremendous pressure to crack down on the thieves, Vishnu managed to give them the slip, and came to Gwalior.

From being a small-time thief to becoming a robber and now a murderer, Vishnu discovered a whole new dimension to himself. He could kill. He started to enjoy killing and went on a murder spree in Gwalior. He raped young girls, murdered elderly couples in their homes, knifed shopkeepers, guards and even beggars sleeping on pavements. Gwalior Police went after him but he escaped to Chambal where he joined a gang of dacoits.

At the time, there weren't many gangs in Chambal. Daku Maan Singh was long gone. Phoolan Devi, Chhabiram and Nirbhay Singh Gujjar had also been shot dead. Only a handful of small gangs operated in the region. Vishnu got them together and turned Chambal into a breeding ground for kidnappers. They anointed him Vishnu Baba.

Vishnu Baba started to kidnap businessmen from Gwalior, Kanpur, Etawah, Etah and Mainpuri. Yet, he had never managed to get his hands on someone as big as Aakash and Shweta. The maximum ransom money his gang had ever extorted was six lakh rupees—for the son of a marble-stone contractor. In five cases of kidnapping, they killed the hostages as they didn't receive the ransom on time.

Vishnu Baba still had no idea who had chained Aakash and Shweta together and left them in Chambal. He had sent word to all the gangs, but none seem to be involved.

Somehow, Vishnu Baba was puzzled by Gadariya. Like a ghost, Gadariya appeared out of nowhere in the dark, and then vanished just as mysteriously. None of the dacoits dared raise their voice against Gadariya, the son of Daku Maan Singh. They feared the spirit of Maan Singh. Unable to destroy this belief about Gadariya, Vishnu Baba preferred to leave him alone and let him wander all around Chambal.

Oftentimes, Vishnu Baba tried to convince his men that Gadariya was just a lunatic. But deep inside, fear gripped him whenever he saw Gadariya. It was as though Gadariya could peer into Vishnu Baba's soul and see the evil lurking in it. Vishnu Baba didn't want any confrontation with Gadariya. He had just lost Guddu due to him. There was something intimidating about him. Maybe he really was possessed by the spirit of Daku Maan Singh.

Vishnu Baba turned to look at the two hostages.

Aakash and Shweta were busy performing their task. With Guddu dead, Vishnu Baba had assigned them the task of cooking. Guddu's body was buried nearby, along with a box of spices that he loved, and his favourite knife that had finally turned on him. In Chambal, most dacoits were buried. Bodies belonging to members of rival gangs were thrown to the dogs and wolves.

Aakash and Shweta were relieved to cook vegetables. Pappu the computerwala had brought a sack full of vegetables for them from the nearby village. This would be a true feast since the dacoits hardly got greens in the wild.

Once the whole gang was high on liquor, Aakash and Shweta served them dinner in steel platters. In minutes, dinner was over. With nothing to do after that, the dacoits trained their lusty eyes on Shweta.

Kallu yelled again. 'Baba, they killed our Guddu. We want revenge. We cannot let them get away with this.'

The whole gang chorused, 'Yes, we want revenge.'

Vishnu Baba looked at them and asked, 'What do you want?'

A drunk Kallu got up and said, 'Guddu won this woman and wanted to sleep with her but they killed him with Gadariya's help. I think Gadariya performed some black magic on our Guddu so he couldn't fight back. We need to fulfil Guddu's last wish. One by one, we'll all have this woman.'

Vishnu Baba raised his hands to silence them. 'You're right but as the leader of the gang, I'll have her first.'

The dacoits hooted and whistled. Vishnu Baba ordered Kallu. 'First break the chain. I can't be screwing her with her husband tied to her.'

Kallu threw aside the steel tumbler and picked up a machete. 'I'll break it.' He walked up to Aakash and Shewta. Shweta trembled with fear. She could see the savage lust in their eyes, and knew that no amount of pleading would work. Aakash tried to block Kallu but the latter smacked him with the butt of the machete before making them sit side by side with the chain on the ground.

Kallu struck the chain repeatedly with the machete. With each strike, sparks flew in the dark but the chain didn't yield to the sharpness of the machete's blade.

Vishnu Baba and the whole gang stood looking at them. Kallu got up irritated. 'I need a hammer.' Bhoora hurriedly fetched a hammer and handed it to Kallu. 'I need to have her after you. I was the one to find them.'

Kallu smiled at him and struck the chain with the hammer. He kept on raining blows on it but the chain didn't break.

'Kallu,' Vishnu Baba shouted to him. 'Why don't you cut that cook's hand and we can have her?'

Picking up the machete again, Kallu moved towards Aakash. 'Brilliant idea, Baba. I'm going to cut his hand in one move. Watch me.'

As Kallu raised the machete, Shweta stood up blocking him and said, 'Please don't do this. Just give us a little time. We might be able to free ourselves from these handcuffs.'

By now, Vishnu Baba had begun to enjoy himself. 'Kallu, stop. If they can do it, let them. We can give them a little time.' Then Vishnu Baba turned to the couple. 'Go ahead, you have ten minutes to free yourselves.'

Kallu stepped back reluctantly.

Vishnu Baba turned to an irate Kallu and said, 'Arrey, this is more fun. Let's cheer them. C'mon, snap out of it! But who has a watch here?'

Bhoora shouted, 'I have one. I'm keeping time.'

Aakash and Shweta looked at each other. They tried to

free themselves, but the handcuffs clung to their wrists with the tenacity of a scorpion's claws. Their eyes filled with tears.

They tried again. Finally, Shweta wailed, 'It's hopeless. We can't do anything.'

Bhoora looked at his watch. 'Three minutes left.' The dacoits watched them like a pack of wolves stalking prey, waiting for the right moment to pounce on it.

Aakash looked at Vishnu Baba. 'We need some oil to grease the handcuffs.' He and Shweta dragged themselves to the makeshift kitchen and poured some dark oil on their hands. After a few seconds, they tried to free their hands again but to no avail.

Bhoora shouted, 'Time's up!'

Kallu raised the machete in the air. 'Let me get the hand, Baba.'

Aakash pleaded, 'We just need a little more time, just a little more time.'

'Enough of your nonsense,' Kallu said, walking towards them. 'This chain won't come off.'

'Please, Vishnu Baba, give us a little more time,' Shweta pleaded.

'I don't like women pleading with me with tears in their eyes,' Vishnu Baba said mockingly. 'It does something to my heart. I can't say no to them but I also need to honour the word I gave my men. Well, I'll give you more time but for that, I need one finger. So decide whose finger it's going to be.'

Spreading his fingers wide, Kallu said to Vishnu Baba in disbelief, 'Only one finger?'

'It's a start,' said Vishnu Baba. 'We need to give them some more time. Look how she's crying.'

Shweta turned to Aakash. 'I'll give them a finger. We can't let them take away your hand.'

'No, I can manage without a finger. Don't worry, we'll get out of this,' Aakash told her, stroking her tear-streaked face.

Kallu came up to them. 'So, have you decided?'

Aakash nodded, placing his palm on the ground. Kallu touched his fingers with the machete, 'So, which one will it be?'

Vishnu Baba called out, 'We'll start with the smallest one.'

Kallu looked at him and said, 'It's no fun chopping a small finger.'

'The fun has just started, Kallu. Do as I say,' Vishnu Baba said.

With a broad grin, Kallu pressed the blade of machete on Aakash's little finger. Aakash cried out in pain. His whole hand was filled with blood. Shweta tried to help staunch the bleeding, but blood splattered all over her face. Kallu picked up the little finger and showed it around to everyone. Then he put it in his mouth and chewed it before spitting it out.

'Okay, you have ten more minutes,' resumed Vishnu Baba.

Aakash's head reeled in pain. He removed his blood-soaked shirt to wrap it around his hand. For the next ten minutes, they struggled to free themselves but drew a blank. Soon, time was up again.

Kallu was ready to have a second go with the machete, but Vishnu Baba stopped him. 'I want to give them one more chance. If they want, they'll get ten more minutes for one more finger.'

Ten minutes later, Aakash was numb with pain. Kallu had chopped off his ring finger. Again, he chewed it and spat it out.

With pain searing his entire being, Aakash lost all sense of time. The entire gang of dacoits was high on adrenaline, bloodlust and rage. The very sight of blood turned them on. Now they wanted the whole hand, but Vishnu Baba wanted the game to progress one step at a time. The sadist in him had come alive.

More liquor started to flow. Aakash knew the dacoits were playing mind games with them, that soon they would chop off his entire hand, and take away his wife. Suddenly, he seemed to be possessed by an unknown spirit—he was determined not to let anyone touch Shweta. He knew that the only chance they had was to run.

Aakash and Shweta were seated near the makeshift kitchen in a faraway corner of the ruins. Behind that was the wild. They knew they wouldn't be any safer in the wild, but they had to escape these savages. In his drunken stupor, Kallu had chucked the machete on the ground. Aakash spotted it. The dacoits were drowning in liquor. Without drawing attention to themselves, Aakash picked it up and whispered to Shweta, 'Run.'

With the dacoits drunk and sleepy, Aakash and Shweta slowly slipped into the darkness. Then they got up and ran.

Kallu saw them sprinting and shouted, 'There they go.' Immediately, the dacoits picked up their rifles and went after them.

Aakash and Shweta charged into the darkness with all their might. They must have covered just a few metres when they suddenly slipped into a hole that sucked them in deeper and deeper.

Finally, they landed on soft sand. When they looked up, they realized that they had fallen into a deep dry well. Kallu and the other dacoits were leaning into the well and yelling menacingly, 'Where will you run from here?'

24

The deep well had uneven, rocky walls. The dacoits believed that ghosts lived in it, so no one ever tried to venture in.

In the past, a team from the archaeology department visited the ruins to evaluate them. They concluded that either they were part of an ancient temple or they could have been an outpost for soldiers during the Mughal Era. The dacoits chased them away. Thereafter, no archaeologist or historian ever set foot in Chambal.

A few years back, the Madhya Pradesh government launched a drive to break down the mud mounds and hills of Chambal, and turn it into flat land. They planted thousands of mango trees to turn the wild into a green forest. None of the trees survived to produce even a single mango. The land was cursed.

Miraculously, Aakash and Shweta survived the fall. For a while, it felt as though every single bone in their body was broken, but gradually the pain subsided.

The machete Aakash had stolen fell close by. He picked it up, and looked up at Kallu and the rest of the dacoits. 'You want to get me? Come get me. C'mon Kallu. I'll chop you into pieces.'

Vishnu Baba came running to the well. Seeing Aakash and Shweta inside, he ordered his men to get the rope and take them out.

Munna threw the rope into the well. 'Baba, they have Kallu's machete so if anyone goes down, he'll strike him.'

Vishnu Baba peered into the well. 'See, we have lowered

the rope for you. You better climb out or I'm going to chop off both your hands.'

'Let your men come down. This time I'm going to hack them to pieces,' Aakash bellowed.

Kallu, who was totally drunk, aimed his rifle into the well. 'I'm going to shoot both of them.'

Vishnu Baba slapped him hard. 'You want to kill them so easily? They are trapped and can't escape. We just need to get them out.'

'I'll go down, Baba. Where's the rope?' Kallu offered.

'Hold back this maniac,' Vishnu Baba shouted to his men. 'He'll lose his head to that cook if he goes down in this state.' Vishnu Baba looked around at his men and called out, 'Chaubey-ji, you don't drink. You're the only sober man around. You go down and bring them up.'

Startled by Vishnu Baba's suggestion, Chaubey-ji, with his huge paunch, nervously suggested, 'He killed Guddu. Don't take him to be a mere cook.'

'Chaubey-ji, you better get down there, or I'm going to cut off your balls,' Vishnu Baba yelled.

Chaubey-ji nervously walked up to the well and held the rope. He looked at the other men and said, 'I hope the rope is strong enough to bear my weight.'

'Look, someone is coming down,' Shweta cautioned Aakash.

Aakash looked up. With the machete in one hand, he started to chant, 'I'm Daku Maan Singh.' The chanting grew louder and louder, reverberating in the well.

Chaubey-ji let go of the rope, and ran to one side. 'I cannot fight Daku Maan Singh. Can't you see the spirit of Maan Singh has possessed him? None of us can fight him.'

Vishnu Baba flew into a rage. 'Munna, you go in,' he shouted.

Munna licked his dry lips with his tongue out of fear, and said, 'Baba, I can't fight Maan Singh. You know about Gadariya. Possessed with Daku Maan Singh's spirit, he killed more than two hundred dacoits with Maan Singh's axe. Leave them alone, Baba.'

'Bloody assholes, you're scared of a name,' Vishnu Baba shouted. Then he turned to Bhoora. 'You get down and bring them up, Bhoora.'

Still holding the liquor bottle in his hand, Bhoora walked up to the well and looked down. 'Come up. Quick,' he ordered Aakash and Shweta.

Irritated beyond measure, Vishnu Baba kicked him hard in the butt. 'How did I get saddled with such cowards?'

Looking up, Aakash shouted at him, 'C'mon, who wants to come down?' He scraped the blade of the machete on the rocky wall. Sparks flew in the dark well. 'Vishnu Baba, you want to come down? Let me see if you really have the balls to rule Chambal!' Aakash laughed loudly.

Vishnu Baba looked at his drunken men and said, 'Let me see how long they can stay in there without food and water.' He pulled out the rope, threw it aside, and walked away.

For a while, Aakash stood inside the well, looking up. The excruciating pain radiated from his hand to every part of his body. He raised his arm, brandishing the machete, and screamed, 'I'm Daku Maan Singh!'

25

The whole bunch of drunken dacoits had fallen asleep across the ruins. None of them wanted to be close to the well lest the spirit of Daku Maan Singh attack them. Frustrated with his lot, Vishnu Baba drank till he passed out as well.

Chained together, Aakash and Shweta sat inside the well, looking up at the distant stars. Almost sixty metres below the earth's surface, they struggled to keep hope alive. Aakash had put up a brave fight, but deep down, he knew that finally the dacoits would get to them. After all, how long could they survive in a deep, dark well without food or water?

Aakash was delirious as he saw images appear in front of him as though the well really was full of spirits. Shweta seemed close to giving up the fight. It was just a matter of time before the dogs and wolves jumped in and tore them apart.

Aakash was sweating profusely. His shirt was totally drenched in blood. He tried to stay awake lest a dacoit slid down the well.

'I'm sorry,' mumbled Shweta. 'Maybe we'll never get out of this hole. Perhaps this will be our burial chamber. I know both of us have been uncouth with each other. Looking back, what were we really fighting about?' She smiled feebly at Aakash; the pain in her soul was unbearable.

'I failed to live up to your expectations. I'm sorry for that,' Aakash said to her.

'Those expectations were the biggest mistakes of my life. What were we doing to each other in the name of shallow values like social standing, recognition, fame and money? Here in the wild, you stood up for me, fought for me, and got your fingers chopped off for me.' Shweta wept copiously as realization dawned on her.

In the dark, Aakash suddenly said, 'I just saw my father. I think he has come to fetch me.'

'Shut up, Aakash!' Shweta screamed. 'You're not leaving me. You can't leave me alone in the darkness of the wild. We'll get out of this together and build a new life.'

Aakash laughed feverishly. Memories flooded his being, creating a collage in front of him.

'You know, my father came from Pakistan to Delhi during Partition,' Aakash mumbled as if narrating the story from the images that came up in front of his eyes. 'He was hardly ten when he started to work in a small eatery in Chandni Chowk. Despite his name being Mahadev Khurana, they all called him a *refugee*—pretty much what you and your brother often call me.

'He started the first onion kachori stall in Chandni Chowk. Soon, it became so famous that people from far and near came to eat his kachoris. That was also the time when truckloads of Punjabis and Sikhs were migrating to the UK and Canada. He also wanted a bright future, so he slipped into London with a group of illegal immigrants.'

Shweta quietly sat by his side, listening to him as if he was telling bedtime stories. He looked at her and smiled. 'I never told you about him. I really love and miss him.' Shweta nodded, trying to forget that they were imprisoned deep inside the earth.

'In London, the first job he got—sweeping and cleaning— was in a small Indian restaurant. Thereafter, he was allowed to clean the kitchen as well, but he was never allowed to cook. He pleaded with them to give him a chance to showcase his skills, but to no avail. For more than two years, he continued to sweep, clean, pick up leftover food, do the dishes and wipe the tables. One day, the chef had an altercation with the owner and quit. Left high and dry in the middle of a busy day, with customers waiting for their orders, the owner asked my father to help in the kitchen. And he made his favourite onion kachoris. That day onwards, the whole of London was running to that restaurant to have his kachoris.'

'Damn! I missed those kachoris,' Shweta said, trying to smile.

'O yes, you did,' Aakash said. 'Soon, he married Keertan, my mother, a typical Punjabi girl. In less than a year, I was born.'

'They sure were in a tearing hurry to have you,' Shweta beamed.

'Yes, my father wanted a family and took a huge loan to start his own restaurant—Curry King—in London. He also came up with unique recipes for Afghani kebabs, Peshawari gosht and chicken tikkas, while the hottest selling item was still his onion kachori. Many other chefs and restaurants tried to copy them, but none of them could get the taste and flavour that he packed in. Back then, in the Punjabi community in London, they used to say that it wasn't the spices but the love that Mahadev put in his kachoris that made them special.'

'So you started assisting him back in London?' Shweta asked.

'Not really, but he would often take me to the restaurant after school. I would sit in the kitchen watching him chop onions, garlic, chillies and vegetables with great finesse. Like any other boy filled with pride for his father, I also felt that there could be no better chef than him. At times, he would make me smell various spices, vegetables and oils, and tell me that the smell was enough to judge an ingredient. Those were my first masterclasses.'

'When did you come to India?' Shweta asked.

Aakash had a faraway look in his eyes. Suddenly they

brimmed with tears. He and Shweta had been married for so many years, yet they never talked about these things. He felt ashamed about bringing up anything about his family, fearing that Shweta would not like such family lore.

Aakash tried to block the pain. He took a deep breath and continued, 'During the London riots, the restaurant was burnt down, and my father was burnt alive. That was the time when the Whites were targeting Indian immigrants. Soon, my heartbroken mother passed away too. I was orphaned and alone in London. The Punjabi community came to my aid and sent me to my maternal grandparents in Amritsar. Thanks to the spirit of Punjab and their sense of community, I discovered a whole new family here. Then there was no looking back.'

'Bloody refugee,' Shweta teased him with tears in her eyes as she rested her head on his shoulder.

Aakash smiled. 'Yes, I'm your refugee. In fact, now we have both become refugees, cast away from the world, in this deep well in the wild.'

'Why would anyone do this to us? Who could it be? Even these dacoits don't know who chained us together,' Shweta moaned.

'Does it matter who did it?' Aakash spoke matter-of-factly. 'We're in a place where even God won't hear our prayers.'

Shweta sobbed softly. 'We can't die in this black hole. Please God, help us! Get us out of here.'

Darkness hung over the well; the wind hissed, reminding them of their death. 'God also needs rest, Shweta. He won't come to our aid. Maybe he wants us to die like this.'

Shweta joined her hands in prayer. 'God, please, if you are there, hear me.' Looking up at the sky, she implored, 'Please God!'

God chose not to respond. Shweta cried in vain till she could sob no more. She sat with her back to the rocky wall and closed her eyes. Her brilliant, logical and calm mind failed her. She was reduced to nothing.

In the darkness outside, a gunshot rang out, echoing through the well. Both Aakash and Shweta sat up. Soon the whole place came alive with gunshots and cries of men. They could hear Vishnu Baba ordering his men to pick up their guns.

A young girl shouted, 'Kill them all!' More shots and cries rent the air. Aakash and Shweta couldn't understand what was going on. They heard the girl's voice again. 'So Chaubey-ji, you seem to be having a good time in Chambal.'

They heard Chaubey-ji pleading for his life. Then the girl said coldly, 'Hey boy, it's your turn to kill them.'

Then Aakash and Shweta heard a gun being cocked. The loud shot was followed by Chaubey's pitiable cry.

'Good work, boy,' the girl said. 'Okay, just look around to see if anyone else is hiding in these ruins.'

Aakash looked at Shweta. 'It could be a police raid. We need to call out for help.' Both of them started to scream their lungs out. 'Help! Help us, please!'

The silhouette of a young girl with knotted hair appeared at the mouth of the well. With a rifle in one hand, she asked, 'Who the hell are you?'

'Vishnu Baba and his gang kidnapped us and threw us in here. Please help us,' Aakash answered.

The girl smiled and said, 'My name is Putli. You don't need to be scared of us. We're friends.' Then she said to someone, 'Hey boy, throw in the rope!'

26

ACP Hemant Roy was still not convinced that a terrorist group had kidnapped Shweta and Aakash. He had investigated many bomb blast cases and terror attacks. Usually, terrorists never asked for a ransom. Were they looking for funds to buy weapons or to expand their base? Something was not right.

The tech team analyzed the video. The writing on the banner behind Shweta and Aakash had been translated from Urdu—it said 'Harkat ul-Ansar', with 'Free Kashmir' written below. Roy was certain that this terrorist group had been decimated. Were they trying to resurrect themselves, and needed funds?

From the topography of the land in the video, he could not come to any conclusion about the hostages' whereabouts. Most of the video had been shot in a tight frame to keep out the surroundings. Still, the tech team magnified the little spots that were visbile, revealing an arid, desert-like region. It was definitely not Kashmir. Perhaps it was a far-flung area close to the Indo-Pak border—Rajasthan, or even Leh in Ladakh.

Roy, along with his team, took over the News World office. He put an embargo on airing news stories on Shweta and Aakash's kidnapping. He didn't want the kidnappers to get any information about their search operations, nor did he want to create panic among the general public. The video on YouTube was also pulled down. He skilfully fobbed off the media, saying that the police couldn't divulge much information as that could endanger the lives of both Shweta and Aakash.

An increasingly impatient Vikram blamed the police for their inefficiency. He wanted to negotiate with the terrorist group. However, there had been no word from them. Even the police were waiting for them to get in touch.

The call came late in the night at the News World office. The caller wanted to speak to the senior-most executive in the upper management. Roy took the call and introduced himself as the MD of the media group.

The caller gave him strict instructions as though he were reading out a set of guidelines. 'The money needs to be delivered in cash before 5.00 a.m. Once we get the money, and are sure that the police are not trying to track us, the hostages will be released twenty-four hours after the ransom has been paid.'

Roy tried to negotiate; they were willing to pay the ransom but they wanted the hostages to be released immediately.

The caller sternly told Roy that he couldn't lay down the rules. He indicated a location for the ransom to be delivered, and warned Roy against trying to track their man, or both the hostages would be killed.

Roy said he needed more time to arrange the cash, trying to prolong the conversation, but the caller hung up. The tech team was busy locating the place from where he had called, and finally traced the call down to Virar. Almost immediately, the SIM card became untraceable. The caller must have destroyed it. There was no way of tracing him now.

While the call was made from Virar, the ransom was to be dropped off in Andheri. Perhaps a whole group of men were involved, or maybe a single abductor would travel from Virar to Andheri.

Roy said, 'Had they wanted it, they could've demanded fifty crores but they settled for just five. This doesn't seem like the work of a professional terrorist group. Seems more like the handiwork of a bunch of thieves. Well, I'm not going to let them get away with this.'

Vikram was quick to admonish him. 'You'd better not risk my sister's life. I can't take chances with them. Let's get her back first. Then you can do whatever you want.'

Roy knew that he couldn't do anything that would jeopardize the lives of the hostages. The need of the hour was to get five crores in cash before 5.00 a.m., and it was already 2.00 a.m.

Vikram offered. 'I'll arrange the cash but on condition that no questions will be asked.'

There was no other way out. Even the treasury department of Mumbai Police didn't have enough cash to cough up such a hefty ransom. They usually kept small amounts to hand out to informants. Roy nodded in approval.

Vikram went out of the building to make some calls.

Roy hated these builder types. A corrupt lot, they would go to any lengths for profit. They hiked the prices of flats in Mumbai to such an extent that it was almost impossible, even for a senior police officer, to ever own a house in the very city that they protected. He knew they hoarded money in cash and were hand in glove with each other.

'It's done,' announced Vikram, walking in after a few minutes. 'We'll get the cash. So who's coming with me to deliver the money?'

Roy shot a glance at him. 'This is strictly a police matter. You will have to stay out of this.'

'She's my sister and I arranged the money, so I'm coming along,' Vikram shouted.

'Next time you raise your voice, I'll put you under arrest and throw you in the lock-up. This is not Gurugram. This is Mumbai, my city. You'd better listen to me, boy,' Roy told him coldly.

Vikram looked at all the policemen and stormed out in rage.

The cash arrived around 3.30 a.m. Vikram handed the cash to Roy, wishing him all the best.

'The hostages will not be released before the next twenty-four hours. So I really don't know whether to trust these kidnappers or not,' Roy said.

'We have no choice but to wait. Hopefully, once they get the cash, they will release them,' said Vikram.

Roy, along with his team, left with the cash. He waited in a private car in Andheri close to the drop-off point. He knew that the kidnappers would also keep watch on the drop-off point. The cash was to be dropped in a large garbage container by the roadside, close to Pushpak Society on Veera Desai Road.

As the clock struck five, Roy signalled to his men to move the cash. Two men dropped large bags of cash into the garbage container and walked away. Roy sat in the car waiting for the bags to be picked up. An entire team of crime branch officials in cars stationed in the area waited for his orders.

Vishnu Baba had made a fool of the Mumbai Police with the video, posing as a terrorist group. With terror attacks on the rise, and India and Pakistan blaming each other for them, doing that had been easy. He had also found people in Mumbai, Delhi and other big cities to work for him. In Mumbai, it was Rajan Kothari, a one-time close aide of the Ravi Pujari gang.

Rajan offered his services to gangsters, Naxals and even terrorist groups in exchange for money. Born and brought up in Mumbai, he knew the city inside out. For his clients, he took care of all the tech support, surveillance, taking pictures, uploading videos on the internet, making calls, collecting ransom, and sending the money back to the clients. His fee was a cool ten per cent of the total loot.

The police team waited but no one came to pick up the bags. Roy messaged his team to hold on to their positions as the kidnappers would also be on the lookout. They waited till 6.30 a.m. but nothing happened. The early morning traffic had started plying on the roads. Soon, garbage trucks would take away the garbage. Roy got out of the car and walked towards the container. He looked inside. The bags were gone.

He was dumbstruck. He had kept a strict eye on the container; no one had even walked past it. Hurriedly, he removed the garbage. Underneath, he saw a gaping hole. The garbage container had been placed directly above a manhole. The kidnappers had come through the manhole like rats, pulled down the bags, and disappeared into the underground maze of sewage lines.

27

All of twenty-eight, Putli was a petite woman, and the only dacoit in Chambal who refused to bow down to Vishnu Baba. She was a true rebel in every sense of the word. Her father Chhabiram, one of the most noble dacoits of the region, was mercilessly killed by the police with the help of Vishnu Baba. Thereafter Putli, until then a simple village girl, made Chambal her home. Hardly five feet five inches tall, and dark complexioned with large eyes and unkempt, curly hair, Putli looked more like a schoolgirl than a dacoit. To avenge her father's murder, Putli always looked for opportunities to attack Vishnu Baba's gang, and possibly kill him.

That night, she had crept up on the ruins with her small band of dacoits and attacked them. While Vishnu Baba managed to escape, she gunned down five of his men. That was good enough for her.

As Aakash and Shweta cried for help, a boy from Putli's gang rushed to the well and peered in. He recognized them immediately. It was Dimple. As Aakash and Shweta climbed out of the well, he hugged them tight and broke down. He told them that the morning after Bhoora beat him senseless and raped his mother, the latter walked into the Chambal River never to come out. Somehow he survived, and vowed to take revenge on Bhoora for killing his father and driving his mother to suicide. So he ran the length and breadth of Chambal till he chanced upon Putli.

Pulti patted the boy proudly, 'He had his first kill. He shot Chaubey-ji in the paunch.'

They walked through the night. Aakash was in terrible pain. A fever wracked his whole body. It was difficult for him to walk, so they stopped to rest at a place. While Aakash lay down on the ground, Shweta recounted everything to Putli—from being chained and tied to a tree, to their meeting with Gadariya and Bhoora and the duel with Guddu.

Putli was impressed that they killed Guddu, one of the best knife-fighters in Chambal.

The Chambal River divided the territories in Chambal. Putli wanted to cross the river. The land on the other side was ruled by Putli. It the dark. The river looked like a freshly tarred road in the middle of the wild. Her men were scared to step into the river as it was infested with alligators. They knew that if Aakash stepped into the river, the alligators would smell the blood dripping from his hand, and would come for them. They would have no chance against a congregation of alligators. Yet they had to cross to the other side for fear of Vishnu Baba coming after them.

As they stood contemplating how to cross the river, the sound of the damru drew closer. Gadariya walked right through them and stepped into the river. He turned to them and said quietly, 'Follow me!'

Gadariya waded through the fast-moving, waist-deep waters. Soon, the water was up to his chin. He held on to his staff. The whole gang followed him quietly. They were scared to even splash about in the water lest they attract alligators. A fearless Gadariya crossed the river and stood on the other side calmly, waiting for each of them to cross over safely. He looked at Aakash's hand, and told Putli to take him to the nearby village where she would find a blacksmith to cut the chain, and perhaps a local doctor who could help with the hand. Then he looked at them with his deep, black eyes and vanished again.

Dimple noted gratefully. 'He's Daku Maan Singh's son. He

can walk on water and glide over hills. I'm sure Maan Singh must have sent him to help us.'

By sunrise they reached the village—a small cluster of hutments and mud houses. Putli ordered her men to fetch the blacksmith and the village doctor. They ate at one of the villagers' houses. Putli paid them in cash despite them refusing to take the money. The villagers knew she was Chhabiram's daughter. Like Maan Singh, Chhabiram was worshipped in many villages. And like her father, Putli never took freebies from the villagers.

To Shweta and Aakash, all the villages looked alike. They couldn't even differentiate between the faces; everyone had the same worn-out face, burnt hair, and dark skin. The women wore cheap cotton sarees and covered their faces with their pallus. The children played in the sun, their laughter adding some cheer to the wild.

It took over an hour for the blacksmith to cut the chain, and another whole hour to remove the handcuffs. Suddenly, Aakash and Shweta were free. The chain had joined them like an umbilical cord they had to live with. Now it was cut. They had learnt to walk together, matching steps, sit together at a comfortable distance so that no one pulled the other person down, and slept close by. The chain restored a sense of togetherness that they had both lost. They wondered if they would ever get so close together again.

By force of habit, Aakash and Shweta sat close together on the charpoy when the village doctor arrived. He applied a paste of herbs over Aakash's amputated fingers, and using an old saree, bandaged the hand. Then he gave him a concoction made from roots. Soon, the hand stopped bleeding; even the pain subsided to an extent.

They slept on the same charpoy with their backs to each other, lying at just the right distance so as not to disturb each other. While they slept, Dimple kept vigil outside, guarding them with a rifle in hand, and a bandolier across his shoulder. The village children gathered to take a look at this little dacoit. Putli told the children that Dimple had killed a big bad dacoit and would soon rule Chambal Valley. The children wanted to touch him. They looked at him in awe, as if he were a celebrity who landed in their village.

Aakash and Shweta slept soundly till late evening. They woke up only when Putli called them to have food. They sat with her gang and ate *bajra* rotis with buttermilk. Their soul felt blissful after the sleep and food. Aakash asked Putli to help them reach the nearest city so that they could return to Mumbai. Putli assured them that she would get them out of the wild, but she had received information that Vishnu Baba, along with a police team, was looking for them—the police force worked for him too. So right away, it would be dangerous to try and move out. Once she was sure that there was no danger, she would take them out.

The whole gang gathered around them and wanted to hear about Mumbai and film stars. Putli's favourite was Shah Rukh Khan. She wanted to meet him. She asked them everything about Shah Rukh and his family. With childlike glee, she sang Shah Rukh's songs. She couldn't stand it if anyone said anything against her favourite actor.

Dimple's favourite was Salman Khan. He loved all his action films. Somehow films brought everyone together, be it gangsters, dacoits, IT whiz kids, journalists or anyone else.

As Aakash and Shweta turned to lie down on the charpoy, they heard someone walking towards them. They got up to see Gadariya holding his staff. He looked at them with his soulful eyes and said, 'It's His will that you are still caught up in this wild. Maybe you had to go through this journey.' Then he sat on a big rock nearby.

Shweta sat upright. 'Do you really think God planned this for us?'

Gadariya smiled. 'Every single thing that happens in this life happens for a reason, as though the soul requires that very experience for its growth. All through our life, we work hard on our bodies to maintain our beauty and strength, and on our brains to sharpen our intellect. But what do we do for our soul? The Almighty works on our soul in strange ways. Only He understands the growth of our souls, and that's what finally matters.'

Aakash laughed, holding out his bandaged hand. 'I lost two fingers. Does that have any meaning?'

'Do you think those fingers were more important than your wife's life and honour?'

Aakash nodded quietly.

'Does that mean our being kidnapped and thrown in this wild also has some meaning?' Shweta asked.

Gadariya smiled at her. 'I'm sure you both will find some meaning in this.'

'I don't understand all this,' Aakash said.

'Okay, tell me, how did you two meet?' Gadariya asked.

Shweta looked at Aakash. 'It was during our college admission in Delhi University. In fact, we got into a fight as I had jumped the queue, and he called me out on that. But even I don't know how we became really good friends, fell in love and got married, and now we're here in Chambal.'

Gadariya laughed. 'This is how everyone meets—by chance. You walk down a street and turn a corner, and you might bump into your life partner. Everything in life is about what's in store for you *round the corner*. We don't have to go out and choose our friends or lovers, we only have to recognize them round that corner.'

'But once people are married, where does love go? In fact,

once they start living together, they become strangers to each other,' said Shweta.

'Well, it is often believed that men fall out of love with their wives after the "conquest", that they have nothing more to really explore. Like primitive hunters, they are constantly on the lookout for fresh prey, but that's not love,' Gadariya said. 'Women largely give in to fear and insecurity. Just love deeply and fearlessly.'

Suddenly, there was a commotion. Putli hurried towards them. 'We need to get out of here fast. Vishnu Baba is close by, along with his men and the police.'

'You should leave with them,' Gadariya said. 'I'll hold them here.'

'You should come with us. What will you do here?' Shweta said.

'I'm the shepherd of Chambal. I can't leave this wild. Now go,' said Gadariya.

Aakash and Shweta ran with Putli and her gang. Dimple went up to Gadariya. 'I'll stay back with you. Maan Singh will help us.'

Gadariya looked at him and tweaked his ears playfully. 'If Maan Singh sees you with a rifle, he won't like it. He hated little boys with rifles. You go with them.'

'How are you going to stop them?' Dimple asked.

Gadariya took out his axe and showed it to him. 'This is Maan Singh's axe. No one in Chambal can stand up to this. Now run along!'

The boy ran, casting occasional glances at Gadariya holding the axe.

Gadariya walked into the darkness and let out a cry. Soon Chambal reverberated with the howling of wolves as they responded to his cry.

28

They lay in a deep crater on top of a rocky hill that was often used as a hideout by Putli. It also provided a good vantage point to engage the enemy in gunfire, with the rocky hill providing ample cover.

The whole gang was ready, with their rifles pointing at the darkness while Aakash and Shweta looked up at the sky. After some initial relief, Aakash's hand began to throb with pain once again. Shweta held on to his other hand and said reassuringly, 'We'll get out of this. We'll fight it out. Everything's going to be fine.' Aakash nodded in agreement.

Putli sat on her haunches with her rifle in one hand. 'It seems Vishnu Baba is bringing together all the gangs of Chambal to search for you. None of his hostages have ever slipped out of his hands. He must have already sent a ransom demand, but now he doesn't have the hostages. He's going mad.'

'His men posed as terrorists in the video they made with us,' Shweta said. 'The police and intelligence agencies must be looking for terrorist groups while we're holed up here in Chambal.'

'Can't we connect with them somehow?' Aakash asked. 'Isn't there a phone in the nearby village, or a smartphone somewhere with an internet connection?'

'Earlier, dacoits would use smartphones, but the police jammed all the networks in Chambal so they can no longer communicate, even with each other. The police still have their wireless while we're left with nothing,' Putli told them.

'So maybe we can go to the nearest police chowki? They can help us,' Shweta said.

Putli cautioned them, 'Don't forget it was a police officer who handed you over to Vishnu Baba. That same Inspector Tewatia, along with his men, is with Vishnu Baba right now, looking for you. You two are a prize catch. By the way, how much ransom did they demand?'

Aakash looked at her and said, 'Five crores.'

Putli whistled loudly. The sound echoed till the far reaches of Chambal before her men asked her to be silent. She said, 'I don't even know how many zeroes that has. Now if I kidnap you, how much should I ask?'

Aakash and Shweta sat up straight.

Putli laughed. 'I'm just joking. I'm not here for money. I'm a baaghi like my father and Daku Maan Singh.'

Aakash and Shweta heaved a sigh of relief. The sudden twist had made them suspicious of Putli. 'How do you get information about other gangs and their activities?' Aakash asked.

'We have our informers in the villages and in the police,' said Putli.

'You said you don't indulge in kidnappings or rob villagers. What do you do as a dacoit?' Shweta asked her.

'We rob other dacoits like Vishnu Baba and the police,' Putli laughed.

'Do you know Gadariya?' Shweta asked her.

'He's like a father-figure to me. After my father was killed, he took care of me. He never let anyone touch me. Finally, I walked out on him and turned into a dacoit to take revenge on Vishnu Baba and improve the lot of the innocent villagers.'

Aakash and Shweta had been so engrossed in sorting out their professional lives. In Chambal, they realized that they had but one life, and it would take just a bullet to put an end to it. In big cities, everyone was chasing illusions, and meeting counsellors and therapists to sort out their lives. They had never felt the cold metal of a gun's barrel on their temples.

The white streak of light pierced the darkness. In a matter of seconds, it spread far and wide. Putli turned to her men, 'We need to get out of here.'

Soon, they were walking through the circuitous routes of Chambal's maze-like expanse. Covered in mud, Aakash and Shweta looked pretty much part of the gang, except they did not carry guns. Dimple walked close by. 'Didi, don't worry. I'll protect you.'

As he walked with them, he kept a hawk-eye vigil for signs of the enemy.

Like a little girl with twinkling toes, Putli effortlessly glided over the rough terrain. A child of this wild, she knew her way around the labyrinth called Chambal.

Aakash was still weak from the blood loss. With every step he took, his hand throbbed in pain. Shweta walked alongside, matching steps with him as though they were still chained together. At times, she would pat him gently on the shoulder, encouraging him to continue. They had walked for almost an hour when the sun emerged from behind a hill and covered them with blinding light. They lost all sense of time.

In Chambal, Aakash and Shweta realized that time was a state of mind, that their happiest moments were few and far between. It was important to value such moments since everything could change in a split second. Chambal had taught them this important lesson.

'Putli, don't you want to lead a normal life? I mean, you can leave all this behind, and settle in a town or a city,' Shweta said.

Putli laughed. 'Once I went to Gwalior to see the city. I went into this new place which was fully air-conditioned and had many shops inside. I loved the air-conditioning so much that I slept there and the police chased me out. This wild is my home; this is my life.'

'Are you married?' Shweta asked her.

Putli burst out laughing. Her laughter criss-crossed Chambal. It followed the many bends of the Chambal River till it came face to face with Bhoora and Kallu and their gang of dacoits, leading them right back to Putli's hideout.

Putli pointed her rifle at them. Both groups had their fingers on the trigger, ready to kill. Bhoora smiled at her. 'Putli, we have nothing against you. These two are Vishnu Baba's property, so we have come to take them.'

Putli stepped forward with her rifle pointed directly at their heads. 'They are under my protection. If you touch them, you won't get out of this place alive.'

Kallu looked at Putli's men. It was a small gang of twelve men and one boy. 'So you've got a boy too. They'll all die, Putli. Then I'm going to do things to you that you'll enjoy.'

Bhoora joined in. 'I did it to the boy's mother, and now he has joined Putli. Dimple, you little bastard, I'll kill you too!'

Dimple screamed, 'Bhoora, I'll have my revenge some day. I'll kill you for what you did to my father and my mother.'

'First get out of here alive, boy,' Bhoora smirked. 'I'll definitely fulfil Guddu's last wish. I'll eat Mumbai's *kulfi falooda* while Kallu, you can taste Chambal's *teekhi mirch*.'

Kallu and the others guffawed.

Putli whistled loudly. More men emerged from the nearby hillocks and mud mounds with their rifles pointed at Kallu's gang.

Putli was no greenhorn. She looked threateningly at Bhoora and Kallu's gang. 'I can kill you all right now and leave your bodies to rot.'

Bhoora, Kallu and their men looked at the rifles pointed at them. They knew they wouldn't be able to get out of there alive.

'Putli, you're making a huge mistake. This will turn the whole Chambal against you. Vishnu Baba has got all the dacoits together. Even the police are with him,' Kallu reminded her.

'Go and tell your Vishnu Baba that Putli has declared war in Chambal. Let's see who has the guts to fight her,' Putli retorted.

A shot rang out in the air as Putli fired from her rifle. Kallu and Bhoora retreated with their men. 'We'll be back, Putli,' said Kallu, conceding only a momentary defeat.

'You better come back with your Vishnu Baba, so I can finish you all off in one go. Run Kallu, run,' Putli fired another shot in the air.

She turned to Aakash and Shweta who were sitting huddled together, and smiled. 'Don't be scared. Putli knows how to keep such dogs away.'

Thirsting for revenge, Dimple looked up at the sky and cried, 'Maan Singh, help me. I'll kill them all.' His war cry echoed through every grain of earth in Chambal.

29

Almost twenty-four hours had passed since the ransom was dropped off. Yet there was no call from the kidnappers. While ACP Hemant Roy had planned to follow the person who would pick up the ransom, the money just disappeared down a hole.

The only possible scenario Roy could think of was that the kidnappers had already killed both the hostages, then fled with the money. He had given strict instructions that not a word about the operation was to be leaked to the media. It was not to be mentioned even on News World, otherwise they could lose whatever little chance they had of rescuing Shweta and Aakash.

It did strike Roy that the ransom call was made from Mumbai, the video was uploaded on YouTube from Mumbai, and even the mail to News World was sent from Mumbai. So either the kidnappers were hiding in Mumbai or they had someone working for them in the city. He could have been the one who collected the ransom.

Roy told his team, 'The way the bags were taken from the manhole underneath makes a few things clear—the person is a pro, has been living in Mumbai for a long time, knows the place, and is familiar with the workings of the police. We'll have to find him.'

'Maybe he has already left Mumbai with all the cash. You should focus on finding Shweta and Aakash,' Vikram intervened.

Roy glared at him and said curtly, 'Once we get this man, he'll lead us to the kidnappers and hopefully we'll rescue both of them.'

He turned to his team and briefed them, 'I don't think he'll personally carry all the cash out of Mumbai. He'll probably use one of the local *hawala* operators to transfer it. Get cracking on all the hawala dealers. I want this man by this evening.'

He turned to look at Vikram and said, 'You must be connected to a lot of hawala dealers in Mumbai. You'd better find out which hawala dealer got five crores in cash this morning and where the money is being transferred. After all, it was your cash.'

He retorted angrily, 'Roy, you have failed to find my sister, but I'll find her. I'll get her back.' With that, he stormed out.

Roy had asked Vikram several times not to meddle in the case, but he didn't seem to understand. Roy even felt that Vikram could be a suspect. So he sought a detailed report on Vikram and his businesses from Delhi Police and Gurugram Police.

According to the reports, Shweta also had a huge share in the family property and business. However, she never evinced any interest in either. There was a strong possibility that Vikram wanted her out so that he could control the entire business. So he staged this whole farce of her being kidnapped by terrorists. Roy didn't want to leave any stone unturned. So he deputed three of his best men to tail Vikram.

Even before the markets opened, the crime branch officials caught up with the hawala operators in Opera House, Zaveri Market, Colaba, Andheri, and right up to Virar. Roy tried to figure out whether the person who had picked up the bags would wait before transferring the money or do it in a hurry.

All known hawala operators were informed about the five-crore cash transfer. A team of police informers were on the field looking for this man. Someone would have surely seen a man coming out of a manhole with huge bags in both hands. Roy needed to find someone who could help identify this man. But he didn't have the luxury of time. With each passing minute, the possibility of the hostages being killed threatened to become a reality.

A thought that never crossed Roy's mind was that the kidnappers could be dacoits from Chambal. Mumbai Police had never stepped into the wild.

30

Exhausted after a long trek through Chambal, Aakash lay down on the rough ground inside a cave on a hillside. His shirt was almost completely red now. The pain in his left hand kicked in again. Shweta gave him a bit of the powder that the village doctor had prepared. After taking it, he went off to sleep.

As darkness covered the wild, Putli's men walked out and let their guard down for a bit. Some relieved themselves while others just sat around, staring at the sky. Occasionally they wondered what lay beyond the starry skies.

Often, they would stare at planes flying over their heads and chuck stones at them, as if they could really hit their targets. Many of them had never sat in a train, tasted a cold drink, eaten a burger, pizza, or even drunk coffee. These were men of the wild. But they knew how to laugh.

When Aakash and Shweta saw them laugh, they were puzzled. 'How could the wretched and the poor laugh so heartily? What was there to laugh about?'

Jagat, one of Putli's aides, told Aakash and Shweta that they laughed simply because they were alive. There was no knowing when a bullet would silence them. People in cities don't laugh, and certainly not loudly. It's considered bad manners. In the wild, Aakash and Shweta learnt to expect *nothing more* of life than life itself. Those who don't laugh disintegrate and perish.

The wild was conducting an autopsy on their soul. Something was happening within them that they couldn't fathom. Bit by bit, their conditioning was being chipped away to unearth something they didn't even know existed within them.

Most people go through life without realizing its essence. They only live as consumers—loyal, disloyal, happy, unhappy, important, unimportant—or as the flavour of the month, year, decade, till finally they are dropped from all lists.

Aakash snored lightly. Shweta and Putli leant against the wall inside the cave. A single wick lit up the place, casting long, dark shadows on the walls. With childlike excitement, Putli looked at Shweta and said, 'Tell me something about Mumbai?'

'It's just another big city,' Shweta said matter-of-factly.

'Do you have your own house there, a *pucca* house, with electricity, TV, fan, air-conditioner and all?' Putli asked.

'Yes,' Shweta nodded. 'We have a beautiful house that overlooks the vast sea but we are trapped in this wild. God knows whether we'll ever get out of here.'

'I'm going to help you get out, but tell me, how big is the sea?'

Shweta smiled indulgently at Putli. 'Imagine the entire Chambal submerged in water till the horizon.'

'Where do people live in Mumbai if the sea is so big?' Putli asked, her eyes wide with curiosity.

Shweta smiled. 'Mumbai is surrounded by the sea but there is enough land there.'

'You're like a heroine. You come on TV and your husband does too,' Putli smiled. 'It's good to see a hero-heroine couple.'

'I'm a journalist and I anchor a news show on TV. Aakash is a chef and he hosts a cookery show on TV,' Shweta corrected her.

'But you two had love-marriage? Please tell me how you met and how the whole romance started,' Putli sat up straight, looking into Shweta's eyes.

Shweta smiled. 'We met during college admissions. In fact,

we got into a fight the very first time we met, but later Aakash came up to me and apologized. After that, I think he took me out for lunch, to share a plate of *chole bhatoore* at a stall behind the college. Soon we started meeting in college. In fact, we had our breakfast, lunch, snacks and chai together.'

'When did you first kiss?' Putli asked excitedly.

Shweta looked at Aakash who was fast asleep, and said, 'I think it was on my birthday when I called him home for the party. I took him to the terrace to show him the view and he just held me close and kissed me. Yes, that was our first kiss. I still remember it so vividly.'

Putli smacked her lips trying to feel the kiss and then told Shweta, 'You know, I've never kissed.'

'What?' Shweta looked shocked. 'You never had a boyfriend? What about all these men in your gang? Isn't there anyone you like?'

Putli shook her head. 'These men work for me and I don't love any of them. Tell me how does it feel while kissing?'

Shweta looked at Putli shyly, and closed her eyes. 'Well, the first kiss is always magical, the second is thrilling, but by the time you reach the third kiss, it becomes routine. After that, most boys are looking to take off the girl's clothes and have sex.'

'Sex?!' uttered Putli, placing a hand on her mouth as if she has uttered a blasphemy. She looked at Shweta and finally asked, 'You have done sex?'

'Of course. We've been married for the last seven years. But after some time, it becomes routine. What about you?'

Putli looked at her and said, 'I haven't kissed yet, so how can I do sex?'

Shweta nodded with a smile.

'How come in all those years you never had a child?' Putli asked Shweta, surprised.

'I didn't want to waste time having a child and taking care of it. I thought we could invest that time into building our careers,' Shweta said.

'What career? I can't believe that you gave up being a mother just to read news on TV,' protested Putli.

'It was more about our freedom to live our lives the way we wanted. A child restricts you,' said Shweta.

Putli smiled. 'What freedom are you talking about? You were chained and tied to a tree in this wild. Maybe if you had a child, this would never have happened to you.'

Shweta turned her head away from Putli. There was some truth to what Putli had just said. Shweta opened her mouth to counter her but words failed her. Finally, she said, 'You won't understand. You're a dacoit with no family, no responsibilities. You are free to do whatever you want.'

Putli shifted closer to her and whispered, 'I know what I want. I want a child of my own. You don't seem to be interested in it so if you don't mind, can I have sex with your husband?'

Shweta looked at her stunned. 'Are you crazy? How can you talk like this? You're a bloody animal.'

'I like him and I'm sure he won't mind sleeping with me. At least I'll have his child if you don't. Otherwise what's the use of all these years of love-making? Let me have him,' Putli persisted.

'Don't you touch him!' Shweta shouted. 'I'll kill you!'

Putli laughed at Shweta's reaction.

Shweta moved closer to Aakash and held his right hand in hers like a little girl clutching her teddy bear for fear of it being snatched away.

Putli called out to her, 'Arrey, I was joking. You got so scared.'

Aakash was still asleep. Shweta looked at his face. For the past many years, they had hated seeing each other's face.

They were the same people who had once loved each other. She kept looking at him for a long time, and then gently ran her fingers through his hair.

Putli continued, 'Dimple was telling me that you two argue and fight a lot. So why are you so protective about him now?'

Shweta looked at Putli and said, 'Yes, we have been nasty to each other. We wanted to file for a divorce and lead our own lives, but got caught in this wild.'

'Okay, I have a solution,' Putli said. 'I'll help you get out of Chambal but on condition that you leave your man with me. I'll take care of him, nurse him back to health, and maybe we'll get married and have lots of children.'

Shweta was speechless as if she had been punched in the guts.

'See, you both had decided to part ways anyway, so I'm just helping you. I'll assure you a safe journey to the nearest city from where you can go back to Mumbai. You can be the TV news heroine again. What do you say?' Putli asked.

Shweta was too shocked to answer.

Putli shrugged her shoulders and continued, 'You can tell the police and your news people that he was killed by dacoits, or better still, that he was eaten by wild dogs and wolves. How does that sound?'

Suddenly, Shweta leapt on Putli and started to punch her. 'You bitch, you're trying to buy my husband in exchange for my freedom! I'm not going to leave him here in the wild with a bunch of animals like you!'

Putli was enjoying this catfight. Hearing the screams and shrieks, her men rushed inside to see them rolling on the ground, with Shweta pulling Putli's hair. They separated the two while pointing their rifles at Shweta. In the commotion, Aakash also woke up with a start. Shweta ran to him and grabbed his hand.

Putli sat in front of Shweta and Aakash. All the rifles were pointed at them. 'In the last so many years, no one has ever attacked me like that. I like your spirit. But think about my proposal. You give me what I want, and I'll give you what you want.'

Aakash turned to Putli and shouted, 'What do you want?'

Putli looked at him and smiled. She took a step closer and caressed his cheeks and ruffled his hair. Shweta grabbed Putli's hand and flung it away.

Putli looked at her. 'You must be my long-lost sister. We have the same temper. We'll have a good time. In the wild, it is said that you cannot fight Putli. If she likes something, she'll take it, even if she has to kill for it.'

31

For the last three hours, ACP Hemant Roy had been grilling Vikram Chaudhary. The police retrieved Shweta's call records and found that she had spoken to Vikram late in the evening before she disappeared. She had also received a few messages but from unknown numbers. The police tried to trace her and Aakash's phones. They searched their penthouse and her office, but drew a blank. Either the phones were taken away by the kidnappers or destroyed. Clearly, the kidnappers were professional and tech-savvy.

Vikram was outraged by the questions being thrown at him. 'Are you crazy? Now that you've failed to get the kidnappers, you're targeting me.'

'We spoke to Shweta's team, and one of the young reporters told us that he had heard her talking on the phone and calling you by your name. The reporter said that Shweta sounded upset and angry. She was threatening to reveal everything. So you better tell me what this is all about, Vikram Chaudhary,' Roy spoke firmly.

'She didn't approve of my relationship with a female reporter in Delhi. She asked me to break off with her,' Vikram cleared the air. 'In fact, she even told me that she had a major fight with her husband Aakash, and that they had decided to file for a divorce. She wanted me to arrange for a good lawyer. Does that answer your question? Now if you're done, I have lots to do.' Vikram got up to leave.

'Did I ask you to get up?' Roy glared at him. 'I'm not done yet.'

Vikram smirked. 'Your whole team fucked up. You lost the ransom money that I gave you, and now you have no leads whatsoever. So you're shooting in the dark. Let me make it clear, she's my sister and if you can't find her, I will.'

Roy smiled with a confidence few police officers have. 'We understand your feelings but we also need to clear our doubts. Tell me something about Shweta's share in your family business.'

Vikram glared at him and at the other police officers in the room. 'So that's what this interrogation is all about? You think that to kick her out of her share, I had her kidnapped and murdered.'

'I never said murdered,' Roy corrected Vikram.

Vikram looked him in the eye. 'ACP Hemant Roy, you failed to rescue my sister. You failed to get her kidnappers. You even failed to trace the ransom money. And now you're trying to save your skin by pinning the blame on me.'

'You haven't answered my question,' said Roy coolly.

'Okay, Shweta holds fifty-one per cent of the shares in the property business. That makes her my boss and the owner of the company. Actually, my father had transferred the shares to my mother. After her death, and according to her will, those shares were transferred to Shweta. Let me also make it clear that Shweta was never interested in the property business. She was crazy about going into war zones and interviewing those militia leaders, Naxals, and making documentaries about poor people without food and water. So all these years, I've been handling the whole business. In fact, she has never taken a single paisa from the company. She prefers to be known as a self-made woman,' Vikram clarified.

'At least you have a strong motive to get her out of the way. What if she ever demanded to take over the company?' Roy asked.

'Yes, I do have a strong motive, but that doesn't mean that I had her kidnapped. You can put my name on top of the suspects' list but I'm not the kidnapper,' Vikram said, getting up in a huff and stomping out.

Roy didn't stop him. He looked at his men and said, 'Keep an eye on him.'

The crime branch team had pulled up all the hawala dealers, but there was no trace of the ransom money. Roy didn't even have a straw to clutch on to. He was sure the person who collected the ransom was still in Mumbai. Seeing the police swing into action, he hadn't taken out the money. Roy was waiting for him to surface.

Late that night, Roy was woken up by SI Shinde. They had nabbed a hawala dealer who had accepted cash worth nearly five crores—four crore five lakh rupees, to be precise. Roy knew the rest was supposed to be the contact's fee.

Roy was back at the crime branch office in a jiffy. The hawala dealer didn't even need to be questioned. ACP Hemant Roy's presence was enough for him to blurt out everything. He told them that he had been asked to deliver the cash to a property dealer in Ghaziabad. He gave them the address.

Roy got a sketch artist to sit with the hawala dealer to have a portrait made of the man who had contacted him. Without wasting time, he got in touch with Ghaziabad Police. Two hours later, Ghaziabad Police raided the property dealer's shop but they didn't find anything. They were informed that the particular shop had never existed, that even the board was put up that morning. Roy knew that all this was a front to receive the ransom money while the kidnappers could be sitting anywhere in Uttar Pradesh, Delhi, Gurugram, or even in Kashmir.

When the portrait was ready, the crime branch team searched through their archives to see if the person had any previous records. Just before dawn, they found him—Rajan Kothari, once a member of the Ravi Pujari gang. He had several criminal cases against him. He had been arrested once, but escaped from court. Since then, he was absconding. He was known to work for terrorist groups.

'If we can get our hands on this Rajan Kothari, we'll get to the kidnappers and maybe the hostages, if they're still alive,' said Roy to his team.

There was not much difference between Mumbai and Chambal. Beneath the designer suits, spit and polish, people were nothing but animals waiting for the right moment to pounce on an opportunity and make off with the spoils.

32

Vishnu Baba and his gang reached Karoli village where Putli, along with Shweta and Aakash, had sought refuge. Inspector Tewatia, along with a police team and other smaller gangs of dacoits, joined Vishnu Baba at the village. Bhoora and Kallu also returned and reported to Vishnu Baba about their run-in with Putli. They knew it would be difficult to search for them in the wild.

Early in the morning, they sat on charpoys, sipping tea. Everyone was waiting for Pahalwan Singh Yadav, minister of state for rural development, Uttar Pradesh (UP). Yadav had hatched a plan to end the dacoit menace in Chambal, and turn the wild into Disneyland—with water sports on Chambal River, a designated zone for five international auto giants who wanted to set up manufacturing units in India, and of course, an international airport. It would turn Chambal into one of the most profitable economic zones in the country. For centuries, no one had been able to tame the wild. Yadav's plan was a winner. Besides getting him votes, it would showcase the vision of a progressive government. So he preferred to have full control over the dacoits in Chambal and their activities.

The three states bordering Chambal—Uttar Pradesh, Madhya Pradesh and Rajasthan—would collaborate on this mega project. The idea was to run a metro into the heart of Chambal from Delhi, bringing in hordes of tourists and businessmen. The only problem was that this plan worked well on paper, and Yadav knew full well that it would remain on paper.

As part of his development programme, Yadav would often visit Chambal and the neighbouring villages. He also came to the wild for adolescent girls. Their screams would never be heard in faraway Uttar Pradesh. Even the so-called new media stayed away from the wild, preferring to operate in familiar territories.

Vishnu Baba had made all the arrangements for the minister. But something else was troubling him. Pappu, the computerwala, had come to inform him about the police raid on the Ghaziabad shop they had set up to receive the ransom. Fortunately, none of their men were captured.

Pappu was their sole contact to the outside world as he lived in Gwalior, and was connected to all their informers and men in other cities. He would often come to visit Vishnu Baba to give him information, or at times, he would pass information to local policemen and villagers working for Vishnu Baba.

'Does Mumbai Police know that they are here in Chambal?' Vishnu Baba asked.

'I don't think so. They still think it's the work of some terrorist group. But if they are able to track down Rajan Kothari, he might spill the beans,' Pappu said.

Vishnu Baba was livid at the turn of events. 'We didn't get the money and those two slipped out of our hands.'

'Baba, it's that Putli who is protecting them,' said Kallu. 'This time, I'll finish off that bitch.'

Vishnu Baba taunted him. 'You did get a chance to do that but what did you do? Came back with your tail between your legs! She's not a little doll. Don't forget, she is Chhabiram's daughter. She could've killed you all, but she let you get away. She mocked you; she told you she could kill you any time and now you stand here and rant.'

'Her men surrounded us or we would've got her,' Bhoora put up a feeble defence.

Vishnu Baba flung his steel tumbler at Bhoora and got up shouting, 'Don't forget, she's a woman. They are a cunning lot. She thinks ten steps ahead of you, while you men have your head in your loins and can never think straight. Next time you go in search of her, she'll chop your heads off and have them sent to me.'

For a few minutes, no one dared utter a word, then Tewatia broke the silence. 'We need to get those two out of her clutches. Once we have them, maybe we can still force them to pay the ransom. I've already started construction work on my house and I am turning it into a three-storeyed house. How else will I pay for all that?'

Vishnu Baba turned to Tewatia and gave him a tight slap. 'Look at these policemen! We don't have a place to stay and they are constructing three-storeyed houses with our money. You prefer to sit on your fat asses and take cuts from our hard work. You are bloody pimps!'

An embarrassed Tewatia looked at his men, got up and walked away.

Vishnu Baba shouted after him, 'Now don't you come to me asking for more money. First get me those two, along with Putli.'

Vishnu Baba looked at the village in the midst of barren land. 'We're out in the open. It could be dangerous. Kallu, please order all the men to spread out.'

Bhoora thrust the village blacksmith in front of Vishnu Baba. 'Baba this one broke their chain and handcuffs. And the village doctor treated the wounds on Aakash's left hand.'

'You broke the chain?' Vishnu Baba asked, looking at the blacksmith.

The poor blacksmith nodded nervously. 'Putli asked me to do it.'

'You all seem to really like Putli. What has she done for

you or the village?'

'Putli is exactly like her father. She even pays for food and tea that the villagers make for her,' said the blacksmith.

Vishnu Baba looked around and said, 'Did you hear that? Putli even pays the villagers for tea.'

His men looked back at him dumbfounded.

'How much did she pay you for breaking the chain?' Vishnu Baba asked.

'Two hundred rupees,' said the blacksmith without looking up.

Vishnu Baba picked up a heavy stick used for steering buffaloes, and hit the man hard with it. 'Those two were my prisoners and you broke their chain!'

He kept hitting the man as he cried in pain. A few villagers came running out of their huts but stood at a distance, afraid to help.

'Did you not ask them who chained them?' asked Vishnu Baba.

The blacksmith was bleeding from his head and mouth. Vishnu Baba hit him in the shin. He cried out again.

'Don't ever come in front of me again or I'll kill you,' yelled Vishnu Baba.

Slowly, the blacksmith got up and limped away in pain.

Vishnu Baba looked at a group of village women and shouted, 'Why are you staring at me? Go and cook food for us!'

Immediately the women disappeared.

Tewatia, along with his team, sat outside a hut. Vishnu Baba shouted at him, 'Ay inspector, ask your men to stand guard. Pahalwan-ji will be here soon.'

Reluctantly, Tewatia gestured to his men to take position. The policemen were hungry, and broken by the humiliation they had to suffer at the hands of these dacoits.

A convoy of jeeps sped towards the village. One of the men announced, 'Pahalwan-ji is here.'

33

Shweta and Aakash melded into the wild. It was here that they found togetherness once again. Shweta made sure to stay by Aakash's side all through the night. She didn't trust Putli. After all, Putli was a dacoit in Chambal, a wild animal. At times, Putli woke up at night to see Shweta watching over Aakash like a guardian angel.

Early in the morning, Putli's men emerged from the cave and hung around the rocky mounds, taking in the vast wilderness—the orphaned child of Mother Nature. They didn't have anything to eat or cook. Putli, who was still inside with Shweta and Aakash, knew that she would have to arrange something or her men would turn into hungry dogs. Aakash told her that he had cooked wild dogs for Vishnu Baba and his gang, so if her men could hunt down a few dogs, that would take care of the whole gang.

For a moment, Putli considered moving to another village but that was miles away. Also, Vishnu Baba, the police and the other gangs of Chambal were on the lookout for her. She was still lost in thought when her close aide Jagat ran to her and said, 'We've just received information that Pahalwan Singh Yadav, along with his whole team, has reached Karoli village. Vishnu Baba, along with Inspector Tewatia and ten other policemen, are already there. They're planning to have a big feast tonight, along with a nautanki.'

Putli jumped up with excitement. 'This is our chance and we should not leave it. There will be enough food for all of us. More importantly, I want Pahalwan Singh Yadav.'

'Who's this Pahalwan?' Aakash asked.

Putli looked at him and smiled. 'He's your ticket to freedom. He's your way out of this wild. He's a minister of the UP government and we'll kidnap him.'

'Are you crazy?' Shweta shouted. 'Already, the police and Vishnu Baba are after us. If you kidnap a minister of state, they'll bring in more forces and attack us. It can endanger our lives.'

'I can't believe your wife comes on TV. She's so dumb,' said Putli, looking at Aakash. 'Well, once we kidnap Yadav, we can force them to give you a safe passage out of Chambal. It'll be an exchange—safe passage for you in exchange for Yadav's life.'

'Are you planning to attack their party in the village?' Aakash asked, looking tense.

'Do you think you can just walk in there, lift up that heavy Yadav and walk out? We'll have to attack with full force. After all, we don't have anything to eat here. There'll be lots of food that we can carry back with us. I'll need both of you in this operation.' Putli sounded like a gang leader who meant business.

'She's nuts, Aakash! She's going to put all of us in danger! There's going to be a lot of security for the minister. Then there is Vishnu Baba's gang and God knows how many more dacoits. This is not a good idea,' Shweta said.

'This is *the* chance we have and if you want to give up, it's up to you. I'll be putting my men in danger for your sake,' Putli told them clearly.

'What makes you think that this plan will work?' Aakash questioned her.

Putli looked at him, surprised. 'Don't you understand? None of the dacoits or the policemen will hurt you as long as Yadav is our hostage.'

'What if we fail to kidnap him? What if your attack fails?

What if we get shot in the bargain? Have you given all this a thought?' Aakash asked.

'No,' Putli replied with the calm of a fearless brigand. 'If you give too much thought to all this, you'll never be able to charge into the battlefield. A warrior rushes into battle and takes it from there. We will also rush in.'

'Why do you need us in this?' Shweta asked.

'I believe they won't shoot you dead. They will want to capture you alive and get the ransom money,' Putli explained. 'Also, there will be lots of food as Yadav loves good food and young girls. So all of us will get to eat a hearty meal.'

Shweta buried her face in her hands. She had never experienced the dearth of basic food. She had never thought she would be fighting to get some food. She could feel her stomach growling, and she knew that by night, she would be mad with hunger. She was dying to eat a chapati with jaggery and chillies.

Putli looked at Aakash and Shweta and asked, 'Can you handle a gun?'

They stared at Putli, dumbstruck.

Putli laughed. 'In Chambal, even a kid can fire a rifle. Look at Dimple; he has become an excellent shot. He can shoot a man from a distance of fifty metres.'

Dimple was embarrassed, like a student unaccustomed to being praised. He picked up his rifle and put it on his shoulder as if he really were a big dacoit in the wild.

Shweta looked at Dimple and said gently, 'He's just a kid. We can't take him for this operation.'

Dimple protested loudly, 'Didi, you know I want to kill that Bhoora and if I get a chance, I'll have my revenge! Come what may, I'm going with you all. The spirit of Daku Maan Singh is with us. He'll protect us.'

Putli walked up to the boy and ruffled his hair. 'You'll have your revenge, Dimple.'

She turned to Aakash and Shweta. 'Chauhan is our best shot. He'll give you a quick lesson on handling the rifle and shooting straight at the target. More importantly, you need a strong heart to kill someone, so better gear up.'

Chauhan, a lanky young man with brown hair, walked up to Aakash and Shweta and thrust a rifle each in their hands. He showed them the bandolier of bullets. He demonstrated how to cock the rifle, point the barrel at the target, and shoot. It was all simple.

Putli looked at Shweta holding the rifle, and lauded her. 'Now you look like a true Chaudhary woman.'

Then she turned to her men and said, 'We must start moving now to reach the village on time.' She turned to Shweta and Aakash. 'Are you two ready?'

They nodded.

Putli hoped to reach the outskirts of the village before sunset so they would have ample time to rest before mounting their attack late at night.

The whole gang began the trek with their rifles slung on their shoulders. In the middle of the gang walked Shweta and Aakash carrying their rifles.

They were now part of a fierce gang of dacoits, out on their first mission.

34

The sun had set when Putli and her gang reached close to Karoli village. Like a reptile, Putli scurried up a mud mound, and surveyed the village. She could see a makeshift stage with charpoys arranged around it. The smell of spicy food floated in the air. She knew Pahalwan Singh loved mutton and whiskey.

She slid down the mound like a little animal raring to go. Most of her men were tired but Putli was excited like a little girl who had seen a butterfly frolicking around her.

Despite being covered in mud from head to toe, Putli's eyes sparkled, as though sensing danger, her soul came alive. In battle, she was not the one to be frightened or lose her nerves. With her rifle slung across her shoulders, she looked like a warrior in camouflage.

'Can you smell it?' Putli whispered excitedly to her men. 'There's going to be good food. We are going to grab it all for ourselves.'

None of the men responded. After the long trek with the sun beating down on them, they were exhausted. They did not have anything except the occasional sip of water. Putli was the only one who seemed as though she'd had an energy bar. Like a seasoned commentator, she described the happenings in the village.

Aakash and Shweta decided to take a nap. Putli crept up on them steathily, like a schoolgirl attempting a prank. She clicked her fingers close to their ears. Immediately, Aakash looked at her, startled. 'I hope you're not too tired to hold your rifles,' said Putli.

Aakash didn't bother to respond and closed his eyes again.

Putli looked around to find everyone sleeping. She shook them hard and said, 'Bloody hell, stop snoring or they'll get to know we're hiding here.'

Putli ran up the mound again to survey the village. It was totally dark. All she could make out was some shadows and a few petro-max lamps around the stage. There was no electricity in the village. Some years back, a few poles were erected, but no wires were ever drawn across them.

For the government, it was too small a village to bother about. Also, providing electricity to a village in Chambal could mean providing unnecessary help to the dacoits. Most men in the village had migrated to nearby cities and towns in search of opportunities. Those left behind were old men, women, young girls, and a few middle-aged men and boys with criminal cases pending against them.

Putli ran around the village limits looking for vantage points to attack and escape. A few jeeps were parked on the outskirts. Armed policemen and Vishnu Baba's men huddled together, cracking lewd jokes. Outside a mudhouse, there were some armed guards. Putli gathered that Yadav and Vishnu Baba were inside. Then she spotted the men cooking food in huge vessels that were brought along by Pahalwan Singh Yadav's convoy.

As Putli moved closer, she spotted Tewatia sitting with two other policemen. He seemed outraged. 'He slapped me in front of everyone! He operates in Chambal because we support him. Otherwise, we can shoot him down any day. After all, we are the police!'

Putli moved behind a stack of dung cakes, and saw Bhoora, Kallu, and some other men discussing the feast. Then she saw Yadav and Vishnu Baba emerge from the mudhouse and walk towards the stage. Two armed guards walked behind them. Yadav was a heavy-set guy who was once a wrestler. Starting out as a thief stealing cycles and buffaloes in his village, Yadav went on to commit bigger crimes. He had eight murder cases and three rape cases pending against him, but nothing had come of it. Now, as a minister of state, he had even co-opted the police into being part of his wild schemes.

Putli realized that it wouldn't be easy to barge into the village with so many armed men patrolling, and kidnap Yadav. She also wanted take back all the delicacies for her men. And if she could lay her hands on their guns and ammunition, it would be perfect.

She saw the nautanki artists getting ready. She loved those folk dramas and remembered watching nautankis as a little girl with her father. She watched as the girls in garish make-up and bright costumes got on stage. The men also started to arrive, and took their seats around the stage. She could see Bhoora, Kallu and the others drinking like there was no tomorrow. A few of them whistled lustily at the girls on stage.

Under the cover of darkness, Putli crawled back to her men. Once again, she climbed on the mud mound from where she could see the stage. She could see Tewatia with his team seated on one side, drinking. Yadav and Vishnu Baba were still busy talking. Yadav looked tense. He called for Tewatia.

Tewatia hurriedly picked up his cap, and ran across to the minister and touched his feet. Yadav held his ear and tweaked it hard. Tewatia somehow managed to suppress a cry. His eyes filled with tears. Putli couldn't hear what they were talking about but she could make out that the minister was upset over something. Maybe Vishnu Baba had told him about the kidnapping fiasco.

Yadav shouted at Tewatia for being irresponsible, and told him to find the Mumbai couple. Tewatia nodded quietly, stepped back, and walked away. Yadav looked at Vishnu Baba and said, 'You guys are sitting here in the wild but outside, the whole country knows about this kidnapping. They think that some terrorists have kidnapped them.'

'We can't let them get away now. If they walk out of Chambal, the whole army will walk in and kill us all. It's better to bury them here so no one will ever find out what happened,' said Vishnu Baba.

Yadav nodded his head thoughtfully. 'Maybe that's the only way left for you. But if Putli helps them escape, I'll not be able to help you in any way. I don't want to be involved in this.'

'Don't worry, I'll catch them and bury them alive,' Vishnu Baba said, handing another glass of liquor to the minister. Then he turned to the artists on the stage and shouted, 'Do you think you are Bollywood heroes? Get started!'

One of the nautanki artists came forward, offered his customary salutations to the minister, and gave a brief introduction to the folktale about Daku Sultana. The dacoits were most interested. Sultana was their hero, their muse, their idol. The entire Chambal worshipped him.

Putli faintly heard the word 'Sultana' and understood that they would be performing his life story. Performing Sultana's story was mandatory in all nautankis. Restless, Putli slid down the mound once again, and went closer to the stage so that she could hear and watch them better. She didn't want to miss this great act. Everyone in Chambal knew the story of Daku Sultana, but they never tired of hearing it again and again.

The act opened with Sultana's birth in a tribal family in a small village in the British era. The little boy grew up in the wild, and like Tarzan, he swung from one tree to another, scaled walls deftly, jumped into rivers and chased wild animals. The boy soon learnt the skills of warfare, and went hunting with his friends and family. In an attack by the British, his entire family was wiped out. From then on, Sultana gave grief to the whole Raj. Soon, he formed a small gang and started to ambush British convoys, kidnap their senior officers, and rob their houses with impunity.

Putli sat there spellbound by the heroics of Sultana when a cold barrel settled on the nape of her neck. For a moment, she froze. Then she regained her calm and said, 'If you want to shoot me, go ahead but please let me watch the whole Sultana act.'

The barrel moved away, and she turned to see Jagat standing behind her. He looked at her and said, 'We've come here to attack them and kidnap the minister, and here you are, watching nautanki.'

'I've checked out everything. There's still time. We need to wait, so I thought why not watch it. You can sit here and watch it too. It's Daku Sultana's story,' Putli said. Jagat settled down next to her.

The story was now at the point when Sultana met a British girl and she fell in love with him. Sultana would take her riding on his favourite horse Badal. Their love became another sore point for the British. In fact, he became a nuisance for the British Empire. Soon, senior detectives from Scotland Yard were called in from London to capture Daku Sultana. But he disappeared into the wild. No one could trace him. An officer from Scotland Yard became obsessed with capturing Sultana and chased him everywhere. Sultana moved from one village to the other. On one occasion, he met a dancing girl called Champa. So the nautanki presented their first dance number based on a folk song. The Scotland Yard officer managed to neutralize a few of Sultana's gang members. During another encounter, a bullet meant for Sultana got his horse, and Badal died.

Everyone sat mesmerized by this epic tale of love, romance,

bravery—of one man's fight against the entire British Empire, with the whole army chasing him. Finally, Daku Sultana was captured and hanged to death at the age of twenty-three. The men sitting around had tears in their eyes. They were so dead drunk that they couldn't even react or clap. The artists came together on the stage, and took a bow, looking for applause. Kallu got up and clapped. Soon the others joined in. They all started to cheer. 'Daku Sultana ki Jai! Daku Sultana ki Jai!'

Yadav ordered, 'Let's have some more song and dance!'

They all knew what the minister meant. Soon a young girl appeared on the stage in revealing clothes. A few musicians from the nautanki played the latest hit numbers on the harmonium to the beat of drums. The young dancer's pelvic thrusts and seductive moves brought out the animals in the drunken men. Soon they crowded around the stage, dancing and drinking. In their excitement, they fired a few shots in the air.

Putli got up and said to Jagat, 'Get everyone ready.' The little girl who was enjoying the nautanki on Sultana Daku just a short while back suddenly turned into a fierce dacoit of Chambal. It was time for her gang to make a move.

A few men had climbed up on the stage. Bhoora tried to tear off the girl's clothes while another pushed him away, and tried to grope the girl. Soon more men got on the stage and started to fight for the girl. Looking at them, Yadav laughed. Vishnu Baba was so drunk that he found it difficult to keep his eyes open.

Tewatia sat quietly drinking after being publicly humiliated by the minister and Vishnu Baba. The policemen joined the dacoits on the stage, dancing wildly with the girl. Kallu tore off the girl's top and pounced on her. Then Bhoora pounced on Kallu. A scuffle ensued.

Putli picked up her rifle and signalled to her men. She

looked at Aakash and Shweta, and asked, 'Are you ready?'

They nodded.

'If you have to kill someone, kill them or they'll kill you,' Putli told them. She started to move in the darkness with the others following her.

Dimple walked close to Aakash and Shweta, and asked in a hushed tone, 'Didi, is this your first attack?'

They looked at him dumbly. He smiled and said, 'Don't be scared. The spirit of Daku Maan Singh is with us. Repeat after me, "I'm Daku Maan Singh!"'

35

The attack was swift and precise. Putli moved in like an eagle suddenly swooping down on an unsuspecting rat. She ordered her men to shoot at will and kill as many dacoits as they could. Her aim was to kidnap Pahalwan Singh Yadav.

Vishnu Baba and his men were too drunk to even find their guns as Putli charged at them. She gestured to the nautanki group to get away. They jumped off the stage and sought refuge in the dark as guns boomed.

Kallu, Bhoora, Munna and the others dacoits whisked Vishnu Baba away to safety. Tewatia preferred to sit in one corner and watch. He instructed his men not to raise their weapons and to let the dacoits settle their own scores.

Putli ordered her men to surround the whole village and not let anyone leave. Jagat, along with Chauhan, took charge of one side while Putli guarded the other.

Shweta and Aakash took up positions too, rifles in hand. They were covering each other but none of them fired a single shot.

Up ahead, Dimple opened fire into the dark, screaming, 'Run, Bhoora, run, or I'll kill you.' Maddened with rage, the little boy kept loading his rifle and firing, offering good cover to Shweta and Aakash.

Would those coffee-house intellectuals, psychologists on TV, or slick city boys understand his plight? Had their mother been raped and thrashed mercilessly in front of their eyes? Who would understand why the boy had taken to arms at such a tender age?

The villagers were screaming and running around in panic. Smoke from the gunfire rose in the air, the smell of gunpowder drowning the aroma of spices and oil. Light from the petro-max lamps cast long shadows, making it difficult to tell who was who.

In this melee, the minister's guards swung into action; they tried to close ranks around Yadav but realized that they were outnumbered by Putli's men. So after putting up a feeble fight, they laid down their arms.

Vishnu Baba managed to escape with his men.

For Putli, Pahalwan Singh Yadav was the prize catch.

The jeeps in the minister's convoy were loaded with all the food, milk, a few cans of desi ghee and two crates of whiskey. The mission was successful. Putli's father would have been proud of her. They had enough food and liquor to last them a few days. Putli walked up to the frightened villagers and gave them some money.

Then Putli approached Yadav and asked, 'Do you recognize me?'

He smiled and told her, 'Girls don't look good with rifles. You should be cooking food and taking care of your children.'

Putli looked him in the eye and using her full strength, hit him in the paunch with her rifle butt. The minister sank to the ground. She bent closer to him and said, 'Look at me, Yadav. Do you recognize me?'

A stunned and breathless Yadav said, 'I'm a state minister. You seem to be mistaken. You can't do this to me or soon the entire state police will be after you.'

Putli looked around and called out, 'O Tewatia, the minister tells me that the whole state police will come running after me. What are you doing here?'

Tewatia rose calmly with his team. 'Actually, we are on duty at the police chowki, not here. Moreover, this area doesn't fall under my jurisdiction, so we don't know what happened here and are not responsible for anything.' He turned to his men and said, 'C'mon, let's get out of here.'

Yadav shouted after him, 'Tewatia, you bastard, I'm going to have you suspended!'

Without turning back, Tewatia walked off with his men.

Yadav was reluctant to get into the jeep. Putli whipped out a knife and pointed the blade at his crotch. 'You better get into the jeep or I'll cut off your balls and throw them to the dogs.'

Meekly, Yadav climbed in and sat amidst the huge vessels of food and cans of desi ghee. Jagat tied his hands and legs. Yadav's guards stood watching helplessy as the convoy sped away.

It was pitch dark. Putli guided the jeeps through the ravines. Brought up by Gadariya, she knew the wild like the back of her hand. Her men trusted her instinctively. They were even ready to lay down their lives for her. The starving gang made one stop close to the river. Putli asked her men to bring down the goodies and soon everyone was having a feast. Aakash and Shweta also ate quietly, sitting by the river.

Chewing on a *puri*, Shweta said, 'Dimple saved our lives. Like a warrior he kept shooting at those dacoits while guarding us all along.'

'He's our little soldier,' Putli said with a smile. 'He must be enjoying the feast. He loves puris.' Putli called out to him, 'Dimple! O re Dimple!'

There was no answer. Putli got up to look for him. She asked her men, 'Where's Dimple?'

Jagat shrugged and said, 'Must be sleeping in one of the jeeps.'

Putli rushed towards the jeeps and looked inside. 'He's not here,' she shouted.

Everyone got up to look for the boy. Aakash and Shweta also looked around the place, but Dimple was nowhere to be found. Soon, every part of Chambal reverberated with just one name: 'Dimple! Dimple! Dimple!'

'I saw Vishnu Baba and his men dragging away a boy,' Yadav said.

Hearing this, Aakash and Shweta rushed towards him. 'That Bhoora will kill him.'

The minister looked at them. 'You must be Shweta and Aakash from Mumbai.' Then he laughed. 'The entire country is talking about you two. Never mind what anyone says but Vishnu Baba managed to fool everyone. Mumbai Police thinks that you've been kidnapped by a terrorist group. They'll never be able to figure out you're here in Chambal.'

Aakash turned to him and shouted, 'Where's the boy, Yadav?'

'I've told you what I know,' said the minister.

Putli shouted something to her men. Within seconds, Yadav found himself kneeling at Putli's feet. She started to hit him mercilessly with her rifle butt. 'If anything happens to that boy, I'm going to kill you!'

Bleeding from his mouth, Yadav pleaded with folded hands. 'Why are you after my life? I've never harmed you. It's that Vishnu Baba who kidnapped these Mumbaiwalas and took your boy. Please let me go. I might even help you get the boy back.'

Putli smacked his face hard. 'Yadav, you still don't recognize me? I'm Chhabiram's daughter.'

The expression on Yadav's face changed.

'You were one of the people involved in killing my father. Later, you ordered his body to be hung from a tree for everyone to see. You got all the reporters to click your picture with his body.' Trembling with rage, Putli put the barrel of the rifle on the minister's forehead. 'Yadav, you deserve to die!'

She was about to pull the trigger when Shweta stopped her. 'Putli, we have to get Dimple back. Till Yadav is alive and with us, we can negotiate with Vishnu to hand over Dimple.'

'You know nothing about this bastard. I was not even seven years old when this man raped me,' Putli screamed, wanting to blow his brains out, but she somehow tore herself away.

Shweta held Putli close. Hugging Shweta tightly, Putli broke down and sobbed uncontrollably.

Jagat, Chauhan and all her men closed in around her. 'Kill him, Putli! Take your revenge! He is the reason why you became a baaghi. Don't think of anything! Just kill him! We'll get Dimple back somehow,' Jagat said.

'Yes, Putli kill him!' cried the others.

'There's no difference between a baaghi and a sadhu. That's what Daku Maan Singh used to say,' Gadariya said as he walked in through the darkness.

Putli ran to him like a little girl to her father. Hugging him tight, she wept. 'He's the one, Baba. He ruined my entire childhood. He killed my father. You know it all.'

'Even if you kill him, nothing is going to change, Putli. You'll still remain in this wild, hounded by the police and your rivals. Finally, you will also be killed,' Gadariya said.

Putli looked at Gadariya with her big dark eyes and said, 'Baba, you took your revenge. You killed more than two hundred men and now you want to stop me.'

'Cautioning against wrongdoing is more important to me today than advising anyone on what is right,' Gadariya told her calmly.

Yadav ran to Gadariya and fell at his feet. 'Please help me. This girl has lost her mind. I know that Vishnu Baba has taken the boy away and I can get him back. Just let me go!'

Putli kicked him in the face. 'Let you go so that you can rape other little girls? You're not going anywhere! I'm going to bury you alive in Chambal.'

Aakash and Shweta said, almost in chorus, 'Think of Dimple. If we have him, we can negotiate to get the boy back.'

Putli screamed hysterically. 'He's already dead! His father was killed and his mother raped and beaten in front of him. He would be better off dead than suffer his whole life like me. I'm not going to spare this man!'

Gadariya pulled out Daku Maan Singh's axe from his waistband and handed it to Putli. 'Okay, kill him.'

Staring at Gadariya in disbelief, Putli grabbed the axe. Aakash and Shweta looked at him and tried to say something, but Gadariya raised his hand to silence them. Turning to Putli, he said, 'Go on! Kill him. Have your revenge.'

Putli turned to the minister, and like an animal in pain, wailed from the depth of her soul. She raised the axe high and brought it down with full force on Yadav's head. Aakash and Shweta closed their eyes. They had already seen enough bloodshed.

There was an eerie silence. Aakash and Shweta opened their eyes to see Putli holding the axe just above the minister's head. Somehow, she couldn't manage to chop it off. She turned away from Yadav, walked up to Gadariya, hugged him and cried.

Gadariya patted her like a father would a child. 'You did the right thing, Putli. This wild is steeped in blood, and today you have changed everything. I'll talk to Vishnu Baba and get the boy back.' He took the axe from her. 'At least give some food to Pahalwan Singh Yadav.'

Tied to a jeep, Yadav ate some food. Putli, along with Shweta and Aakash, ate with Gadariya, sitting on the riverbank.

'So after killing more than two hundred men, have you turned non-violent?' Aakash asked.

Gadariya looked at him and said, 'Yes, I'm against inhuman violence, but I'm not against taking the right action. I prompted you to fight and kill Guddu, or else he would've killed you and taken away your wife. There are times when one has to act, use violence. Then it is no longer mindless violence, but action that helps and saves others.'

'I don't understand you,' Putli said while eating.

'Never mind, but you behaved in the right manner. Your mind and your heart know what's right. The mind may waver; the heart does not.'

'What would Maan Singh have done to him?' Putli asked.

Gadariya looked at them and said, 'Daku Maan Singh would have beheaded him, and hung his head from a tree in the village square to teach every rapist a lesson.'

Putli looked at him. With her hair falling over her shoulders, she looked like a goddess ready to pronounce a judgement. 'What would you have done had this minister raped your daughter?'

Gadariya looked at her sternly. 'You are my daughter. What makes you think I've ever seen you differently?'

Suddenly, everyone became silent. Gadariya got up and said, 'We'll get the boy back.'

Then he disappeared into the darkness.

36

Ghaziabad Police, along with the crime branch of Delhi Police, conducted raids at various places in UP. They arrested many local criminals and interrogated them to get some information on the kidnappings but found nothing. The media was going ahead at full steam, carrying stories on police inaction and the failure of the powers that be to rescue Shweta and Aakash.

Newspapers and TV channels outdid each other with their daily spins. One anchor said that they had information that Shweta and her husband were being held hostage in Pak-Occupied Kashmir. Another reporter wrote that a terrorist group had taken them to Afghanistan.

Late at night, ACP Hemant Roy received information about Rajan Kothari's hideout. He, along with a team of crime branch officials, set out to pick him up. Unlike other gangsters who preferred to live in chawls, shanties and slums that provided them ample cover, Rajan lived on the tenth floor of a high-rise building in Lokhandwala in Andheri West.

Roy had the layout of the flat. He spread it on the ground. 'It's a three BHK with a single entry and exit. We just need to barge in and get him. He might be armed, so be prepared. No matter what, we need him alive. He's the only lead we have if we are to rescue Shweta and her husband.'

It was a meticulously planned operation. Roy was known for that. He cordoned off the building. The team was divided into three groups. The one led by Roy took the lift directly to

the tenth floor. Another one took the staircase to make sure
that Rajan didn't get away from there, while the third blocked
all entrances and exits to the building. Roy made sure there
would be no collateral damage.

It was already 12.30 a.m. A haven for TV actors, film
personalities and strugglers, Lokhandwala never seemed to sleep.
Groups of young boys and girls hung out, discussing the latest
film, or ripping apart the best film directors and actors. The
police made sure to move them as far away as possible from the
building. Most of them carried smartphones and were always
looking for an opportunity to turn anything into a film. A live
police operation would be fabulous. Maybe they could sell it
to news channels. But Roy didn't want any of them to be a
nuisance.

As the lift door opened, Roy and his team headed straight
for Rajan's flat. The flat number was 1010. Roy knew that most
gangsters were superstitious, and spent huge amounts of money
for astrologically compatible car and house numbers. They even
wore a variety of stones on different fingers for prosperity or
to ward off the evil eye. Little did they realize that evil lurked
within their souls.

The team stood on either side of the door while Roy rang
the doorbell like a casual visitor. Soon he heard footsteps shuffling
inside. Since most criminals in Mumbai recognized Roy, he
quickly pushed another man in front of the peephole. He heard
the latch turn, and then the door being opened. Through the
slightly ajar door, he heard someone say, 'Who's it?'

In a split second, Roy kicked open the door. The man
staring back at them was not Rajan. Roy shouted at him, 'This
is the police! Where's Rajan Kothari?' The man who looked like
a house-help pointed to a room.

Roy saw a door shut and heard hurried footsteps inside

the room. He signalled to his men to move towards the room while instructing the help to leave the flat.

Roy and his men were pressed against the wall on either side of the door. They knew that Rajan could shoot them through the door, and didn't want to take chances. They had to catch him alive. Roy knocked on the door with the butt of his pistol. 'Rajan, it would be better if you surrendered. There's no way you can escape from here. If you resist, we might have to shoot you down.'

Roy heard the window slide open. Rajan seemed to have an escape plan and could slip out. He banged open the door and saw Rajan precariously perched over the large French window. He turned to look at Roy while the other officers pointed their guns at him.

'You'd better get down. There's no way out of here. If you help us trace the kidnapped journalist and her husband, you might be let off with a lighter sentence, or you know it's a bullet in the back or the head.'

Suddenly, Rajan fished out a pistol and opened fire on Roy's team. In a reflex response, the team shot at him. His body was riddled with more than seven bullets when he fell from the tenth-floor window to the concrete ground.

37

The lone neem tree stood like a giant in the barren land on the outskirts of Karoli village. Almost fifty metres away stood both parties. On one side was Putli's gang with Pahalwan Singh Yadav and on the other side was Vishnu Baba.

'Where's the boy?' Putli asked.

Vishnu Baba pointed to the neem tree. 'Your little boy is sitting on top of that tree. The moment the minister reaches the tree, the boy will jump off the tree and run to you.'

'What the hell is this? Some kind of joke?' Shweta shouted at him.

Vishnu Baba smirked. 'You know I like playing my little games. You have to believe me when I say the boy is on the tree.'

Shweta called out, 'Dimple, if you can hear us, raise your hand so we can see you!'

A shaky little hand emerged from the canopy. Putli and Shweta looked at each other, relieved.

'We can't see his face. What if he's not Dimple? What if they've planted some other village boy?' Aakash said. 'Let me talk to him.' Aakash called out to the boy. 'Dimple, we can't see you. Can you stand on one of the branches so we can see your face?'

Gingerly, Dimple stood up. His face was streaked with tears. He looked scared.

'Let him stand under the tree. He doesn't need to be on it,' Shweta suggested.

Vishnu Baba smiled. 'I don't trust Putli. What if she shoots the minister before he reaches us? The boy will remain on the tree and jump only when Pahalwan Singh reaches it.'

Shweta looked at Putli and nodded. 'We can handle it. At least we know that it is Dimple on the tree. Let's get on with it!'

Putli shouted to the boy, 'Don't worry, Dimple! We'll get you! Just wait till the minister reaches the tree, then jump and run over to us.'

The boy seems to be shaking his head as if to say no.

Putli said, 'Don't be scared. We all are here. If they try to shoot, I'm going to shoot each one of them. I'm there, Dimple. Now just wait till I call out.' She saw the boy sit carefully on the branch.

Vishnu Baba called out, 'There's only one catch. If the boy jumps before the minister reaches the tree, we'll shoot him.' He signalled Bhoora who had a rifle pointed at the tree.

Putli shot back, 'If you touch that boy, I'm going to kill you all. That's a promise, Vishnu.'

Vishnu Baba laughed loudly. 'Make sure Pahalwan-ji is safe. That will keep you alive, Putli, or I'm going to hack you to pieces.'

Gadariya stood quietly on a hillock, watching everything. Then he raised his head to the heavens and said, 'Get this little boy out of this wild!'

Shweta looked at Putli and said, 'Let's get this done with this.'

Putli nodded. 'Okay, let the minister start walking. The moment he reaches the tree, Dimple will jump down and walk towards us.'

'Let him come then,' Vishnu Baba said.

Barefoot, Pahalwan Singh Yadav started to shuffle his feet. Vishnu Baba and his men cheered him on, 'Pahalwan-ji! Come on, keep walking!'

Putli and her gang waited with bated breath for the minister to reach the neem tree.

The bulky man broke into a run. As he approached the tree, Putli shouted, 'Dimple, jump!' She saw the boy moving his hand above the branches as if indicating that he couldn't jump. Putli saw his hand and said encouragingly, 'C'mon, you're a brave boy. It's not very high. You can jump.'

The minister had started running towards Vishnu Baba, but Dimple had still not jumped from the tree.

Shweta also called out to Dimple, but he didn't jump. 'Don't be scared. You won't get hurt. Come on, you can do it!'

Slowly, he stood up on the branch trying to show them something. Suddenly, a shot rang out. The bullet hit the branch on which Dimple was standing.

Putli, Shweta, Aakash and all the men ran towards the tree! The boy was hanging by a rope tied around his neck. He had rags stuffed in his mouth. His legs were flaying. He was gasping for breath.

Vishnu Baba and his men helped the minister climb into a jeep and drove off. Turning back to Putli, Bhoora shouted, 'He wanted to kill me to avenge himself. I've killed him. Take his body and bury him.'

Jagat and the other men fired at the jeep speeding away. At one turn, it was just swallowed up by the narrow winding alleys of the wild.

Putli ran to Dimple, crying aloud, 'I'm here, Dimple! I'm here! You're going to be fine!' Putli turned to her men and shouted, 'Cut the rope!'

She could feel the boy's body getting colder with each passing second. As the rope was cut, she lay him on the ground and looked at him. The boy didn't react. His eyes were wide open, staring at her. She shook him hard. 'Get up, Dimple! Get up!'

Aakash checked Dimple's pulse. There was no pulse. He bent down close to his heart. There was no heartbeat. He forced open the boy's mouth and tried to give him mouth-to-mouth resuscitation. There was no reaction. He started to hammer Dimple in the chest to revive him. There was no movement. The tug of the rope on the neck had broken it, crushing the windpipe.

Aakash gently put down the boy's head on the hard ground and looked at Putli. 'He's gone.'

Putli screamed in disbelief, 'No, he can't be dead! I promised him I'd keep him safe.'

Shweta put her hand gently on Putli's shoulder. 'He's gone.'

Putli looked at her men standing with their heads bowed down. Like an animal abandoned by its mother in the wild, Putli shrieked and wailed. She held Shweta tight and wept. 'That Bhoora killed his father, and raped his mother. He wanted to avenge their deaths, but see, they killed him too. He's gone!'

Another cry shattered the wild. The axe flew through the air and struck Pahalwan Singh Yadav's neck, flinging him down from the moving jeep. Vishnu Baba and others saw Gadariya running down the hillock towards them.

'He's going to kill us all!! Let's get out of here! He's possessed by the spirit of Daku Maan Singh. We cannot fight him!' Bhoora cried out.

Vishnu Baba raised his rifle and pointing at Gadariya, said, 'Today, I'm going to show you all that Gadariya is no ghost. I'll kill him with one shot.'

Gadariya's plaintive cry awakened the soul of the wild. The wolves and dogs charged down the hillocks towards the jeep. Seeing them, Vishnu Baba lowered his rifle and shouted, 'Speed up!'

Gadariya came down to the minister who was now writhing in pain with the axe stuck on his neck. The pack of dogs and wolves waited for Gadariya's orders. Vultures circled the sky.

Gadariya bent down and pulled out the axe. Blood spurted from the minister's neck. He tried to speak, but blood oozed from his mouth. He folded his hands pleadingly.

'She was a child when you raped her. Had her father Chhabiram or Daku Maan Singh been here, they would've chopped off your head!' Gadariya cried. Then he raised the axe and brought it down on the minister's neck with full force. The head rolled to one side. The body convulsed for a few seconds before becoming still.

Gadariya picked the head up by the hair. Before walking away, he turned to the dogs and the wolves. Then pointing to the minister's lifeless body, he said coldly, 'There, have your fill.'

Shweta held Putli tight as she wept like a child. Aakash managed to keep his emotions in check. 'We'll have to give him a proper burial.'

Putli wiped away her tears with her hand. In the distance, she saw a figure coming towards them. As the figure drew closer, she realized it was Gadariya. He was drenched in blood. In one hand, he held the axe, and in the other, Pahalwan Singh Yadav's severed head. He came up to her and threw the head at her feet. Then he walked up to the boy. He took his hand in his, mumbled a few words and put it down. He kissed him on the head and disappeared into the wild.

Jagat, Chauhan and others began to dig a grave under the tree. Aakash and Shweta stood staring at Yadav's severed head. The wild had ripped apart their souls, and made them experience life and death in ample measure.

They lowered the little boy into the pit. This was the second boy that Shweta and Aakash were burying in Chambal. Their killer Bhoora was still alive and roaming free. Jagat recited some prayers. Then everyone poured mud into the pit till Dimple was completely covered.

Putli sat close to the grave for a while. Then she turned to Shweta and Aakash and said, 'We all are meant to die here. Our lives are worthless. But you don't belong here. We have jeeps, so Jagat will drop you off to the nearest city. From there, you can go back to your Mumbai.'

Shweta looked at Putli. 'So you want us to run away? Dimple called me didi. I'm not leaving Chambal till I avenge his murder. He was my little brother, and I am not going to let his killers go scot free. He wanted to avenge his father and mother's deaths. It's time I finish his unfinished task.'

Aakash looked stunned. 'Are you out of your mind, Shweta? You can't go out and fight those dacoits! Putli is right. You need to get out of this wild and get back to your life in Mumbai.'

'What life?' screamed Shweta. 'What life are you talking about? Do we really have a life? We work, make money, buy things and then we work again, make money again, and buy more things. For the first time in my life, I've felt so strongly about something. Finally, I've found a purpose to my life—to avenge Dimple's murder.'

'Are you saying that you're going to join a gang of dacoits, that you're going to wield a gun like them, and slaughter like them?' Aakash asked.

'We're already are one of them. We have already carried guns, but now I'll carry the gun to kill the killers,' Shweta said. 'If you want, you can leave. I'm staying back.'

Aakash nodded helplessly. Blood was oozing from the wound in his hand.

'You need proper medical help, Aakash. You should leave this place,' Shweta said.

Aakash raised his hand to look at the dirty bandage soaked in blood, and said, 'We were thrown in this together. We'll get out of this together.'

38

Dusk fell over Chambal. The earth and the sky merged into an endless stretch of ashen grey. Putli, along with her gang, reached the cave in the hills. They sat under the grey sky, waiting for darkness to cover the land like a heavy shroud.

Aakash came down with a high fever. Shweta removed the dirty bandage and tried to clean the wound with some water. They didn't have any medicines. Putli told her to sprinkle some sugar over the wounds as that would stop the bleeding. In villages, they use sugar to cover small cuts and wounds. They had managed to grab a load of ration from Pahalwan-ji's welcome feast.

Shweta sprinkled water on his forehead and feet to bring down the temperature. For a while, Aakash seemed to move in and out of delirium, mumbling incoherently. At times, he stared at Shweta as if he didn't recognize her. Slowly, he began to speak about his favourite recipes, about their crumbling relationship.

'Aakash, I think you should leave. Putli has organized everything. Her men will take you in the jeep to a nearby hospital. You need proper medical care,' Shweta said, stroking his face lovingly.

He smiled at her. 'Now that you've found a purpose in life, you want to discard me.'

'C'mon Askash, it's not like that,' protested Shweta. 'Our life was leading nowhere. Even our relationship was practically over. This wild has awakened something in my soul that I never felt before. I'm no longer afraid of dying.'

Aakash held her hand and nodded. 'I don't want to die

alone in a fancy penthouse on the sixty-fifth floor. No one will even get to know of it.' They both smiled.

'Okay, you'd better get rest,' Shweta told him.

Aakash nodded. He closed his eyes, and taking a deep breath, said, 'When I open my eyes, I want to see you right here in front of me. If I die here, I would at least like to do so holding your hand.'

'Nothing's going to happen to you. It's just a small wound,' Shweta tried to make light of it.

'True, it's just a small wound. I only lost two fingers,' he laughed. 'But I can still hold a knife and I can still cook.'

Shweta smiled at him.

'Honestly, did you never like my cooking?' Aakash asked.

Shweta titled her head as if in deep thought, and said, 'Well, I hate your favourite Spice-o-Clay Fish but I love your pasta. All in all, I enjoy whatever you cook.'

'Now I can make you some nice bajra rotis and hot chilli chutney too,' Aakash joked.

'That would be perfect, but right now you'd better rest,' Shweta said.

'Are you sure you want to do this?' Aakash asked, holding her hand.

Shweta nodded like a battle-hardened soldier. 'Yes, I do.'

Aakash looked at her, and said playfully, 'Now I can proudly say that my wife is Daku Shweta Chaudhary, *Chambal ki Sherni*.' Then he took a deep breath and closed his eyes. Soon, he was asleep.

Shweta walked up to Jagat and Chauhan. It was time for her to learn about guns. Chauhan handed her a pistol and showed her how to dismantle it and reassemble it in less than a minute. Jagat, one of the best marksmen in Putli's gang, gave her tips on shooting with a long-range rifle.

Jagat and Chauhan taught Shweta the ways of Chambal. She needed to learn how to use a knife. She had already used it on Guddu but now, Jagat taught her how to hold the knife properly while facing the opponent so that the least area of her body was exposed to any attack. The way the arm moved with the whole body was crucial in a knife fight, along with some luck.

One needs a heart of steel to stab someone below the ribs, and then move the knife up right till the heart, slicing through it—a skill few have. Most people go for the heart, and hit the ribs or the stomach instead. The technique is to stab, twist and move the knife inside, tearing the body apart.

Putli quietly walked up to Aakash and lay close to him. In his sleep, Aakash thought she was Shweta and hugged her tight, and started to kiss her all over. Suddenly, he opened his eyes to see Putli in his arms. She smiled at him coyly. 'I like the way you kiss.'

Aakash sat up startled. 'What the hell are you doing here?'

'I wanted to lie close to you,' said Putli. 'We dacoits in Chambal have no life. Look at what happened to Dimple. He was hardly ten years old. What will happen to me? One day, I'll also get killed. I don't want to go on like this. Yes, I wanted to be a baaghi and take revenge on those who killed my father and raped me. Now that Pahalwan is dead, I feel hollow and purposeless. Maybe I too need a family. Why don't you marry me?'

Aakash tried to push Putli away. 'But I'm already married, and I'm not a dacoit.'

Putli caressed his cheek. 'Your wife has gone crazy. She wants to take Dimple's revenge to its logical conclusion by killing Bhoora. I'm telling you, she'll die here in Chambal. Maybe then the two of us can get married and have a family. She never gave you any children but we can have ten–twelve kids.'

'I think you have gone crazy. I'm married to Shweta and we've vowed to be together for life,' Aakash reminded Putli.

Putli smiled at him mockingly. 'Do you call this a marriage? You two don't even love each other. You keep fighting and arguing, and will continue to do so all your life. Do you really want such a life? Even if you get out of here alive, she's going to divorce you. She'll blame you for everything and then you'll lose everything. This is the chance of a lifetime. You have everything to gain and start a new life.'

Aakash looked at her stunned. 'I don't know whether we'll get out of here alive, but I know I'll never leave her.'

Putli looked at him and smiled. 'The wild does things to people. Maybe both of you have lost your minds.' Saying that, she got up and walked away.

39

With Rajan Kothari dead, Mumbai Police lost a vital lead. He was the single point of contact with the kidnappers. Despite repeated warnings from ACP Hemant Roy, he was shot, and plunged to his death. Within minutes, OB vans landed up at the spot in Andheri and reporters started their own investigation.

They said that the crime branch had raided Kothari's flat, and shot him at point blank range. Vikram Chaudhary told them that Kothari was a vital link in the kidnapping of Shweta Chaudhary and her husband Aakash Khurana. News channels upped the ante. Several questions were raised—'Why did they kill him? What prompted the police to take such a drastic step? Why did they not capture him alive?' Rookie reporters declared Roy and his team to be trigger-happy policemen who wanted to add to their already impressive number of encounters.

At the press conference, the commissioner of police tried to placate the unruly media with *samosas,* pastries and cold drinks, but they were hungry for spicy bytes, hungrier than the dogs and wolves of Chambal. Everyone was talking to everyone and anyone, looking for something exclusive.

ACP Hemant Roy told the media that the police had vital information that they couldn't share, but that they were following up on every lead to rescue Aakash and Shweta.

The press conference over, the commissioner and Roy sat across leftover snacks and discarded paper plates. 'How could you be so careless as to shoot him dead?' the commissioner asked.

'Sir, he took out a pistol to shoot at the police team. They responded and shot him in self-defence,' Roy explained.

The commissioner took a deep breath. He knew these things happened on the spur of the moment.

'Now what?' the commissioner asked.

'Sir, forensics and the crime branch have gone through each and everything in Rajan's flat. There was no trace of any cash there. We found a laptop and the cyber cell is working on it. We also found two glasses in which Rajan and another person must have had a couple of drinks. On one glass, there were lipstick marks, so maybe Rajan's girlfriend was over, or he had brought another girl to the flat. We're doing a door-to-door in the whole building, and analyzing fingerprints taken from the glass. I hope we'll find some leads soon,' Roy informed the commissioner.

The commissioner looked him in the eye and said, 'Roy, don't give me hope. Hope is illusory. You never know when it vanishes. Give me results. We don't have time; we don't even know whether Shweta and her husband are alive or dead. We have to crack this soon.'

'Sir, it'll be done,' assured Roy.

'Good,' said the commissioner and got up to leave. Roy saluted the man. There was no time to waste.

By the time Roy reached office, the cyber cell had gained access to the contents of Rajan's laptop. They were busy trying to get to his personal email. That took a few hours. Then they came across the video that was uploaded on YouTube and circulated to the media, the exchange of emails on the ransom and the hostages. Roy noticed that most mails were from Gwalior.

'There must be a sleeper cell of the terrorist group in Gwalior,' quipped SI Bhonsle.

'How did you come up with this theory?' Roy asked.

'Recently, I watched a movie about these terror cells. Anyone around us—our neighbours, friends, associates—could belong to a terrorist group,' said an almost fear-mongering Bhonsle.

Roy knew that the police were deeply influenced by movies. Like the policemen in movies, they all wanted to be heroes.

'What about the fingerprint report? Have we found a match yet?' Roy asked.

'We're looking into it. Rajan's girlfriend doesn't seem to have a criminal record, so we're trying a larger database of Aadhaar cards. We hope to find something soon,' said an officer.

'Don't give me hope; give me results,' Roy repeated the commissioner's words.

40

'So you decided to stay back in the wild,' Gadariya walked through the darkness and sat down on a rock close to Shweta.

'I can't just stand around and watch all this. I have to do something,' she said.

With great effort, Aakash opened his eyes. 'How do you know this is the right thing? All through, you wanted to get out of the wild and suddenly you put your life on hold to take revenge for Dimple.'

Gadariya listened quietly. Putli came and sat close to his feet. Gadariya put his hand on her head as though blessing her.

'Sometimes, we just have to do things without thinking too much. At times, our actions are more in the nature of questions, not answers. So I don't know if I'm right or wrong,' Shweta said.

Gadariya kissed Putli's head. 'There are times when we must follow our inner voice. Let her do what she believes in. Maybe that's why you were thrown into the wild. Nothing happens by chance; everything happens for a reason.'

'You stopped us from killing Pahalwan Singh Yadav, but then you went ahead and killed him,' Aakash pointed out.

'I did what a father would've done,' Gadariya replied.

'These two seem to be falling in love all over again,' Putli remarked.

'You've been trying to lure my husband into marrying you,' said Shweta, looking at Putli accusingly.

Putli laughed. 'You really think I can get married and have kids of my own? I am a dacoit in the wild! One fine day, a bullet will snuff out my life. I'm happy to see you two together.'

'I think we've just started to understand each other better,' Shweta said.

'To understand is to forgive everything. When you forgive, you forget, and when you forget, there is no bitterness, no guilt. The past is dead and the future is far away. Live in the present, in that moment, to experience love. Love is the only thing that matters. All else is meaningless,' Gadariya said.

Aakash and Shweta looked at each other with a feeling they never experienced before; it revealed itself after all the superficiality of life had been cast aside.

Gadariya fished out a comb from his waistband. 'See what I've got for you, Putli.'

Putli asked Gadariya, 'Will you comb my hair?'

Gadriya slid the comb gently through her wiry hair.

'What's the most important thing in a relationship?' Shweta asked.

'Respect, honesty and love are the three pillars of a relationship. If even one is missing, the whole relationship crumbles,' Gadariya said, trying to untangle Putli's hair. 'You'd better start washing your hair or no one will marry you.'

Putli burst into laughter. Gadariya patted her on the head. That's when Jagat walked in. 'We have information that tomorrow Vishnu Baba and his gang are going to Morena for the Maha Puja. But the whole place will be swarming with police.'

Putli got up. 'The day has come. We'll attack them at the Maha Puja.'

She turned to Shweta, 'It's time for you to take revenge.'

41

Dawn was still a few hours away. The wild slept like a baby. Shweta and Aakash had been talking through the night. They had never opened up to each other like this before. The wild had washed away their fears, insecurities, pride and bitterness. Like two travellers who shared the experience of the wild, they wanted to move on, hand in hand.

With her head on Aakash's chest, Shweta said softly, 'I don't know if I'll ever get out of here but I love you and would like to spend my whole life with you.'

'I'm coming with you too. We're in this together,' said Aakash.

Resting her chin on his chest, Shweta looked at Aakash. 'My dear chef, you're down with a fever. It's better for you to rest. I can handle these wild animals.'

'The place will be crawling with police and dacoits,' Aakash sounded concerned.

Shweta caressed his face. 'Only God decides our fate.'

'Don't get carried away by what Gadariya says,' Aakash cautioned Shweta. 'This is not a place where you can swan in flashing your press card. You'll be going there as a dacoit, as their rival, and they'll be waiting for you. We can still walk away from all this.'

'That's what we always do. We always find a way to escape,' Shweta said.

For a moment, both were quiet.

'There's something I've never told you,' said Shweta, breaking the silence.

'What? That you can shoot as well?' Aakash said jokingly.

'No, it's about me and my family,' Shweta said, closing her eyes. 'Right after I finished college, we had a huge party in our house. I invited Madhu, a close friend, and we really had a great time. Everyone was drunk and dancing. That night, my brother Vikram and his friends, who were high on cocaine, forcibly took Madhu to Vikram's room and gang-raped her. Paralyzed with terror and too drunk to help, I just passed out.'

Shweta broke down. Aakash held her close as she sobbed. 'That night, Madhu died while they were raping her. When they came to their senses, Vikram and those boys dumped her body at a construction site. Then they poured cement and concrete on her, forever wiping out all traces of her existence. One of Vikram's friends secretly made a video of the whole thing and showed it to me.'

Choking with grief, Shweta continued, 'I desperately wanted to report this to the police but thinking of my family's reputation, I decided against it. So I walked out of the house and the family business, and took up my first job in a news channel. Thereafter, I never spoke to Vikram. All these years, I've been tormented by the shame and guilt of having failed Madhu. By not doing right by her, I also became party to the crime.'

'Her parents kept calling me up to find out about her whereabouts, and each time I said I had no idea. I lied shamelessly. Vikram spun a yarn—Madhu had eloped with one of her boyfriends. For weeks, the police kept looking for her, but drew a blank. I destroyed that video and Vikram warned his friend that he'd kill him if he ever spoke about it to anyone.'

Aakash held her close.

'I was spineless! A coward! I didn't have the guts to report my own brother—a rapist and a murderer! How could I betray Madhu's trust?'

Ridden with guilt, Shweta wailed. 'All these years, despite being feted as a fearless journalist, the news anchor known to expose the truth, I have lived with this terrible truth that I withheld from the world. So I vented all my anger and frustration on you.'

'What about Vikram?' Aakash asked.

'Today he's a powerful businessman. No one can touch him. God knows how many more girls he and his henchmen have raped and killed. The day before we disappeared from Mumbai, I called him to say that I was going to report him to the police. That very night, we found ourselves here in Chambal,' Shweta said.

'Could Vikram have had us kidnapped?'

'I have no idea, but he was scared and nervous. He pleaded with me. He said that it was a huge mistake, that he also needed to be given a second chance, that I couldn't go against my own brother and family. I told him categorically that my mind was made. And then we found ourselves chained and abandoned in the wild.'

'I'm with you, Shweta. Once we're back in Mumbai, we'll reveal the truth about Vikram. But what's this revenge all about? You really want to go out and fight those dreaded dacoits?' Aakash asked.

'There was a time I betrayed my friend, but not anymore. This is for that little boy who guarded both of us with his life, but was killed mercilessly by his father's killer and mother's rapist. I can't be a coward all my life,' Shweta said.

Aakash looked at her. 'I won't stop you.'

Shweta sat up. 'Gadariya was right—the only thing worth fighting for is love.'

Aakash held her hand. 'You've really turned into a philosopher.'

'We'd better get some sleep. I'll be leaving at dawn,' Shweta said.

'You're not going anywhere without me. I'm fine and I can fight them all,' Aakash said, trying to get up. But he felt weak. Let alone get up, he found it difficult to even sit.

Shweta helped him lie down. 'Sleep, you'll feel better. Then you can fight.' Shweta moved closer to him. They hugged each other tight and closed their eyes.

Aakash slipped into deep slumber. For the rest of the night, Shweta stayed awake, staring at the sky. Her mind was a clean slate. She no longer feared anything, not even the possibility of being killed. Something was driving her to action, to redeem herself. She focused on the task at hand.

With the faint glow of dawn, a hand gently shook Shweta's shoulder. She saw Putli standing next to her. As she got up, Putli handed her a rifle and walked away, telling her men to get the jeeps ready. Shweta realized that she could be killed, that this could be the last time she was seeing Aakash. She bent down to kiss him on the forehead. Tears ran down her face and were about to fall on Aakash's face, but she hurriedly wiped them away.

She looked at his bandaged hand. The bleeding had stopped. Despite the fever, he seemed to be free from pain. She smiled at him and gently ruffled his hair. Then she walked away.

42

The fingerprints on the glass with lipstick marks in Rajan Kothari's flat turned out to be those of Amrita Singhal, a newbie actress living in Lokhandwala. Kothari's neighbours and the security guards of the building confirmed that they had seen her often, visiting Rajan in his flat.

She was auditioning for an ad when the police picked her up and brought her to the crime branch office. ACP Hemant Roy grilled her, but was unable to find anything substantial. Amrita said she was friendly with Rajan but had no idea about the nature of his work. Rajan had told her that he was an investor and worked at the stock market.

She told Roy that Rajan wanted to invest in films and had promised to produce her film—by far the easiest and most common ploy some men used to exploit aspiring actresses.

Roy tried his best to break the girl. He told her that Rajan was involved with a terrorist group and that if the police found her involved in it too, she could be in jail for the rest of her life. She broke down, pleaded and begged to be let off. She swore she didn't know anything. Only when Roy was convinced that she was telling the truth did he let her go. He warned her not to leave Mumbai or she could be arrested.

Meanwhile, the cyber cell found the IP address from which Rajan had received the email with the video. It belonged to a prestigious boarding school in Gwalior. The only explanation was that someone from the staff was involved with the terrorist group.

'I told you, Sir. It's a sleeper cell,' SI Bhonsle proudly reiterated his earlier claim.

Roy disagreed. Right from the start, he had serious doubts about the involvement of a terrorist group. Now the leads pointed to Gwalior. The city had not witnessed any terror attacks in the recent past. It could be a good place for a terrorist group to operate from. Yet Roy was not convinced.

'Get me a detailed map of the region on Google,' Roy asked the cyber team.

A large map of the region opened up on screen. He could see Gwalior and a small town close by. He asked the team to zoom in. He could now see Jhansi surrounded by smaller towns. And then he spotted a large wasteland—Chambal.

'Most dacoits were wiped out from Chambal,' Roy said. 'We had reports that a few small gangs operated from nearby cities and towns, using Chambal as a hideout.'

He looked at his team and said, 'What if they were kidnapped by a gang from Chambal? Most of these small gangs take to kidnapping for a ransom and that's what they asked for.'

SI Bhonsle interjected, 'But Sir, from the video, it was clear that they were terrorists.'

'Nowadays, even a schoolboy can create such reels on their smartphones,' Roy said. 'It could've been a smokescreen used by this gang as they didn't want to reveal their true identity to the police. Possibly, they're only interested in the ransom and the freedom to carry on the kidnappings without anyone pointing fingers at them or discovering their hideout in Chambal.'

He realized that Chambal bordered three states—Madhya Pradesh, Uttar Pradesh and Rajasthan. Once again, he looked at Gwalior—among the biggest cities near Chambal.

43

Baldev Singh Tomar, who had won an MP's seat from Morena in the recent elections, had organized a Maha Puja at the local party headquarters. The top brass was invited, along with the dacoits of Chambal who also did Tomar's bidding. Mahant Swami Jagdeeshwar Maharaj from Allahabad was to conduct the puja. There was heavy police patrol everywhere after the murder of Pahalwan Singh Yadav in Chambal.

The puja was to start around 10.00 a.m. and culminate by sunset with the distribution of food and clothes to the poor. Later at night, a grand feast was organized for party workers, with free liquor, mutton, chicken and dancing girls.

Putli, along with Shweta and her gang, reached Morena around noon. They were all armed to the teeth, but to get to the Maha Puja was no mean task. They would have to fight armed policemen, dacoits and political goons. To make things easier, Putli organized police uniforms for everyone. As always, she divided the gang into three teams—one led by Jagat, another by Chauhan and the third with Putli, Shweta and three other men. The plan was to enter from different gates and move close to Vishnu Baba and his gang. Once the mission was accomplished, the jeeps waiting in the open grounds near the local party headquarters would whisk them away to safety.

The Maha Puja was underway. Along with his eleven close disciples, Swami Jagdeeshwar was conducting a *hawan*. The grounds were overrun with beggars, lepers and street kids, lining up for free food and clothes.

During the puja, Baldev Singh Tomar sat close to Swami-ji, while other senior party workers sat in the row behind him. Vishnu Baba and his gang sat on one side. The leaders of Tomar and Gujjar gangs were also there. Also seated close by were many local businessmen who had funded the election campaign and hundreds of rank-and-file party workers, college students and local men and women.

Tewatia was keeping an eye on the crowd. After the killing of Pahalwan Singh Yadav, he had been let off with a warning instead of being suspended, as Karoli village didn't fall in his jurisdiction. However, in Morena, he was responsible for the law and order of the town.

Putli's gang masqueraded as policemen on duty, trying to control the burgeoning crowd. Slowly, they moved inside. Shweta, along with Putli, walked in confidently. Being women in police uniforms, no one questioned them. Soon, they were close to where the hawan was being conducted.

Putli took out her pistol and fired at Vishnu Baba. The bullet pierced his shoulder; blood splattered everywhere. Shweta covered her face with a piece of cloth and moved swiftly through the crowd, looking for Bhoora. A stampede ensued, with politicians, locals and sadhus running for cover. Jagat, Chauhan and their men went after the other dacoits.

Tewatia spotted Putli in a police uniform. 'You won't be able to get out of here, you bitch!' He ordered his men to surround her.

Putli took out a crude bomb from a pocket and hurled it at the crowd. Soon, smoke filled the place. She instructed her men to move swiftly.

Shweta noticed Bhoora trying to slip out. She ran after him and hit him hard in the head with her rifle butt. Bhoora fell down, blood spilling out of the wound. Her eyes were enough for him to recognize her. He laughed deliriously. 'You too have joined Putli's gang?'

Shweta brought down her rifle on Bhoora's head again. She grabbed him by the collar and dragged him to the jeep that was waiting for them.

Caught in the smoke, Tewatia and the police team jostled with the unruly crowd desperate to get out.

Within minutes, the mission was accomplished. Seconds later, Putli, her gang and Shweta sped away from Morena.

Soon, they reached Kutwar, the village where Bhoora had thrashed and raped Dimple's mother in front of Shweta and Aakash. The setting sun looked like a giant red disc that had spun out of orbit and was descending rapidly on Earth.

In Morena, the police rushed the injured to the hospital. While trying to flee, Baldev Singh Tomar was shot in the leg while Swami Jagdeeshwar tripped on his dhoti and fell headlong into the *hawan kund*, badly burning his face.

Putli and her gang summoned the entire village to the public square. Bhoora was made to stand on a platform before the people's court. Then Putli turned to address the villagers.

'This man, Bhoora, not only killed Dimple's father who was a policeman, but also raped his mother and forced her to commit suicide. He then joined Vishnu's gang and killed the little boy Dimple by hanging him from a tree,' Putli said. 'Now you tell me, how should he be punished?'

The villagers discussed it among themselves, and arrived at a unanimous verdict, 'Kill him.'

One of the village elders stepped forward and said, 'You all are right in what you're saying, but if you kill him here, Vishnu Baba and his gang will terrorize us. Then the police will also come after us.'

Shweta screamed at him, 'Where were you when Dimple's

mother was being raped? Or when his father was killed? None of you came forward because you were scared of getting involved.'

'This is Dimple's village too, and this is where this wretched man will get his punishment. If anyone comes asking, tell them Putli killed him,' Putli said to the villagers loudly.

Putli turned to look at Bhoora and said, 'So Bhoora, do you want to say something?'

Bhoora looked at her defiantly and spat on the ground. 'What's come over this Mumbaiwali? If you kill me, the police will come after you. Let me go and I'll drive you safely out of this Chambal.'

Shweta hit him in the stomach with her rifle butt. 'Bastard! I was sent here to kill you.'

Putli looked at the villagers and said, 'The court hereby sentences Bhoora to death.' Putli turned to Bhoora and said, 'Stand against the wall.'

Plaster was peeling off the brick wall. Bhoora stood nervously in front of it. Putli signalled to Shweta, saying, 'He's all yours.'

Shweta took position a few metres away from Bhoora. She removed the rifle from her shoulder, took aim and fired. The first bullet hit the brick wall.

Bhoora begged for mercy. 'Please let me go. Please.'

The second bullet hit him in the neck. Then Shweta kept pressing the trigger till she had emptied all the bullets in him. Bhoora slumped down leaving telltale marks of blood on the wall. A fly flew into the hole in his head and settled on the blood. Soon, more would cover the corpse.

Putli looked around. 'It'll get dark soon. So it's better if you all stay inside your huts. Let the dogs and wolves finish him up.' Then she turned to Shweta and asked, 'How do you feel?'

'Like a baaghi,' Shweta nodded quietly.

They hugged each other and cried.

44

Aakash lay alone in the dark. He ate the bajra roti Shweta had left near him, and drank some water from an old plastic bottle. The fever wracked his body. His head reeled with weakness.

All his anger, bitterness and resentment towards his wife, and all the superfluous things they had been chasing, appeared trivial after what they had gone through. Suddenly, he felt a rush of joy as he had never experienced before.

He lost track of time; it didn't really matter. He was told so often that time is money and he laughed it off.

He had no idea how long he lay there in the dark. Then he heard the rattling sounds. He saw some blinding lights as though the angels of death had come to take him away. Then he heard her calling for him, 'Aakash! Aakash!'

He opened his eyes to see Shweta jumping off one of the jeeps, and running towards him. She hugged him tight and said, 'We're free! We're free! Now we can go back to our lives.'

He looked at her and smiled, running his fingers through her unkempt hair and mumbled, 'I love you, my Daku Rani.' They laughed and kissed.

As the headlights of the jeeps were switched off, Putli walked up to them. 'Your wife would make a great dacoit. Can I keep her here in Chambal?' Putli said, laughing. 'You should have seen how she led the attack, moved deftly through the huge crowd, and grabbed Bhoora.'

'You had your revenge?' Aakash asked Shweta.

Shweta nodded. 'He got what he deserved.'

'Well, it's time you both got out of Chambal. Soon, the police will bring in more men to comb the valley. Early in the morning, we'll drop you on the highway. From there, Jagat will take you in a jeep to Etawah. It's a big city and you can board a train to Mumbai or some place nearby. I'll give you enough cash to take care of everything,' Putli said.

Shweta looked at her. 'Thank you, Putli. You have done a lot for us. I'm sorry I misunderstood you earlier.'

Putli smiled. 'Well, I'm still ready to marry him if you leave him here.'

'I'm not leaving without him,' Shweta smiled back.

So Putli turned around and looked wistfully at the horizon before retracing her steps back to her men.

Shweta lay close to Aakash, hugging him. 'You still have a fever.'

'I'm just too hot to handle, girl,' Aakash teased, turning towards her. They giggled like they used to when they had fallen in love.

Then the heavens opened up and started to shower blessings on them. Putli and her men danced and frolicked as the drizzle turned into a downpour. That night, on the hard dusty ground, under the driving rain, Aakash and Shweta made love like never before.

45

Putli didn't want to take chances. So, well before sunrise, she instructed Aakash and Shweta to get into one jeep, while her men readied to get into the other. Gadariya appeared from nowhere to bid Shweta and Aakash goodbye. Putli hugged him and cried like a child.

Gadariya could sense her pain. Torn between her life in the wild and all the lives she would never live, Putli had settled for the former. Running his fingers through her knotted hair, he said, 'You're the daughter of the wild, Putli. You belong here, and I'm going to find you a suitable boy.'

Wiping her tears, Putli walked up to Shweta and Aakash. 'Take care of yourselves and don't throw away this second chance at life.'

'We'll miss you, Putli,' said Shweta, choking with emotion.

Aakash looked at Putli and smiled, 'If you ever feel like leaving Chambal, you know where to find us.'

Putli fought back her tears. 'I'm happy here. Maybe the next time you visit, you'll find my grave somewhere in the wild.'

'Whatever happens to us, happens for us,' said Gadariya, holding Putli's hand gently.

'We need to get going,' said Jagat. 'Soon the sun will be out.'

Everyone got into their respective jeep. Gadariya raised his hand in farewell. Against the dark grey before dawn, two jeeps sped away into the wild.

The one in front had Shweta and Aakash with Jagat behind the wheel, along with two men mounting vigil. Right behind them were Chauhan and three men ready to fend off any attack from the rear. Slowly, the sun came up.

'Once we are on the highway, it would take roughly two hours to reach Etawah. It is surrounded by many big towns and cities like Etah, Mainpuri and Shikohabad. Aligarh is not far off either. Etawah has a big railway station. Hopefully, from there, you'll get a direct train to Mumbai,' said Jagat.

'What's the date today?' Shweta asked.

Jagat shrugged and looked at the other men. None of them seemed to know. Neither she nor Aakash knew how many days they had been in Chambal. It was as though they stepped into a time machine that took them to a faraway land, and now they were returning to their original time and place. Shweta smiled as if none of this mattered anymore.

Aakash and Shweta could see the wild they were leaving behind, and with it, countless hillocks, mud mounds and never-ending ravines spreading out till the horizon. In the dull, flat, barren wild of Chambal, they did what they had never done in Mumbai—they travelled within themselves. Who kidnapped them, chained them, and threw them in the wild seemed insignificant.

They waited to hit the highway where they would soon see trucks, tempos, luxury cars, motorbikes and more—all trappings of 'civilization'—competing with each other to stay ahead of the curve. They buried their heads between their knees to keep off the harsh light and rest a while.

A loud shot interrupted their reverie. Their jeep swerved off the dirt road. Was it a tyre burst or a shot fired from a gun? Soon, multiple shots were fired at the jeeps. Jagat pressed on the accelerator but with a flat tyre, the jeep tilted dangerously to one side.

'Keep low and don't look up,' Jagat warned Aakash and

Shweta. He told the other men to move out and take position around the jeep. Jagat shouted for Chauhan driving the other jeep to move away. He didn't have enough time as a Molotov cocktail flew through the air and landed on the jeep Chauhan was driving. Soon, it was engulfed in flames and exploded; Chauhan and all the men were burnt alive.

Jagat was looking around but couldn't spot the enemy. They seem to be hiding behind the mud mounds or atop the hillocks. Then bullets whizzed through the air, blowing apart the heads of the men keeping vigil.

Now only Jagat was left with Shweta and Aakash. They hid behind the jeep. Jagat was trying to figure out the cover of the enemy when another Molotov cocktail landed on their jeep. The jeep caught fire, forcing the three to come out in the open. In that instant, a shot rang out and caught Jagat on his thigh. He dropped his rifle and fell to the ground.

Aakash picked up his rifle and looked around. He saw men charging at them from all directions. Then he saw Vishnu Baba with his arm in a sling. He walked towards them and stopped right in front of Jagat. Without even looking at Shweta and Aakash, he said, 'Kallu, chop off his head.'

In a swift stroke, Kallu brought down the machete on Jagat's neck. His head rolled away in the dust. Vishnu Baba smiled and looked at Shweta and Aakash. 'So finally I have caught up with you. But now I want that Putli. This time she'll come to me herself.' Vishnu Baba took a step back and said, 'Kallu, grab the girl.'

Aakash tried to raise the rifle in his hand. With one hand, Kallu snatched it away. He grabbed Shweta by her hair and started to drag her.

'Don't worry about me, Aakash. I'll be fine,' cried Shweta. With all the rifles pointed at them, Aakash couldn't do a thing. Vishnu Baba looked at him and said, 'Now listen to me carefully, Mr Cook. You'd better go back to that Putli and tell her to come to my place. Maybe in exchange for her, I'll let your wife go.'

With that, Vishnu Baba walked away, kicking Jagat's head down a dry and rocky slope.

46

ACP Hemant Roy, with a team of crime branch officials and two IT experts from the cyber cell, reached the sprawling Gwalior Public School. One of the most prestigious boarding schools in the country, it was a part of the Gwalior Fort and was funded by the royal family of Gwalior. Children of top businessmen, politicians, filmmakers and bureaucrats studied here.

Yashpal Bhardwaj, the school principal and director, was shocked to learn that the school premises and computers had been used to send out emails regarding the kidnapping of Shweta and her husband.

This was a kidnapping case that had taken the entire nation by storm. Everyone had their own theory. Even a roadside tea-seller had a plausible theory on their disappearance. Only the police seemed to be baffled. After all, they were the ones responsible for not only getting them back alive but also apprehending the kidnappers.

'I can assure you that no staff member is involved in this kidnapping. We have done a thorough background check on each and every one here,' Bhardwaj assured Roy.

Roy nodded. 'I understand what you're saying. Still, I would like to meet all the staff members. In fact, I would like to start with the computer teacher himself.'

For the next two hours, Roy and his team grilled the staff members while IT experts worked on the computers to find other possible clues that could lead them to the kidnappers.

Finally, Roy was convinced that the staff members were indeed not involved in this case.

'Could be the work of an outsider,' Roy told the principal. 'Do you have many outsiders coming in and using the computers?'

'We don't allow outsiders to walk into our computer labs,' said Bhardwaj. Suddenly, he remembered, 'Recently, we had our school Sports Day. That's the only time when a whole lot of outsiders come in. Along with parents, there are daily wage workers, including sweepers, gardeners, local security, a videographer and photographer…'

Roy interjected. 'I would like to meet this videographer and photographer.'

'He has been a regular at the school, and covers most of the school programmes and functions. I think his name is Pappu. He's too naïve to be involved in something like this,' Bhardwaj said.

'I would like to meet this Pappu,' said Roy.

'Don't worry, ACP-saab, I'll ask my head clerk to give him a call, and he'll be here soon,' Bhardwaj said.

'Make sure he doesn't mention anything about the police. Tell him that you have some programme and want him to take photographs,' Roy suggested.

'Sure.'

'Meanwhile, let me check with my IT experts if they have found something,' Roy said politely and left the principal's office.

Roy walked into the computer lab. Students in uniform were hurrying to their classes. He made sure that they didn't get a whiff of what was going on in their school.

In the computer lab, the IT experts had dug out many photographs from Sports Day. As Roy looked at the photographs, he said, 'This means the photographer used the lab and these computers. He could be the one who also sent out the mail.'

At that moment, the head clerk walked in. 'Sir, I have tried Pappu Bhaiyya's number but it's not available. Maybe he has gone out to photograph some function in a nearby village. He's the one who covers all marriages, birthday parties, baby showers and school annual days. The moment I get through to him, I'll let you know.'

'He's the one,' Roy said. 'Please give me the number, the address of his studio, house…everything. We have to track him down right now!'

47

Only eight men were left in Putli's gang. Her two trusted lieutenants Jagat and Chauhan had been killed, along with five other men. Putli sat facing Aakash, who looked distraught with pain. The whole day, he had walked through the wild, losing his way many times before Gadariya found him and brought him to Putli.

'Shweta is going to be fine,' Putli said. 'This time, they want me, so they won't do anything to her. I'll go and get her back.'

'I'm coming with you,' Aakash said feverishly.

'You're not in a position to even walk properly. Let me handle this.'

'That Kallu groped her all over, and I couldn't do a thing. They chopped off my fingers. Now it's my turn,' said Aakash gritting his teeth in rage.

Gadariya pulled out his axe and handed it to Aakash. 'You'll need this.'

Taken aback, Putli looked at Gadariya. 'What are you doing, Baba? He can't even pick up the axe.'

With his right hand, Aakash grabbed the axe by its handle and looked at them. 'I'm fine. I can hold it *and* I can move it.' He swung the axe in a deep arc as it made a swishing sound in the air.

Putli got up and called out to her men, 'Grab your guns. We need to move out now.'

The sun was already setting. She wondered whether to surrender to get Shweta back or attack Vishnu Baba.

Putli walked up to Gadariya and looked at him. 'Do you have anything to say to me?'

Gadariya gently touched her face and placing his hand on her head, blessed her. 'You'd better start washing your hair. If you look like this, no one will marry you.' They both had tears in their eyes. Putli hugged him.

'I hope I'm doing the right thing,' said Putli, pulling herself together.

With his hand still over her head, Gadariya said, 'If Chhabiram was here, he would've been proud of you.'

Aakash slung a couple rifles on his shoulders, along with a bandolier of bullets. As a chef, he had been particular about the aroma, texture, presentation and taste of the dish. That seemed like another life on another planet. He hardly felt like a chef right now. On the brink of death, life seems to acquire a new meaning.

Putli got into the jeep and called out to Aakash, who seemed lost in thought. He picked up the axe and tucked it into the waist of his tattered trousers. He still wore the same blood-soaked shirt. Only he could no longer make out one spot from the other. Nothing seemed to bother him anymore except that he had to get Shweta back even if that meant he would have to kill someone.

Soon, dusk turned into darkness. Night came down on them like a hammer on a nail.

In the middle of the night, they reached the Chambal River, and abandoned the only jeep Putli had now. From there, they walked to the river. Single-mindedly, they all waded through the dark, murky waters without a care about the hungry alligators in the river.

They moved out of the river and started a long trek to Vishnu Baba's hideout. Gone were the times when Aakash was plagued with fear. He walked into the darkness purposefully, without the fear of death. All he knew was that he had to save Shweta. Even his own life didn't matter to him anymore.

∞

At 10.00 a.m., ACP Hemant Roy, along with his team and Gwalior Police, arrived at Pappu's shop, but it was closed. They broke open the shutter and searched the premises. They found the banner the terrorist group had used in the video, carelessly wrapped up and kept in a corner. Some Pathani suits and camouflage clothing were stuffed into a large plastic bag. Roy instantly realized that these were worn by the kidnappers in the video. Could it be possible that they were not terrorists?

They turned the shop upside down but didn't find anything else. One thing was certain. This Pappu was involved with the kidnappers. He was the one who had made the video and mailed it to the media houses. Once they nabbed him, everything else would fall into place.

Roy, along with the police teams, barged into his house and searched the place. They found a thick wad of cash, along with a trunk filled with small arms and ammunition. Pappu was not just a photographer.

'What kind of criminals here take to kidnapping for a ransom?' Roy asked SI Deenanath Srivastava of Gwalior Police.

He answer was simple, 'The dacoits of Chambal.'

48

As Aakash approached Vishnu Baba's hideout, thoughts of Shweta tormented him like a knife tearing into his soul. 'Was she alive? Had they tortured her? Had they raped her?'

Putli, along with her men, slowly climbed up a hillock close to the ruins. She instructed her men to take position at different places. She crept down the hillock to take a closer look. There was no sign of Shweta.

She approached the ruins cautiously. She couldn't see any of Vishnu's gang members. She took off her rifle from her shoulder and pointed it in front, and slid down into the open. Suddenly, bullets came flying at her from all sides. She was hit on a shoulder joint. It made her fall flat on her back.

Soon, Vishnu's men emerged out of hiding. He knew that Putli would try to attack him, and he wanted to surprise her. Only he forgot that she was Chhabiram's daughter and had been brought up and trained by Gadariya, the shepherd of Chambal. As Vishnu's men came out into the open, her men came out of hiding and killed four of them instantly.

The ruins turned into a battlefield as Putli's men rained bullets on Vishnu's men. Aakash charged down with his rifle but it got jammed. Unable to shoot, he threw it away and fished out the axe. As he swung the axe, he transformed into something else. He forgot where he was, what he was doing; he kept swinging, cutting and chopping with the axe, with Vishnu's men falling all around him. Finally, he stopped. Drenched in blood from head to toe, Aakash stood with the bloodied axe in his hand in the midst of bodies.

Kallu picked up the machete and charged towards him. Aakash focused on Kallu's arm holding the machete. As he came closer and raised his arm to strike, Aakash swung the axe and with one swift stroke, chopped off his arm. This was the man who had chopped off his fingers, chewed them and spat them out. There was no remorse, no guilt and no doubt as Aakash raised the axe, and struck him on the neck. The axe got stuck in the thick, log-like neck. Aakash put his foot on Kallu's chest, pulled out the axe, and then struck him again. In a matter of seconds, Kallu's head rolled on the dusty ground.

Vishnu Baba ran inside the ruins only to be blocked by Putli. He turned to see Aakash standing behind him with the axe. 'Where's Shweta?' Aakash asked him.

'She's down in the well. *Kaali-Mata ki kasam*, no one has touched her. I'll help her out,' Vishnu Baba pleaded.

Aakash turned away as Vishnu faced Putli. She raised her rifle and shot him in the abdomen, to make sure that he didn't die instantly, but slowly bled to death. She then used the rifle butt to hammer his head. With every strike, Putli invoked her father, 'Baba, this is for you.'

Aakash ran to the dry well where Shweta and he were once held captive till Putli rescued them. Shweta lay at the bottom, with her hands tied behind her, and cloth stuffed in her mouth. Aakash lowered a rope and climbed down. He pulled the cloth out of her mouth and untied her. They couldn't help but hug and cry.

Putli kept hitting Vishnu like a woman possessed. She didn't notice when Vishnu took out the long knife and stabbed her in the ribs. The blade pierced her heart and then he pulled it out. Putli dropped to the ground. She looked almost dead with her eyes wide open.

Vishnu stood triumphantly over her. Then he raised his hand to stab her again. At that very instant, Putli turned the rifle on him and shot him in the head. The head exploded like a watermelon, splattering tissue, bones and grey matter all over the walls of the ruins.

On hearing the gunshot, Aakash and Shweta ran towards Putli. She was bleeding profusely. Shweta cradled her in her arms. Soon, blood started to trickle from her ears. Putli tried to speak but blood spurted from her mouth. She looked at Shweta and Aakash with a feeble smile. She took their hands and placed them on top of each other. Then she stiffened and went limp.

49

ACP Hemant Roy had instructed his team and the local police to keep an eye on Pappu's family. Early in the morning, they followed Pappu's mother to a government hospital right into an isolation ward for patients suffering from tuberculosis. Roy walked in to find Pappu lying on a bed. With the police closing in on him, Pappu had got himself admitted in the tuberculosis ward. Few would suspect he was there. His mother would bring him food, and he slept there peacefully, while the police spent sleepless nights looking for him. It took one slap from ACP Hemant Roy for Pappu to blurt everything out.

❧

Back in Chambal, Gadariya, along with Aakash and Shweta, gave Putli and her loyal brigade a proper burial. 'Finally, she's free,' Gadariya said, tears flowing down his cheeks. Then he looked at Aakash and Shweta and said, 'It's time for you to leave.'

Aakash drove the jeep, with Gadariya showing the way. As they reached the outer limits of Chambal, Gadariya got down and waved them off. 'Remember everything, and each one you met here, and all those who died here.'

Aakash and Shweta watched in silence as Gadariya climbed over the hillocks. Suddenly, they saw a cloud of dust on the road. Some police jeeps were heading towards them.

ACP Hemant Roy got off even before his jeep had come to a halt. He ran towards Aakash and Shweta, and introduced himself. Aakash and Shweta were relieved to see the police. Then they saw Gadariya standing over a hillock looking at them.

'Who's that?' asked Roy.

'He's Gadariya, the shepherd, who showed us the way,' replied Aakash.

One of the local policemen blurted out, 'I've heard this Gadariya is the son of Daku Maan Singh.'

'But he was killed by rival gangs,' another constable piped up.

'That's right. What you see there is the spirit of Gadariya that roams in the wild,' said the policeman.

They looked up again to see Gadariya, but by then he had vanished.

50

A press conference was held by Mumbai Police. National and international media flocked to it for an exclusive scoop. ACP Hemant Roy explained the entire operation executed by Mumbai Police to rescue Aakash and Shweta from the kidnappers.

Corroborating Roy's report, Shweta told the media that they were kidnapped by unknown people in Mumbai, and were later handed over to dacoits in Chambal. Aakash thanked Mumbai Police for all their effort to bring them back. Neither Aakash nor Shweta uttered a word about their experiences in the wild. Those were too personal.

Vikram Chaudhary proclaimed loudly, 'Mumbai Police pocketed the five crore rupees that I had forked out as ransom money. In fact, I'm convinced that there was never any demand for ransom and that ACP Hemant Roy cooked up the whole story to pocket the money.'

The media went berserk as if a piece of meat had been thrown at hungry wolves. Roy tried to answer their questions to the best of his ability, but the media didn't seem satisfied.

Finally, Shweta spoke again, 'I'm the majority stakeholder in my family's construction business, so the ranson money my brother so painstakingly organized actually belongs to me. And I don't care where the money disappeared. What matters is that I'm back here with my husband. I have never been interested in my family business, but now I'll have to look into it more closely to see what's what.'

Vikram yelled, 'That's is why I wanted you away from

the business. I begged and borrowed to rescue you from your kidnappers, and this is how you pay me back.'

Shweta stared hard at him. Taking a deep breath, she said, 'For years, I've been living a lie. I've been a coward. I never spoke out before as I was too conscious of my family's reputation.'

She went on to tell the media about the rape and murder of her close friend Madhu at their house in Gurugram in the hands of Vikram and his friends.

Vikram protested loudly saying that it was all a lie. He was immediately taken into custody by the crime branch, while another team went after his friends.

Shweta turned to ACP Roy, 'You can arrest me for withholding information.'

'No, it was me who forced her to not divulge the details about this,' Aakash called out.

Roy smiled at them and said, 'It's good both of you have come to your senses.'

It was late in the evening when Aakash and Shweta reached Ambar Apartments. As they walked into the lobby, a security guard saluted them, 'Madam-ji, I prayed everyday for your return and finally, God has answered my prayers.'

Aakash and Shweta smiled at him. They had often seen him in the lobby, but never noticed him, or ever enquired about his well-being.

'What's your name?' Shweta asked.

'Maan Singh,' replied the guard. 'My father was a fan of Daku Maan Singh, and decided to name me after him.'

Aakash and Shweta looked stunned. 'So you know about Chambal?' Aakash asked.

The guard smiled and said, 'Sir-ji, I was born in Morena and spent my entire childhood there.'

∽

Gadariya stood over a hillock. Looking at the stars above, he cried. The dogs and wolves of the wild too cried with him.

∞

But let there be spaces in your togetherness,
And let the winds of the heavens dance between you.

Love one another, but make not a bond of love:
Let it rather be a moving sea between the shores of your souls.
Fill each other's cup but drink not from one cup.
Give one another of your bread but eat not from the same loaf.
Sing and dance together and be joyous,
but let each one of your be alone,
Even as the strings of the lute are alone though
they quiver with the same music.

Give your hearts, but not into each other's keeping.
For only the hand of Life can contain your hearts.
And stand together yet not too near together:
For the pillars of the temple stand apart,
And the oak tree and the cypress grow not in each other's shadow.

—Kahlil Gibran, *The Prophet*